TWIST ME

TWIST ME: BOOK 1

ANNA ZAIRES

D0754070

♠ MOZAIKA PUBLICATIONS ♠

Copyright © 2014 Anna Zaires
http://annazaires.com/

Published by Mozaika Publications, an imprint of Mozaika LLC.
www.mozaikallc.com

Cover by Najla Qamber Designs
www.najlaqamberdesigns.com

e-ISBN: 978-1-63142-000-9
ISBN: 978-1-63142-003-0

PROLOGUE

*B*ood.
It's everywhere. The pool of dark red liquid on the floor is spreading, multiplying. It's on my feet, my skin, my hair... I can taste it, smell it, feel it covering me. I'm drowning in blood, suffocating in it.

No! Stop!

I want to scream, but I can't draw in enough air. I want to move, but I'm restrained, tied in place, the ropes cutting into my skin as I struggle against them.

I can hear her *screams, though. Inhuman shrieks of pain and agony that slice me open, leaving my mind as raw and mangled as her flesh.*

He lifts the knife one last time, and the pool of blood turns into an ocean, the rip current sucking me in—

I wake up screaming his name, my sheets soaked through with cold sweat.

For a moment, I'm disoriented... and then I remember.

He will never come for me again.

EIGHTEEN MONTHS EARLIER

I'm seventeen years old when I first meet him.

Seventeen and crazy about Jake.

"Nora, come on, this is boring," Leah says as we sit on the bleachers watching the game. Football. Something I know nothing about, but pretend I love because that's where I see him. Out there on that field, practicing every day.

I'm not the only girl watching Jake, of course. He's the quarterback and the hottest guy on the planet—or at least in the Chicago suburb of Oak Lawn, Illinois.

"It's not boring," I tell her. "Football is a lot of fun."

Leah rolls her eyes. "Yeah, yeah. Just go talk to him already. You're not shy. Why don't you just make him notice you?"

I shrug. Jake and I don't run in the same circles. He's got cheerleaders climbing all over him, and I've been watching him long enough to know that he goes for tall blond girls, not short brunettes.

Besides, for now it's kind of fun to just enjoy the attraction. And I know that's what this feeling is. Lust. Hormones, pure and simple. I have no idea if I'll like Jake as a person, but I certainly love how he looks without his shirt. Whenever he walks by, I feel my heart beating faster from excitement. I feel warm inside, and I want to squirm in my seat.

I also dream about him. Sexy dreams, sensual dreams, where he holds my hand, touches my face, kisses me. Our bodies touch, rub against each other. Our clothes come off.

I try to imagine what sex with Jake would be like.

Last year, when I was dating Rob, we nearly went all the way, but then I found out he slept with another girl at a party while drunk. He groveled profusely when I confronted him about it, but I couldn't trust him again and we broke up. Now I'm much more careful about the guys I date, although I know not all of them are like Rob.

Jake might be, though. He's just too popular not to be a player. Still, if there's anybody I'd want to have my first time with, it's definitely Jake.

"Let's go out tonight," Leah says. "Just us girls. We can go to Chicago, celebrate your birthday."

"My birthday is not for another week," I remind her, even though I know she's got the date marked on her calendar.

"So what? We can get a head start."

I grin. She's always so eager to party. "I don't know.

What if they throw us out again? Those IDs are just not that good—"

"We'll go to another place. It doesn't have to be Aristotle."

Aristotle is by far the coolest club in the city. But Leah was right—there were others.

"Okay," I say. "Let's do it. Let's get a head start."

Leah picks me up at 9 p.m.

She's dressed for clubbing—dark skinny jeans, a sparkly black tube-top, and over-the-knee high-heeled boots. Her blond hair is perfectly smooth and straight, falling down her back like a highlighted waterfall.

In contrast, I'm still wearing my sneakers. My clubbing shoes I hide in the backpack that I intend to leave in Leah's car. A thick sweater hides the sexy top I'm wearing. No makeup and my long brown hair in a ponytail.

I leave the house like that to avoid any suspicion. I tell my parents I'm going to hang out with Leah at a friend's house. My mom smiles and tells me to have fun.

Now that I'm almost eighteen, I don't have a curfew anymore. Well, I probably do, but it's not a formal one. As long as I come home before my parents start freaking out —or at least if I let them know where I am—it's all good.

Once I get into Leah's car, I begin my transformation.

Off goes the thick sweater, revealing the slinky tank-top I have on underneath. I wore a push-up bra to maximize my somewhat-undersized assets. The bra straps are cleverly designed to look cute, so I'm not embarrassed to have them show. I don't have cool boots like Leah's, but I did manage to sneak out my nicest pair of black heels. They add about four inches to my height. I need every single one of those inches, so I put on the shoes.

Next, I pull out my makeup bag and pull down the windshield visor, so I can get access to the mirror.

Familiar features stare back at me. Large brown eyes and clearly defined black eyebrows dominate my small face. Rob once told me that I look exotic, and I can kind of see that. Even though I'm only a quarter Latino, my skin always looks lightly tanned and my eyelashes are unusually long. Fake lashes, Leah calls them, but they're entirely real.

I don't have a problem with my looks, although I often wish I were taller. It's those Mexican genes of mine. My abuela was petite and so am I, even though both of my parents are of average height. I wouldn't care, except Jake likes tall girls. I don't think he even sees me in the hallway; I'm literally below his eye level.

Sighing, I put on lip gloss and some eye shadow. I don't go crazy with makeup because simple works best on me.

Leah cranks up the radio, and the latest pop songs fill the car. I grin and start singing along with Rihanna.

Leah joins me, and now we're both belting out S&M lyrics.

Before I know it, we arrive at the club.

We walk in like we own the place. Leah gives the bouncer a big smile, and we flash our IDs. They let us through, no problem.

We've never been to this club before. It's in an older, slightly rundown part of downtown Chicago.

"How did you find this place?" I yell at Leah, shouting to be heard above the music.

"Ralph told me about it," she yells back, and I roll my eyes.

Ralph is Leah's ex-boyfriend. They broke up when he started acting weird, but they still talk for some reason. I think he's into drugs or something these days. I'm not sure, and Leah won't tell me out of some misplaced loyalty to him. He's the king of shady, and the fact that we're here on his recommendation is not super-comforting.

But whatever. Sure, the area outside is not the best, but the music is good and the crowd is a nice mix of people.

We're here to party, and that's exactly what we do for the next hour. Leah gets a couple of guys to buy us shots. We don't have more than one drink each. Leah—because she has to drive us home. And me—because I don't metabolize alcohol well. We may be young, but we're not stupid.

After the shots, we dance. The two guys who bought

us drinks dance with us, but we gradually migrate away from them. They're not that cute. Leah finds a group of college-age hotties, and we sidle up to them. She strikes up a conversation with one of them, and I smile, watching her in action. She's good at this flirting business.

In the meantime, my bladder tells me I need to visit the ladies' room. So I leave them and go.

On my way back, I ask the bartender for a glass of water. I am thirsty after all the dancing.

He gives it to me, and I greedily gulp it down. When I'm done, I put down the glass and look up.

Straight into a pair of piercing blue eyes.

He's sitting on the other side of the bar, about ten feet away. And he's staring at me.

I stare back. I can't help it. He's probably the most handsome man I've ever seen.

His hair is dark and curls slightly. His face is hard and masculine, each feature perfectly symmetrical. Straight dark eyebrows over those strikingly pale eyes. A mouth that could belong to a fallen angel.

I suddenly feel warm as I imagine that mouth touching my skin, my lips. If I were prone to blushing, I would've been beet-red.

He gets up and walks toward me, still holding me with his gaze. He walks leisurely. Calmly. He's completely sure of himself. And why not? He's gorgeous, and he knows it.

As he approaches, I realize that he's a large man. Tall and well built. I don't know how old he is, but I'm guessing he's closer to thirty than twenty. A man, not a boy.

He stands next to me, and I have to remember to breathe.

"What's your name?" he asks softly. His voice somehow carries above the music, its deeper notes audible even in this noisy environment.

"Nora," I say quietly, looking up at him. I am absolutely mesmerized, and I'm pretty sure he knows it.

He smiles. His sensuous lips part, revealing even white teeth. "Nora. I like that."

He doesn't introduce himself, so I gather my courage and ask, "What's your name?"

"You can call me Julian," he says, and I watch his lips moving. I've never been so fascinated by a man's mouth before.

"How old are you, Nora?" he asks next.

I blink. "Twenty-one."

His expression darkens. "Don't lie to me."

"Almost eighteen," I admit reluctantly. I hope he doesn't tell the bartender and get me kicked out of here.

He nods, like I confirmed his suspicions. And then he raises his hand and touches my face. Lightly, gently. His thumb rubs against my lower lip, as though he's curious about its texture.

I'm so shocked that I just stand there. Nobody has ever done that before, touched me so casually, so possessively. I feel hot and cold at the same time, and a tendril of fear snakes down my spine. There is no hesitation in his actions. No asking for permission, no pausing to see if I would let him touch me.

He just touches me. Like he has the right to do so. Like I belong to him.

I draw in a shaky breath and back away. "I have to go," I whisper, and he nods again, watching me with an inscrutable expression on his beautiful face.

I know he's letting me go, and I feel pathetically grateful—because something deep inside me senses that he could've easily gone further, that he doesn't play by the normal rules.

That he's probably the most dangerous creature I've ever met.

I turn and make my way through the crowd. My hands are trembling, and my heart is pounding in my throat.

I need to leave, so I grab Leah and make her drive me home.

As we're walking out of the club, I look back and I see him again. He's still staring at me.

There is a dark promise in his gaze—something that makes me shiver.

2

*T*he next three weeks pass by in a blur. I celebrate my eighteenth birthday, study for finals, hang out with Leah and my other friend Jennie, go to football games to watch Jake play, and get ready for graduation.

I try not to think about the club incident again. Because when I do, I feel like a coward. Why did I run? Julian had barely touched me.

I can't fathom my strange reaction. I had been turned on, but ridiculously frightened at the same time.

And now my nights are restless. Instead of dreaming of Jake, I often wake up feeling hot and uncomfortable, throbbing between my legs. Dark sexual images invade my dreams, stuff I've never thought about before. A lot of it involves Julian doing something to me, usually while I'm helplessly frozen in place.

Sometimes I think I'm going crazy.

Pushing that disturbing thought out of my mind, I focus on getting dressed.

My high school graduation is today, and I'm excited. Leah, Jennie, and I have big plans for after the ceremony. Jake is throwing a post-graduation party at his house. It will be the perfect opportunity to finally talk to him.

I'm wearing a black dress under my blue graduation gown. It's simple, but it fits me well, showing off my small curves. I'm also wearing my four-inch heels. A little much for the graduation ceremony, but I need the added height.

My parents drive me to the school. This summer I'm hoping to save enough money to buy my own car for college. I'm going to a local community college because it's cheaper that way, so I'll still be living at home.

I don't mind. My parents are nice, and we get along well. They give me a lot of freedom—probably because they think I'm a good kid, never getting in trouble. They're mostly right. Other than the fake IDs and the occasional clubbing excursions, I lead a pretty sedate life. No heavy drinking, no smoking, no drugs of any kind—although I did try pot once at a party.

We arrive and I find Leah. Lining up for the ceremony, we wait patiently for our names to be called. It's a perfect day in early June—not too hot, not too cold.

Leah's name is called first. Luckily for her, her last name starts with 'A.' My last name is Leston, so I have to stand for another thirty minutes. Fortunately, our graduating class is only a hundred people. One of the perks of living in a small town.

My name is called and I go to receive my diploma. Looking out onto the crowd, I smile and wave to my parents. I'm pleased that they look so proud.

I shake the principal's hand and turn to go back to my seat.

And in that moment, I see him again.

My blood freezes in my veins.

He's sitting in the back, watching me. I can feel his eyes on me, even from a distance.

Somehow I make my way down from the stage without falling. My legs are trembling, and my breathing is much faster than normal. I take a seat next to my parents and pray that they don't notice my state.

Why is Julian here? What does he want from me? Taking a deep breath, I tell myself to calm down. Surely he's here because of someone else. Maybe he has a brother or a sister in my graduating class. Or some other relative.

But I know I'm lying to myself.

I remember that possessive touch, and I know he's not done with me.

He wants me.

A shudder runs down my spine at the thought.

I don't see him again after the ceremony, and I'm relieved. Leah drives us to Jake's house. She and Jennie are chattering the entire way, excited to be done with high school, to start the next phase of our lives.

I would normally join in the conversation, but I'm too disturbed by seeing Julian, so I just sit there quietly. For some reason, I hadn't told Leah about meeting him in the club. I only said that I had a headache and wanted to go home.

I don't know why I can't talk to Leah about Julian. I have no problem spilling my guts about Jake. Maybe it's because it's too difficult for me to describe how Julian makes me feel. She wouldn't understand why he frightens me.

I don't really understand it myself.

At Jake's house, the party is in full swing when we arrive. I am still resolved to talk to Jake, but I'm too freaked out from seeing Julian earlier. I decide that I need some liquid courage.

Leaving the girls, I walk over to the keg and pour myself a cup of punch. Sniffing it, I determine that it definitely has alcohol, and I drink the full cup.

Almost immediately, I start to feel buzzed. As I had discovered in the past few years, my alcohol tolerance is virtually nonexistent. One drink is just about my limit.

I see Jake walking to the kitchen, and I follow him there.

He's cleaning up, throwing away some extra cups and dirty paper plates.

"Do you want some help with that?" I ask.

He smiles, his brown eyes crinkling at the corners. "Oh, sure, thanks. That would be awesome." His sun-streaked hair is a little long and flops over his forehead, making him look particularly cute.

I melt a little inside. He's so handsome. Not in the disturbing Julian way, but in a pleasantly comfortable sense. Jake is tall and muscular, but he's not all that big for a quarterback. Not big enough to play ball in college, or at least that's what Jennie once told me.

I help him clean up, brushing some chip crumbs off the counter and wiping up the punch that had spilled on the floor. The entire time, my heart is beating faster from excitement.

"Nora, right?" Jake says, looking at me.

He knows my name!

I give him a huge grin. "That's right."

"That's really awesome of you to help, Nora," he says sincerely. "I like throwing parties, but the cleaning is always a bitch the next day. So now I try to clean a little during, before it gets really nasty."

My grin widens further, and I nod. "Of course."

That makes total sense to me. I love the fact that he seems so nice and thoughtful, so much more than just a jock.

We start chatting. He tells me about his plans for next year. Unlike me, he's going away to college. I tell him I'm planning to stay local for the next two years to save money. Afterwards, I want to transfer to a real university.

He nods approvingly and says that it's smart. He'd thought about doing something like that, but he was lucky enough to get a full-ride scholarship to the University of Michigan.

I smile and congratulate him. On the inside, I'm jumping up and down in joy.

We're clicking. We're really clicking! He likes me, I can tell. Oh, why hadn't I approached him before?

We talk for about twenty minutes before someone comes into the kitchen looking for Jake.

"Hey, Nora," Jake says before he goes back to the party, "are you doing anything tomorrow?"

I shake my head, holding my breath.

"How about we go see a movie?" Jake suggests. "Maybe grab dinner at that little seafood place?"

I grin and nod like an idiot. I'm too afraid to say something stupid, so I keep my mouth shut.

"Great," Jake says, grinning back at me. "Then I'll pick you up at six."

He goes back to being the party host, and I rejoin the girls. We stay for another couple of hours, but I don't talk to Jake again. He's surrounded by his jock friends, and I don't want to interrupt.

But every now and then, I catch him looking my way and smiling.

I'm floating on air for the next twenty-four hours. I tell Leah and Jennie all about what happened. They're excited for me.

In preparation for our date, I put on a cute blue dress

and a pair of high-heeled brown boots. They're a cross between cowboy boots and something a bit dressier, and I know I look good in them.

Jake picks me up at six o'clock sharp.

We go to Fish-of-the-Sea, a popular local joint not too far from the movie theater. It's a nice sit-down place, not too formal.

Perfect for a first date.

We have a great time. I learn more about Jake and his family. He asks me questions too, and we discover that we like the same types of movies. I can't stand chick flicks for some reason, and I really enjoy cheesy end-of-the-world stories with lots of special effects. So does Jake, apparently.

After dinner, we go see a movie. Unfortunately, it's not about an apocalypse, but it's still a pretty good action film. During the movie, Jake puts his arm around my shoulders, and I can barely suppress my excitement. I hope he kisses me tonight.

When the movie is done, we go for a walk in the park. It's late, but I feel completely safe. The crime rate in our town is negligible, and there are plenty of streetlights.

We're walking and Jake is holding my hand. We're discussing the movie. Then he stops and just looks at me.

I know what he wants. It's what I want, too.

I look up at him and smile. He smiles back, puts his hands on my shoulders, and leans down to kiss me.

His lips feel soft, and his breath smells like the minty

gum he was chewing earlier. His kiss is gentle and pleasant, everything I hoped it would be.

Then, in a blink of an eye, everything changes.

I don't even know what happened or how it happened. One minute, I'm kissing Jake, and the next, he's lying on the ground, unconscious. A large figure is looming over him.

I open my mouth to scream, but I can't get more than a peep out before a big hand covers my mouth and nose.

I feel a sharp prick on the side of my neck, and my world goes completely dark.

3

I wake up with a pounding headache and queasy stomach. It's dark, and I can't see a thing.

For a second, I can't remember what happened. Did I have too much to drink at a party? Then my mind clears, and the events of last night come rushing in. I remember the kiss and then... Jake! Oh dear God, what happened to Jake?

What happened to me?

I'm so terrified that I just lie there, shaking.

I am lying on something comfortable. A bed with a good mattress, most likely. I'm covered by a blanket, but I can't feel any clothes on my body, just the softness of cotton sheets against my skin. I touch myself and confirm that I'm right: I'm completely naked.

My shaking intensifies.

I use one hand to check between my legs. To my huge relief, everything feels the same. No wetness, no soreness, no indication that I've been violated in any way.

For now, at least.

Tears burn my eyes, but I don't let them fall. Crying wouldn't help my situation now. I need to figure out what's going on. Are they planning to kill me? Rape me? Rape me and then kill me? If it's ransom they're after, then I'm as good as dead. After my dad got laid off during the recession, my parents can barely pay their mortgage as is.

I hold back hysteria with effort. I don't want to start screaming. That would attract their attention.

Instead I just lie there in the dark, every horrifying story I've seen on the news running through my mind. I think of Jake and his warm smile. I think of my parents and how devastated they'll be when the police tell them I'm missing. I think of all my plans, and how I will probably never get a chance to attend a real university.

And then I start to get angry. Why did they do this? Who are they, anyway? I assume it's 'they' instead of 'he' because I remember seeing a dark figure looming over Jake's body. Someone else must've grabbed me from the back.

The anger helps hold back the panic. I'm able to think a little. I still can't see anything in the dark, but I can feel.

Moving quietly, I carefully start exploring my surroundings.

First, I determine that I'm indeed lying on a bed. A big bed, probably king-sized. There are pillows and a blanket, and the sheets are soft and pleasant to the touch. Likely expensive.

For some reason, that scares me even more. These are criminals with money.

Crawling to the edge of the bed, I sit up, holding the blanket tightly around me. My bare feet touch the floor. It's smooth and cold to the touch, like hardwood.

I wrap the blanket around me and stand up, ready to do further exploration.

At that moment, I hear the door opening.

A soft light comes on. Even though it's not bright, I'm blinded for a minute. I blink a few times, and my eyes adjust.

And I see him.

Julian.

He stands in the doorway like a dark angel. His hair curls a little around his face, softening the hard perfection of his features. His eyes are trained on my face, and his lips are curved in a slight smile.

He's stunning.

And utterly terrifying.

My instincts had been right—this man is capable of anything.

"Hello, Nora," he says softly, entering the room.

I cast a desperate glance around me. I see nothing that could serve as a weapon.

My mouth is dry like the desert. I can't even gather enough saliva to talk. So I just watch him stalk toward me like a hungry tiger approaches its prey.

I am going to fight if he touches me.

He comes closer, and I take a step back. Then another and another, until I'm pressed against the wall. I'm still huddling in the blanket.

He lifts his hand, and I tense, preparing to defend myself.

But he's merely holding a bottle of water and offering it to me.

"Here," he says. "I figured you must be thirsty."

I stare at him. I'm dying of thirst, but I don't want him to drug me again.

He seems to understand my hesitation. "Don't worry, my pet. It's just water. I want you awake and conscious."

I don't know how to react to that. My heart is hammering in my throat, and I feel sick with fear.

He stands there, patiently watching. Holding the blanket tightly with one hand, I give in to my thirst and take the water from him. My hand shakes, and my fingers brush against his in the process. A wave of heat rolls through me, a strange reaction that I ignore.

Now I have to unscrew the cap—which means I have to let go of the blanket. He's observing my dilemma with interest and no small measure of amusement. Thankfully, he's not touching me. He's standing less than two feet away and simply watching me.

I press my arms tightly against my body, holding the blanket that way, and unscrew the cap. Then I hold the blanket with one hand and lift the bottle to my lips to drink.

The cool liquid feels amazing on my parched lips and tongue. I drink until the entire bottle is gone. I can't remember the last time water tasted so good. Dry mouth must be the side effect of whatever drug he used to get me here.

Now I can talk again, so I ask him, "Why?"

To my huge surprise, my voice sounds almost normal.

He lifts his hand and touches my face again. Just like he did at the club. And again, I stand there helplessly and let him. His fingers are gentle on my skin, his touch almost tender. It's such a stark contrast to the whole situation that I'm disoriented for a moment.

"Because I didn't like seeing you with him," Julian says, and I can hear the barely suppressed rage in his voice. "Because he touched you, laid his hands on you."

I can barely think. "Who?" I whisper, trying to figure out what he's talking about. And then it hits me. "Jake?"

"Yes, Nora," he says darkly. "Jake."

"Is he—" I don't know if I can even say it out loud. "Is he... alive?"

"For now," Julian says, his eyes burning into mine. "He's in the hospital with a mild concussion."

I'm so relieved I slump against the wall. And then the full meaning of his words hits me. "What do you mean, for now?"

Julian shrugs. "His health and wellbeing are entirely dependent on you."

I swallow to moisten my still-dry throat. "On me?"

His fingers caress my face again, push the hair back behind my ear. I'm so cold I feel like his touch is burning my skin. "Yes, my pet, on you. If you behave, he'll be fine. If not…"

I can barely draw in a breath. "If not?"

Julian smiles. "He'll be dead within a week."

His smile is the most beautiful and frightening thing I've ever seen.

"Who are you?" I whisper. "What do you want from me?"

He doesn't answer. Instead, he touches my hair, lifts a thick brown strand to his face. Inhales, as though smelling it.

I watch him, frozen in place. I don't know what to do. Do I fight him now? And if so, what would that accomplish? He hasn't hurt me yet, and I don't want to provoke him. He's much larger than me, much stronger. I can see the thickness of his muscles under the black T-shirt he's wearing. Without my heels on, I barely come up to his shoulder.

While I contemplate the merits of fighting someone who probably outweighs me by a hundred pounds, he makes the decision for me. His hand leaves my hair and tugs at the blanket I'm holding so tightly.

I don't let go. If anything, I clutch it harder. And I do something embarrassing.

I beg.

"Please," I say desperately, "please, don't do this."

He smiles again. "Why not?" His hand is continuing to pull at the blanket, slowly and inexorably. I know he's doing it this way to prolong the torture. He could easily rip the blanket away from me with one strong tug.

"I don't want this," I tell him. I can barely draw in air through the constriction in my chest, and my voice comes out sounding unexpectedly breathy.

He looks amused, but there's a dark gleam in his eyes. "No? You think I couldn't feel your reaction to me in the club?"

I shake my head. "There was no reaction. You're wrong..." My voice is thick with unshed tears. "I only want Jake—"

In an instant, his hand is wrapped around my throat. He doesn't do anything else, doesn't squeeze, but the threat is there. I can feel the violence within him, and I'm terrified.

He leans down toward me. "You don't want that boy," he says harshly. "He can never give you what I can. Do you understand me?"

I nod, too scared to do anything else.

He releases my throat. "Good," he says in a softer tone. "Now let go of the blanket. I want to see you naked again."

Again? He must've been the one to undress me.

I try to plaster myself even closer to the wall. And still don't let go of the blanket.

He sighs.

Two seconds later, the blanket is on the floor. As I had suspected, I don't stand a chance when he uses his full strength.

I resist the only way I can. Instead of standing there and letting him look at my naked body, I slide down the wall until I'm sitting on the floor, my knees drawn up to my chest. My arms wrap around my legs, and I sit there like that, trembling all over. My long, thick hair streams down my back and arms, partially covering me.

I hide my face against my knees. I'm terrified of what he'll do to me now, and the tears burning my eyes finally escape, running down my cheeks.

"Nora," he says, and there is a steely note in his voice. "Get up. Get up right now."

I shake my head mutely, still not looking at him.

"Nora, this can be pleasurable for you or it can be painful. It's really up to you."

Pleasurable? Is he insane? My entire body is shaking with sobs at this point.

"Nora," he says again, and I hear the impatience in his voice. "You have exactly five seconds to do what I'm telling you."

He waits, and I can almost hear him counting in his head. I'm counting too, and when I get to four, I get up, tears still streaming down my face.

I'm ashamed of my own cowardice, but I'm so afraid of pain. I don't want him to hurt me.

I don't want him to touch me at all, but that is clearly not an option.

"Good girl," he says softly, touching my face again, brushing my hair back over my shoulders.

I tremble at his touch. I can't look at him, so I keep my eyes down.

He apparently objects to that, because he tilts my chin up until I have no choice but to meet his gaze with my own.

His eyes are dark blue in this light. He's so close to me that I can feel the heat coming off his body. It feels good because I'm cold. Naked and cold.

Suddenly, he reaches for me, bending down. Before I can get really scared, he slides one arm around my back and another under my knees.

Then he lifts me effortlessly in his arms and carries me to the bed.

He puts me down, almost gently, and I curl into a ball, shaking. He starts to undress, and I can't help watching him.

He's wearing jeans and a T-shirt, and the T-shirt comes off first.

His upper body is a work of art, all broad shoulders, hard muscles, and smooth tan skin. His chest is lightly dusted with dark hair. Under some other circumstances, I would've been thrilled to have such a good-looking lover.

Under these circumstances, I just want to scream.

His jeans are next. I can hear the sound of his zipper being lowered, and it galvanizes me into action.

In a second, I go from lying on the bed to scrambling for the door—which he'd left open.

I may be small, but I'm fast on my feet. I did track for ten years and was quite good at it. Unfortunately, I hurt my knee during one of the races, and now I'm limited to more leisurely runs and other forms of exercise.

I make it out the door, down the stairs, and I'm almost to the front door when he catches me.

His arms close around me from behind, and he squeezes me so hard that I can't breathe for a moment. My arms are completely restrained, so I can't even fight him. He lifts me, and I kick back at him with my heels. I manage to land a few kicks before he turns me around to face him.

I'm sure he's going to hurt me now, and I brace myself for a blow.

Instead, he just pulls me into his embrace and holds me tightly. My face is buried in his chest, and my naked body is pressed against his. I can smell the clean, musky scent of his skin and feel something hard and warm against my stomach.

His erection.

He's fully naked and turned on.

With the way he's holding me, I'm almost completely helpless. I can neither kick nor scratch him.

But I can bite.

So I sink my teeth into his pectoral muscle and hear him curse before he yanks on my hair, forcing me to release his flesh.

Then he holds me like that, one arm wrapped around my waist, my lower body tightly pressed against him. His other hand is fisted in my hair, holding my head arched back. My hands are pushing at his chest in a futile attempt to put some distance between us.

I meet his gaze defiantly, ignoring the tears running

down my face. I have no choice but to be brave now. If I die, I want to at least retain some dignity.

His expression is dark and angry, his blue eyes narrowed at me.

I am breathing hard, and my heart is beating so fast I feel like it might jump out of my chest. We look at each other—predator and prey, the conqueror and the conquered—and in that moment, I feel an odd sort of connection to him. Like a part of myself is forever altered by what's happening between us.

Suddenly, his face softens. A smile appears on his sensuous lips.

Then he leans toward me, lowers his head, and presses his mouth to mine.

I am stunned. His lips are gentle, tender as they explore mine, even as he holds me with an iron grip.

He's a skilled kisser. I've kissed quite a few guys, and I've never felt anything like this. His breath is warm, flavored with something sweet, and his tongue teases my lips until they part involuntarily, granting him access to my mouth.

I don't know if it's the aftereffects of the drug he gave me or the simple relief that he's not hurting me, but I melt at that kiss. A strange languor spreads through my body, sapping my will to fight.

He kisses me slowly, leisurely, as though he has all the time in the world. His tongue strokes against mine, and he lightly sucks on my lower lip, sending a surge of liquid heat straight to my core. His hand eases its grip on my hair and cradles the back of my head instead. It's almost like he's making love to me.

I find my hands holding on to his shoulders. I have no idea how they got there, but I'm now clinging to him instead of pushing him away. I don't understand my own reaction. Why am I not cringing away from his kiss in disgust?

It just feels so good, that incredible mouth of his. It's like kissing an angel. It makes me forget the situation for a second, enables me to push the terror away.

He pulls away and looks down on me. His lips are wet and shiny, a little swollen from our kiss. Mine probably are too.

He no longer seems angry. Instead, he looks hungry and pleased at the same time. I can see both lust and tenderness on his perfect face, and I can't tear my eyes away.

I lick my lips, and his eyes drop down to my mouth for a second. He kisses me again, just a brief brush of his lips against mine.

Then he picks me up again and carries me upstairs to his bed.

4

When I look back on this day, my behavior doesn't make sense to me. I don't understand why I didn't fight him harder, why I consented in this twisted way. It wasn't a rational decision on my part —it wasn't a conscious choice to cooperate in order to avoid pain.

No, I am acting purely on instinct.

And my instinct is to submit to him.

He puts me down on the bed, and I just lie there. I'm too worn out from our earlier struggle, and I still feel woozy from the drug.

There is something so surreal about what's happening that my mind can't process it fully. I feel like I'm watching a play or a movie. It can't possibly be me in this situation. I can't be this girl who was drugged and kidnapped, and who is letting her kidnapper touch her, stroke her all over her body.

We're lying on our sides, facing each other. I can feel

his hands on my skin. They're slightly rough, callused. Warm on my frozen flesh. Strong, though he's not using that strength right now. He could subdue me with ease, like he did before, but there is no need. I'm not fighting him. I'm floating in a hazy, sensual fog.

He's kissing me again, and caressing my arm, my back, my neck, my outer thigh. His touch is gentle, yet firm. It's almost like he's giving me a massage, except I can feel the sexual intent in his actions.

He kisses my neck, lightly nibbling on the sensitive spot where my neck and shoulder join, and I shiver from the pleasurable sensation.

I close my eyes. It's disarming, that surprising gentleness of his. I know I should feel violated, but instead, I feel oddly cherished.

With my eyes closed, I pretend that this is just a dream. A dark fantasy, like the kind I sometimes have late at night. It makes it more palatable, the fact that I'm letting this stranger do this to me.

One of his hands is now on my buttocks, kneading the soft flesh. His other hand is traveling up my belly, my rib cage. He reaches my breasts and cups the left one in his palm, squeezes it lightly. My nipples are already hard, and his touch feels good, almost soothing. Rob has done this to me before, but it's never been like this. It's never felt like this.

I continue to keep my eyes shut as he rolls me onto my back. He's partially on top of me, but most of his weight is resting on the bed. He doesn't want to crush me, I realize, and I feel grateful.

He kisses my collarbone, my shoulder, my stomach. His mouth is hot, and it leaves a moist trail on my skin.

Then he closes his lips around my right nipple and sucks on it. My body arches, and I feel tension low in my belly. He repeats the action with my other nipple, and the tension inside me grows, intensifies.

He senses it. I know he does because his hand ventures between my thighs and feels the moisture there. "Good girl," he murmurs, stroking my folds. "So sweet, so responsive."

I whimper as his lips travel down my body, his hair tickling my skin. I know what he intends, and my mind blanks out when he reaches his destination.

For a second, I try to resist, but he effortlessly pulls my legs apart. His fingers pat me gently, then pull apart my nether lips.

And then he kisses me there, sending a surge of heat through my body. His skilled mouth licks and nibbles around my clitoris until I'm moaning, and then he closes his lips around it and lightly sucks.

The pleasure is so strong, so startling that my eyes fly open.

I don't understand what's happening to me, and it's frightening. I'm burning inside, throbbing between my legs. My heart is beating so fast I can't catch my breath, and I find myself panting.

I start struggling, and he laughs softly. I can feel the puffs of air from his breath on my sensitive flesh. He easily holds me down and continues what he's doing.

The tension inside me is becoming unbearable. I'm

squirming against his tongue, and my motions seem to be bringing me closer to some elusive edge.

Then I go over with a soft scream. My entire body tightens, and I'm swamped by a wave of pleasure so intense that my toes curl. I can feel my inner muscles pulsing, and I realize that I just had an orgasm.

The first orgasm of my life.

And it was at the hands—or rather the mouth—of my captor.

I'm so devastated that I just want to curl up and cry. I squeeze my eyes shut again.

But he's not done with me yet. He crawls up my body and kisses my mouth again. He tastes differently now, salty, with a slightly musky undertone. It's from me, I realize. I'm tasting myself on his lips. A hot wave of embarrassment rolls through my body even as the hunger inside me intensifies.

His kiss is more carnal than before, rougher. His tongue penetrates my mouth in an obvious imitation of the sexual act, and his hips settle heavily between my legs. One of his hands is holding the back of my head, while another one is between my thighs, lightly rubbing and stimulating me again.

I still don't really resist, although my body tenses as the fear returns. I can feel the heat and hardness of his erection pushing against my inner thigh, and I know he's going to hurt me.

"Please," I whisper, opening my eyes to look at him. My vision is blurred by tears. "Please… I've never done this before—"

His nostrils flare, and his eyes gleam brighter. "I'm glad," he says softly. Lowering his head, he kisses me again before shifting his mouth to my ear. "Now tell me you want me," he murmurs, his warm breath wafting over my neck before he lifts his head to stare down at me.

Breathing shallowly, I hold his gaze, shaken by the strange compulsion to obey.

"Tell me, Nora," he repeats, his tone turning darker, more commanding, and to my shock, my mouth forms the words.

"I—I want you."

He smiles. "Good girl." Then he shifts his hips a little and uses his hand to guide his shaft toward my opening.

I gasp as he begins to push inside. I'm wet, but my body resists the unfamiliar intrusion. I don't know how big he is, but he feels enormous as the head of his cock slowly enters my body.

It begins to hurt, to burn, and I cry out, clutching at his shoulders.

His pupils expand, making his eyes look darker. There are beads of sweat on his forehead, and I realize he's actually restraining himself. "Relax, Nora," he whispers harshly. "It will hurt less if you relax."

I'm trembling. I can't follow his advice because I'm too nervous—and because it hurts so much, having even a little bit of him inside me.

He continues to press, and my flesh slowly gives way, reluctantly stretching for him. I'm writhing now, sobbing, my nails scratching at his back, but he's relentless, working his cock in inch by slow inch.

Then he pauses for a second, and I can see a vein pulsing near his temple. He looks like he's in pain. But I know that it's pleasurable for him, this act that's hurting me so much.

He lowers his head, kissing my forehead. And then he pushes past my virginal barrier, tearing through the thin membrane with one firm thrust. He doesn't stop until his full length is buried inside me, his pubic hair pressing against my own.

I almost black out from the pain. My stomach twists with nausea, and I feel faint. I can't even scream; all I can do is try to take small, shallow breaths to avoid passing out. I can feel his hardness lodged deep inside me, and it's the most agonizingly invasive thing I've ever experienced.

"Relax," he murmurs in my ear, "just relax, my pet. The pain will pass, it will get better…"

I don't believe him. It feels like a heated pole has been shoved inside my body, tearing me open. And I can't do anything to escape, to make it hurt less. He's so much larger than me, so much stronger. All I can do is lie there helplessly, pinned underneath him.

He doesn't move his hips, doesn't thrust, even though I can feel the tension in his muscles. Instead, he gently kisses my forehead again. I close my eyes, bitter tears streaming down my temples, and feel the light brush of his lips against my eyelids.

I don't know how long we stay there like this. He's raining soft kisses on my face, my neck. His hands embrace me, caress my skin in a parody of a lover's touch. And all the while, his cock is buried deep inside me, its uncompromising hardness hurting me, burning me from within.

I don't know at what point the pain starts to change. My treacherous body slowly softens, begins to respond to his kisses, to the tenderness in his touch.

The evil bastard senses it. And he slowly begins to move, partially withdrawing from my body and then working himself back in.

Initially, his movements make it worse, only adding to my agony. And then he reaches between our bodies with one hand, and uses one finger to press against my clit, keeping the pressure light and steady. His thrusts move my hips, causing me to rub against his finger in a rhythmic way.

To my horror, I feel the tension gathering inside me again. The pain is still there, but so is the pleasure. I'm writhing in his arms, but now I'm fighting myself as well. His thrusts get harder, deeper, and I'm screaming from the unbearable intensity. The pain and the pleasure mix, until they're indistinguishable from one another—until I exist in a world of pure, overwhelming sensation. And then I explode, the orgasm ripping through my body with such force that my vision darkens for a moment.

Suddenly, I can hear him groaning against my ear and feel him getting even thicker and longer inside me.

His cock is pulsing and jerking deep within me, and I know that he found his release as well.

In the aftermath, he rolls off me and gathers me to him, holding me close.

And I cry in his arms, seeking solace from the very person who is the cause of my tears.

Afterwards, my mind is foggy, my thoughts strangely jumbled. He carries me somewhere, and I lie limply in his arms, like a rag doll.

Now he's washing me. I'm standing in the shower with him. I'm vaguely surprised that my legs can hold me upright.

I feel numb, detached somehow.

There is blood on my thighs. I can see it mixing with the water, running down the drain. Also, there's something sticky between my legs. His semen, most likely. He hadn't used protection.

I might now have an STD. I should be horrified by the thought, but I just feel numb. At least pregnancy isn't something I have to be concerned about. As soon as I got serious with Rob, my mom insisted on taking me to the doctor to get a birth control implant in my arm. As a nursing assistant at a nonprofit women's clinic, she saw far too many teenage pregnancies and wanted to make sure the same thing didn't happen to me.

I'm so grateful to her right now.

While I'm pondering all this, Julian washes me thoroughly, shampooing and conditioning my hair. He even shaves my legs and armpits.

Once I'm squeaky clean and smooth, he shuts off the water and guides me out of the shower.

He dries me with a towel first and then himself. Afterwards, he wraps me in a fluffy robe and carries me to the kitchen to feed me.

I eat what he puts in front of me. I don't even taste it. It's a sandwich of some kind, but I don't know what's in it. He also gives me a glass of water, which I gulp down eagerly.

I vaguely hope that he's not drugging me, but I don't really care if he is. I'm so tired I just want to pass out.

After I'm done eating and drinking, he leads me back to the bathroom.

"Go ahead, brush your teeth," he says, and I stare at him. He cares about my oral hygiene?

I do want to brush my teeth, though, so I do as he says. I also use the restroom to pee. He considerately leaves me alone for that.

Then he takes me back to the room. Somehow the bed now has fresh sheets on it, with no traces of blood anywhere. I'm thankful for that.

He kisses me lightly on the lips, leaves the room, and locks the door.

I'm so exhausted that I walk over to the bed, lie down, and instantly fall asleep.

---

5

*W*hen I wake up, my mind is completely clear. I remember everything, and I want to scream.

I jump out of bed, noticing that I'm still wearing the robe from last night. The sudden movement makes me aware of a deep inner soreness, and my lower body tightens at the memory of how I got to be that sore. I can still feel his fullness inside me, and I shudder at the recollection.

I am sickened and disgusted with myself. What is wrong with me? How could I have let Julian have sex with me and told him that I want him? How could I have consented and found pleasure in his embrace?

Yes, he's good-looking, but that's no excuse. He's evil. I know it. I sensed it from the very beginning. His outer beauty hides a darkness inside.

I have a feeling he's only begun to reveal his true nature to me.

Yesterday I had been too frightened, too traumatized to pay attention to my surroundings. I'm feeling much better today, so I carefully study this room.

There is a window. It's covered by thick ivory shades, but I can still see a little sunlight peeking through.

I rush to it, pulling open the shades, and blink at the sudden bright light. It takes a few seconds for my eyes to adjust, and then I look outside.

The bottom drops out of my stomach.

The window is not hermetically sealed or anything like that. In fact, it looks like I could easily open it and climb out. This room is on the second floor, so I could maybe even make it to the ground without breaking anything.

No, the window is not the problem.

It's the view outside.

I can see palm trees and a white sandy beach. Beyond it, there is a large body of water, blue and shimmering in the bright sun.

It's beautiful and tropical.

And about as different as possible from my little town in the Midwest.

I'm cold again. So cold that I'm shivering. I know it's from stress because the temperature must be somewhere in the eighties.

I'm pacing up and down the room, occasionally pausing to look out the window.

Every time I look, it's like a punch to the stomach.

I don't know what I'd been hoping. I honestly hadn't had a chance to think about my location. I'd just sort of assumed that he would keep me somewhere in the area, maybe near Chicago where we'd first met. I'd thought that all I had to do in order to escape is find a way out of this house.

Now I realize it's far more complicated than that.

I try the door again. It's locked.

A few minutes ago, I had discovered a small bathroom attached to this room. I used it to take care of my basic needs and to brush my teeth. It had been a nice distraction.

Now I'm pacing like a caged animal, growing more terrified and angry with every minute that passes.

Finally, the door opens, and a woman comes inside.

I'm so shocked that I simply stare. She's fairly young —maybe in her early thirties—and pretty.

She's holding a tray of food and smiling at me. Her hair is red and curly, and her eyes are a soft brown color. She's bigger than me, probably at least five inches taller, with an athletic build. She's dressed very casually, in a pair of jean shorts and a white tank top, with flip-flops on her feet.

I think about attacking her. She's a woman, and I have a small chance of winning against her in a fight. I have no chance against Julian.

Her smile widens, as though she's reading my mind.

"Please don't jump me," she says, and I can hear the amusement in her voice. "It's quite pointless, I promise. I know you want to escape, but there is really nowhere to go. We're on a private island in the middle of the Pacific Ocean."

The sinking feeling in my stomach worsens. "Whose private island?" I ask, though I already know the answer.

"Why, Julian's, of course."

"Who is he? Who are you people?" My voice is relatively steady as I speak to her. She doesn't make me nervous the way Julian does.

She puts down the tray. "You'll learn everything in due time. I'm here to take care of you and the property. My name is Beth, by the way."

I take a deep breath. "Why am I here, Beth?"

"You're here because Julian wants you."

"And you don't see anything wrong with that?" I can hear the hysterical edge in my tone. I don't understand how this woman is going along with that madman, how she's acting like this is normal.

She shrugs. "Julian does whatever he wants. It's not for me to judge."

"Why not?"

"Because I owe him my life," she says seriously and walks out of the room.

I eat the food Beth brought me. It's pretty good actually, even though it's not traditional breakfast food. There is grilled fish in some kind of mushroom sauce and roasted potatoes with a side of green salad. For dessert, there's some cut-up mango. Local fruit, I'm guessing.

Despite my inner turmoil, I manage to eat everything. If I were less of a coward, I would resist by refusing to eat his food—but I fear hunger as much as I fear pain.

So far he hasn't really hurt me. Well, it did hurt when he put his cock inside me, but he hadn't been purposefully rough. I suspect it would've hurt the first time regardless of the circumstances.

The first time. It suddenly dawns on me that it had been my first time. Now I'm no longer a virgin.

Strangely, I don't feel like I lost anything. The thin membrane inside me had never held any particular meaning for me. I never intended to wait until marriage or anything else like that. I regret that my first time was with a monster, but I don't mourn the loss of the 'virgin' designation. I would've gladly gone all the way with Jake, if I'd only had a chance.

Jake! My stomach lurches. I can't believe I haven't thought about him since Julian told me he was safe. The guy I've been crazy about for months had been the furthest thing from my mind when I was in the arms of my captor.

Hot shame burns inside me. Shouldn't I have been thinking of Jake last night? Shouldn't I have been picturing his face when Julian touched me so intimately? If I truly wanted Jake, shouldn't he have been the one on my mind during my first sexual encounter?

I'm suddenly filled with bitter hatred for the man who did this to me—the man who shattered my illusions about the world, about myself. I'd never thought much about what I would do if I got kidnapped, how I would react. Who thinks about stuff like that? But I guess I'd always assumed I would be brave, fighting to my last breath. Isn't that what they do in all the books and movies? Fight, even when it's useless, even when doing so means getting hurt? Shouldn't I have done that too? Yes, he's stronger than me, but I didn't have to give in so easily—and I certainly didn't have to admit I want him. He didn't tie me up; he didn't threaten me with a knife or a gun. All he'd done was chase me down when I tried to run.

That run had been the grand total of my resistance thus far.

I don't recognize this person who had given in so easily. And yet I know she's me. A part of me that had never come to light before. A part of me that I would've never known if Julian hadn't taken me.

Thinking about this is so upsetting that I focus on my captor instead. Who is he? How can someone afford to have an entire private island? How does Beth owe him her life? And, most importantly, what does he intend to do with me?

A million different scenarios run through my mind, each one more horrifying than the next. I know there's such a thing as human trafficking. It happens all the time, especially to women from poorer countries. Is that the fate that awaits me? Am I going to end up in a brothel somewhere, drugged out of my mind and used daily by dozens of men? Is Julian simply sampling the merchandise before he delivers it to its final destination?

Before panic can take over my mind, I inhale deeply and try to think logically. While the human trafficking is a possibility, it doesn't seem likely to me. For one thing, Julian appears to be very possessive of me—far too possessive for someone just testing out the merchandise. And besides, why bring me here, to his private island, if he's just planning to sell me?

My pet, he had called me. Is that just a meaningless endearment, or is that how he sees me? Does he have some fetish that involves keeping women captive? I think about it for a while, and decide that he probably does. Why else would a wealthy, good-looking man do this? Surely he has no problem getting dates the usual way. In fact, I might've gone out with him myself if I hadn't gotten that strange vibe from him in the club.

If he hadn't touched me like he owned me.

Is that his thing? Ownership? Does he want a sex slave? If so, why did he choose me? Was it because of my reaction to him at the club? Did he guess that I would be a coward, that I would let him do whatever he wanted to me? Did I somehow bring this upon myself?

The thought is so sickening that I push it away and get up, determined to explore my prison further.

The door is still locked, which doesn't surprise me. I'm able to open the window, and warm, ocean-scented air fills the room.

I can't open the screen on the window, though. I would need to do that in order to climb out. I don't try too hard. If Beth is to be believed, escaping from this room wouldn't help me at all.

I look for something that could be used as a weapon. There's no knife, but there's a fork left over from my meal. Beth would probably notice if I hide it. Still, I take a chance and do it, concealing the utensil behind a stack of books on a tall bookshelf that lines one of the walls.

Next I explore the bathroom, hoping to find a bottle of hairspray or something else along those lines. But there's only soap, toothbrush, and toothpaste. In the shower stall, I find body wash, shampoo, and conditioner—all nice, expensive brands. My captor is clearly not stingy.

Then again, anyone who owns a private island can probably afford a fifty-dollar shampoo. He might even be able to afford a thousand-dollar shampoo, if such a thing exists.

The fact that I'm thinking about shampoo amazes me. Shouldn't I be screaming and crying? Oh, wait, I did that yesterday. I guess there's only so much crying a person can do. I seem to be all out of tears, at least for now.

After exploring every nook and cranny of the room, I get bored, so I take one of the books from the bookshelf. A Sidney Sheldon novel, something about a woman betrayed who seeks revenge on her enemies.

It's engrossing enough that I'm able to mentally escape my prison for the next couple of hours.

Beth comes and brings me lunch. She also brings me some clothes, folded in a stack.

I'm glad. I've been wearing the bathrobe all morning, and I would like to dress normally.

When she puts the clothes on the dresser, I again think about tackling her and trying to escape. Maybe using the fork I've got stashed away.

"Nora, give me the fork," she says.

I jump a little and give her a startled look. Could she actually be a mind-reader?

And then I realize that she's simply looking at the empty tray and noticing that the utensil is missing.

I decide to play dumb. "What fork?"

She lets out a sigh. "You know what fork. The one you hid behind the books. Give it to me."

Another one of my assumptions proven wrong. I don't know why I'd thought I had any privacy.

I look up at the ceiling, studying it carefully, but I can't see where the cameras are.

"Nora..." Beth prompts.

I retrieve the fork and throw it at her. I think I'm secretly hoping it spears her in the eye.

But Beth catches it and shakes her head at me, as though disappointed in my behavior. "I was hoping you wouldn't act this way," she says.

"Act what way? Like a victim of kidnapping?" I really, really want to hit her right now.

"Like a spoiled brat," she clarifies, putting the fork in

her pocket. "You think it's so awful, being here on this beautiful island? You think you're suffering by being in Julian's bed?"

I stare at her like she's a lunatic. Does she honestly expect me to be okay with this situation? To meekly go along with this and never utter a word of protest?

She stares back at me, and for the first time, I notice some lines on her face. "You don't know the real meaning of suffering, little girl," she says softly, "and I hope you never find out. Be nice to Julian, and you just might be able to continue living a charmed life."

She leaves the room, and I swallow to get rid of the sudden dryness in my throat.

For some reason, her words make my hands shake.

6

*I*t's evening now. With every minute that passes, I'm starting to get more and more anxious at the thought of seeing my captor again.

The novel that I've been reading can no longer hold my interest. I put it down and walk in circles around the room.

I am dressed in the clothes Beth had given me earlier. It's not what I would've chosen to wear, but it's better than a bathrobe. A sexy pair of white lacy panties and a matching bra for underwear. A pretty blue sundress that buttons in the front. Everything fits me suspiciously well. Has he been stalking me for a while? Learning everything about me, including my clothing size?

The thought makes me sick.

I am trying not to think about what's to come, but it's impossible. I don't know why I'm so sure he'll come to me tonight. It's possible he has an entire harem of women stashed away on this island, and he visits each one only once a week, like sultans used to do.

Yet somehow I know he'll be here soon. Last night had simply whetted his appetite. I know he's not done with me, not by a long shot.

Finally, the door opens.

He walks in like he owns the place. Which, of course, he does.

I am again struck by his masculine beauty. He could've been a model or a movie star, with a face like his. If there was any fairness in the world, he would've been short or had some other imperfection to offset that face.

But he doesn't. His body is tall and muscular, perfectly proportioned. I remember what it feels like to have him inside me, and I feel an unwelcome jolt of arousal.

He's again wearing jeans and a T-shirt. A gray one this time. He seems to favor simple clothing, and he's smart to do so. His looks don't need any enhancement.

He smiles at me. It's his fallen angel smile—dark and seductive at the same time. "Hello, Nora."

I don't know what to say to him, so I blurt out the first thing that pops into my head. "How long are you going to keep me here?"

He cocks his head slightly to the side. "Here in the room? Or on the island?"

"Both."

"Beth will show you around tomorrow, take you

swimming if you'd like," he says, approaching me. "You won't be locked in, unless you do something foolish."

"Such as?" I ask, my heart pounding in my chest as he stops next to me and lifts his hand to stroke my hair.

"Trying to harm Beth or yourself." His voice is soft, his gaze hypnotic as he looks down at me. The way he's touching my hair is oddly relaxing.

I blink, trying to break his spell. "And what about on the island? How long will you keep me here?"

His hand caresses my face, curves around my cheek. I catch myself leaning into his touch, like a cat getting petted, and I immediately stiffen.

His lips curl into a knowing smile. The bastard knows the effect he has on me. "A long time, I hope," he says.

For some reason, I'm not surprised. He wouldn't have bothered bringing me all the way here if he just wanted to fuck me a few times. I'm terrified, but I'm not surprised.

I gather my courage and ask the next logical question. "Why did you kidnap me?"

The smile leaves his face. He doesn't answer, just looks at me with an inscrutable blue gaze.

I begin to shake. "Are you going to kill me?"

"No, Nora, I won't kill you."

His denial reassures me, although he could obviously be lying.

"Are you going to sell me?" I can barely get the words out. "Like to be a prostitute or something?"

"No," he says softly. "Never. You're mine and mine alone."

I feel a tiny bit calmer, but there is one more thing I have to know. "Are you going to hurt me?"

For a moment, he doesn't answer again. Something dark briefly flashes in his eyes. "Probably," he says quietly.

And then he leans down and kisses me, his warm lips soft and gentle on mine.

For a second, I stand there frozen, unresponsive. I believe him. I know he's telling the truth when he says he'll hurt me. There's something in him that scares me— that has scared me from the very beginning.

He's nothing like the boys I've gone on dates with. He's capable of anything.

And I'm completely at his mercy.

I think about trying to fight him again. That would be the normal thing to do in my situation. The brave thing to do.

And yet I don't do it.

I can feel the darkness inside him. There's something wrong with him. His outer beauty hides something monstrous underneath.

I don't want to unleash that darkness. I don't know what will happen if I do.

So I stand still in his embrace and let him kiss me. And when he picks me up again and takes me to bed, I don't try to resist in any way.

Instead, I close my eyes and give in to the sensations.

He's again gentle with me. I should be terrified of him—and I am—but my body seems to enjoy the dual sensation of fear and arousal. I don't know what that says about me.

I lie there with my eyes closed as he takes off my clothes, layer by layer. First he unbuttons the front of the dress, like he's unwrapping a present. His hands are strong and sure; there's no hint of awkwardness or hesitation in his movements. He's clearly had a lot of practice with women's clothing.

After the dress is unbuttoned, he pauses for a second. I sense his gaze on me, and I wonder what he's seeing. I know I have a good body; it's slim and toned, even though it's not as curvy as I would like.

He trails his fingers down my stomach, making me tremble. "So pretty," he says softly. "Such lovely skin. You should always wear white. It suits you."

I don't respond, just squeeze my eyes tighter. I don't want him looking at me, don't want him enjoying the sight of my body in the undergarments he picked out for me. I wish he would just fuck me and get it over with, instead of engaging in this twisted parody of lovemaking.

But he has no intention of making it easy for me.

His mouth follows the same path as his fingers. It feels hot and moist on my belly, and then he moves lower, to where my legs are instinctively squeezed tightly together. He doesn't seem to like that, and his hands are rough as they pull my thighs apart, his fingers digging into my tender flesh.

I whimper at the hint of violence, and try to relax my legs to avoid angering him further.

His grip eases, his hands becoming gentler. "My sweet, beautiful girl," he whispers, and I can feel his hot breath on my sensitive folds. "You know I'll make it good for you."

And then his lips are on me, and his tongue is swirling around my clit, his mouth sucking and nibbling. His hair brushes against my inner thighs, tickling me, and his hands hold my legs spread wide open. I twist and cry out, the pleasure so intense that I forget everything but the incredible heat and tension inside me.

He brings me close to the edge, but doesn't let me go over. Every time I feel my orgasm approaching, he stops or changes the rhythm, driving me crazy with frustration. I find myself pleading, begging, my body arching mindlessly toward him. When he finally lets me reach the peak, it's such a relief that my entire body spasms, shuddering and twisting from the intensity of the release.

For some reason, I start crying when it's over. Tears leak from the outer corners of my eyes and run down my temples, soaking into my hair and then the pillow. He appears to like it because he crawls up my body and kisses the wet trails on my face, then licks them.

His large hands stroke my body, rubbing my skin,

caressing me all over. It would be soothing if it weren't for the hardness of his cock prodding at my entrance.

I'm not fully healed inside, so it hurts again when he starts to push in. Even though I'm wet from the orgasm, he can't slip into me easily, not without tearing me open. Instead, he has to go slowly, working himself in gradually until I have a chance to adjust to the intrusion.

I bite my lower lip, trying to cope with the burning, too-full feeling. Would I ever be able to accept him easily? Would I ever experience pleasure without pain in his arms?

"Open your eyes," he orders in a harsh whisper.

I obey him, even though I can barely see through the veil of tears.

He's staring at me as he slowly begins to move inside me, and there's something triumphant in his gaze. The heat of his body surrounds me, his weight presses me down on the bed. He's inside me, on top of me, all around me. I can't even escape into the privacy of my mind.

And in that moment, I feel possessed by him, like he's taking more than just my body. Like he's laying claim to something deep within me, bringing out a side of me that I never knew existed.

Because in his arms, I experience something I have never felt before.

A primitive and completely irrational sense of belonging.

~

He takes me twice more during the night. By morning I'm so sore I feel raw inside—and yet I've had so many orgasms I lost count.

He leaves me at some point in the morning. I'm so exhausted I'm not even aware of his departure. I sleep deeply and dreamlessly, and when I wake up, it's already past noon.

I get up, brush my teeth, and take a shower. On my thighs, I can see dried bits of semen. He didn't use a condom this night either.

I wonder again about STDs. Does Julian care about this at all? He probably isn't worried about catching anything from me, given my lack of experience, but I'm certainly worried about getting it from him. Lifting my left arm, I peer at the tiny mark where my birth control implant was inserted. Thank God for my mom's pregnancy paranoia. If I didn't have it... I shudder at the thought.

Right after I exit the bathroom, Beth comes into my room carrying another food tray and more clothes. This time, it's more traditional breakfast food: an omelet with vegetables and cheese, a piece of toast, and fresh tropical fruit.

She's again smiling at me, apparently determined to ignore the fork incident. "Good morning," she says cheerfully.

My eyebrows rise. "And good morning to you too," I say, my voice thick with sarcasm.

At my obvious attempt to needle her, Beth's smile

widens further. "Oh, don't be such a grump. Julian said you get to leave the room today. Isn't that nice?"

It actually is nice. It would give me a chance to explore my prison a bit, to see if this place is really an island. Maybe there are other people here besides Beth —people who would be more sympathetic to my plight.

Alternatively, maybe I'll find a phone or a computer. If I could just send a text or an email to my parents, they could pass it along to the police and then I might be rescued.

At the thought of my family, my chest feels tight and my eyes burn. They must be so worried about me, wondering what happened, whether I am still alive. I'm an only child, and my mom always said she'd die if anything happened to me. I hope she didn't mean it.

I hate him.

And I hate this woman, who's smiling at me right now.

"Sure, Beth," I say, wanting to claw at her face until that smile turns into a grimace. "It's always nice to leave a small cage for a bigger one."

She rolls her eyes and sits down on a chair. "So dramatic. Just eat your food and then I'll show you around."

I think about not eating just to spite her, but I am hungry. So I eat, polishing off all the food on the tray.

"Where is Julian?" I ask between bites. I'm curious how he spends his days. So far, I've only seen him in the evenings.

"He's working," Beth explains. "He has a lot of business interests that require his attention."

"What kind of business interests?"

She shrugs. "All kinds."

"Is he a criminal?" I ask bluntly.

She laughs. "Why would you assume that?"

"Um, maybe because he kidnapped me?"

She laughs again, shaking her head as though I said something funny.

I want to hit her, but I restrain myself. I need to learn more about my surroundings before I try anything like that. I don't want to end up locked up in the room if I can avoid it. My chances of escape are much better if I have more freedom.

So I just get up and give her a cold look. "I'm ready to go."

"Then put on a swimming suit," she says, gesturing toward the clothes she had brought, "and we can go."

Before we walk out, Beth shows me the rest of the house. It's spacious and tastefully furnished. The decor is modern, with just a hint of tropical influence and subtle Asian motifs. Light hues predominate, although here and there, I see an unexpected pop of color in the form of a red vase or a bright blue dragon sculpture. There are four bedrooms—three upstairs and one downstairs. The kitchen on the first floor is particularly striking, with top-of-the-line appliances and gleaming granite countertops.

There is also one room that Beth says is Julian's office. It's on the first floor, and it's apparently off-limits to anyone but him. That's where he supposedly takes care of his business affairs. The door is closed when we walk past it.

After we're done with the house tour, Beth spends the next two hours showing me the island. And it's definitely an island—she didn't lie to me about that.

It's only about two miles across and a mile wide. According to Beth, we're somewhere in the Pacific Ocean, with the nearest populated piece of land over five hundred miles away. She emphasizes that fact a couple of times, as though she's afraid I might take it into my head to try to swim away.

I wouldn't do that. I'm not a strong enough swimmer, nor am I suicidal.

I would try to steal a boat instead.

We go up to the highest point of the island. It's a small mountain—or a large hill, depending on one's definition of these things. The view from there is amazing—all bright blue water wherever the eye can see. On one side of the island, the water is a different shade of blue, more turquoise, and Beth tells me it's a shallow cove that's great for snorkeling.

Julian's house is the only one on the island. It's sitting on one side of the mountain, a little ways back from the beach and somewhat elevated. That's the most sheltered location, Beth explains; the house is protected from both strong winds and the ocean there. It has apparently survived a number of typhoons with minimal damage.

I nod, as though I care. I have no intention of being here for the next typhoon. The desire to escape burns brightly within me. I didn't see any phones or computers when Beth was showing me the house, but that doesn't mean they're not there. If Julian is able to work from the island, then there's definitely internet connectivity. And if they're foolish enough to let me roam this island freely, I will find a way to reach the outside world.

We end the tour at the beach near the house.

"Want to go for a swim?" Beth asks me, stripping off her shorts and T-shirt. Underneath, she's wearing a blue bikini. Her body is lean and toned. She's in such great shape that I wonder about her age. Her figure could belong to a teenager, but her face seems older.

"How old are you?" I ask straight out. I would never be so tactless under normal circumstances, but I don't care if I offend this woman. What do social conventions matter when you're being held captive by a pair of crazy people?

She smiles, not the least bit upset at my impolite question. "I'm thirty-seven," she says.

"And Julian?"

"He's twenty-nine."

"Are you two lovers?" I don't know what makes me ask this. If she's in any way jealous of my position as Julian's sexual plaything, she's certainly not showing it.

Beth laughs. "No, we're not."

"Why not?" I can't believe I'm being so forward. I've been raised to always be polite and well-mannered, but there's something liberating about not caring what people think. I have always been a people-pleaser, but I don't want to please this woman in any way.

She stops laughing and gives me a serious look. "Because I'm not what Julian needs or wants."

"And what is that?"

"You'll learn someday," she says mysteriously, then walks into the water.

I stare after her, curiosity eating at me, but she appears to be done talking. Instead, she dives in and starts swimming with a sure athletic stroke.

It's hot outside, and the sun is beaming down on me. The sand is white and looks soft, and the water is sparkling, tempting me with its coolness. I want to hate this place, to despise everything about my captivity, but I have to admit that the island is beautiful.

I don't have to go swimming if I don't want to. It doesn't seem like Beth is going to force me. And it seems wrong to enjoy myself at the beach while my family is undoubtedly worried sick about me, grieving about my disappearance.

But the lure of the water is strong. I've always loved the ocean, even though I've been to the tropics only a couple of times in my life. This island is my idea of paradise, despite the fact that it belongs to a snake.

I deliberate for a minute, then I take off my dress and kick off my sandals. I could deny myself this small pleasure, but I'm too pragmatic. I have no illusions about my status here. At any moment, Julian and Beth could lock me up, starve me, beat me. Just because I've been treated relatively well so far doesn't mean it will continue to be that way. In my precarious situation, every moment of joy is precious—because I don't know what the future holds for me, whether I will ever again experience anything resembling happiness.

So I join my enemy in the ocean, letting the water wash away my fear and cool the helpless anger burning in the pit of my stomach.

We swim, then lounge on the hot sand, and then swim again. I don't ask any more questions, and Beth seems content with the silence.

We stay on the beach for the next two hours and then finally head back to the house.

---

7

*T*his time, Julian is supposed to join me for dinner. Beth sets a table for us downstairs and prepares a meal of local fish, rice, beans, and plantains. It's her Caribbean recipe, she tells me proudly.

"Are you having dinner with us?" I ask, watching as she carries the plates over to the table.

I'm showered and dressed in the clothes Beth provided for me. It's another white lacy bra-and-panties set and a yellow dress with white flowers on it. On my feet, I'm wearing white high-heeled sandals. The outfit is sweet and feminine, very different from the jeans and dark tops I normally wear. It makes me look like a pretty doll.

I still can't believe they're letting me walk around the house freely. There are knives in the kitchen. I could steal one and use it on Beth at any point. I'm tempted, even though my stomach churns at the thought of blood and violence.

Perhaps I'll do it soon, once I've had a chance to learn a bit more about this place.

I'm learning something interesting about myself. I apparently don't believe in grand, but pointless gestures. A cool, rational voice inside me tells me that I need a plan, a way to get off the island before I try anything. Attacking Beth right now would be stupid. It could result in my being locked up or worse.

No, this is much better. Let them think I'm harmless. I stand a much greater chance of escape that way.

For the past hour, I've been sitting in the kitchen, watching Beth prepare food. She's very good, very efficient. Spending time with her is distracting me from thoughts of Julian and the night to come.

"No," she says, answering my question. "I'll be in my room. Julian wants some alone time with you."

"Why? Does he think we're dating or something?"

She grins. "Julian doesn't date."

"No kidding." My tone is beyond sarcastic. "Why date when you can kidnap and use force instead?"

"Don't be ridiculous," Beth says sharply. "Do you really think he has to force women? Even you can't be that naive."

I stare at her. "You mean to tell me he doesn't make a habit of stealing women and bringing them here?"

Beth shakes her head. "You're the only person besides me who has ever been here. This island is Julian's private sanctuary. Nobody knows it even exists."

A chill runs down my spine at those words. "So why

am I so lucky?" I ask slowly, my pulse picking up. "What makes me worthy of this great honor?"

She smiles. "You'll find out someday. Julian will tell you when he wants you to know."

I'm sick of all this 'someday' bullshit, but I know she's too loyal to my captor to tell me anything. So I try to learn something else instead. "What did you mean when you said you owe him your life?"

Her smile fades and her expression hardens, her face settling into harsh, bitter lines. "That's none of your business, little girl."

And for the next ten minutes while she's finishing setting the table, she doesn't speak to me at all.

After everything is ready, she leaves me alone in the dining room to wait for Julian. I'm both nervous and excited. For the first time, I'm going to have a chance to interact with my captor outside the bedroom.

I have to admit to a kind of sick fascination with him. He frightens me, yet I'm unbearably curious about him. Who is he? What does he want from me? Why did he choose me to be his victim?

A minute later, he walks into the room. I'm sitting at the table, looking out the window. Before I even see him, I feel his presence. The atmosphere turns electric, heavy with expectation.

I turn my head, watching him approach. This time, he's wearing a soft-looking gray polo shirt and a pair of white khaki pants. We could be having dinner at a country club.

My heart is beating rapidly in my chest, and I can feel blood rushing through my veins. I'm suddenly much more aware of my body. My breasts feel more sensitive, my nipples tightening underneath the lacy confines of my bra. The soft fabric of the dress brushes against my bare legs, reminding me of the way he touched me there. Of the way he touched me everywhere.

Warm moisture gathers between my thighs at the memory.

He comes up to me and bends down, giving me a brief kiss on the mouth. "Hello, Nora," he says when he straightens, his beautiful lips curved in a darkly sensual smile. He's so breathtaking that I'm unable to think for a moment, my mind clouded by his nearness.

His smile widens, and he walks over to sit down across the table from me. "How was your day, my pet?" he asks, reaching for a piece of fish and putting it on his plate. His movements are confident and oddly graceful.

It's hard to believe that evil wears such a beautiful mask.

I gather my wits. "Why do you call me that?"

"Call you what? My pet?"

I nod.

"Because you remind me of a kitten," he says, his blue eyes glittering with some strange emotion. "Small, soft, and very touchable. You make me want to stroke you just to see if you will purr in my arms."

My cheeks get hot. I feel flushed all over, and I hope my skin tone hides my reaction. "I'm not an animal—"

"Of course you're not. I'm not into bestiality."

"Then what are you into?" I blurt out, then cringe internally. I don't want to make him mad. He's not Beth. He scares me.

Fortunately, he just looks amused at my daring. "At the moment," he says softly, "I'm into you."

I look away and reach for the rice, my hand shaking slightly.

"Here, let me help you with that." He takes the plate from me, his fingers briefly brushing against mine. Before I can say anything, my plate is filled with a healthy portion of everything that's on the table.

He puts the plate back in front of me, and I stare at it in dismay. I'm too nervous to eat in front of him. My stomach is all tied into knots.

When I look up, I see that he has no such problem. He's eating with gusto, clearly enjoying Beth's cooking.

"What's the matter?" he asks between bites. "You're not hungry?"

I shake my head, even though I was ravenous before he came.

He frowns, putting down his fork. "Why not? Beth said you spent the day at the beach and swam quite a bit. Shouldn't you be hungry after all that exercise?"

I shrug. "I'm okay." I'm not about to tell him that he's the cause of my lack of appetite.

His eyes narrow at me. "Are you playing games with

me? Eat, Nora. You're already slim. I don't want you to lose weight."

I gulp nervously and start to pick at the food. There's something about him that makes me think it would be unwise to oppose him on this issue.

On any issue, really.

My instincts are screaming that this man is as dangerous as they come. He hasn't really been cruel to me, but there is cruelty within him. I can sense it.

"Good girl," he says approvingly after I eat a few bites.

I continue eating, even though I don't really taste the food and I have to force each bite past the restriction in my throat. I keep my eyes trained on my plate. I have an easier time eating if I don't see his piercing blue gaze.

"So Beth tells me you had a nice day swimming," he comments after I've had a chance to eat about half of my portion.

I nod in response and look up to find him staring at me.

"What do you think of the island?" he asks, as though genuinely interested in my opinion. He's studying me with a thoughtful look on his face.

"It's pretty," I tell him honestly. Then, pausing for a second, I add, "But I don't want to be here."

"Of course." He looks almost understanding. "But you'll get used to it. This is your new home, Nora. The sooner you come to terms with that, the better."

My stomach lurches, and I feel like the food that I just ate is in danger of coming up. I swallow convulsively, trying to control the sick feeling inside me. "And my family?" The words come out low and bitter. "How are they supposed to come to terms with it?"

Some emotion flickers briefly across his face. "What if they didn't think you were dead?" he asks quietly, holding my gaze. "Would that make you feel better, my pet?"

"Of course it would!" I can hardly believe what I'm hearing. "Can you do that? Can you let them know I'm alive? Maybe I can just call them and—"

He reaches out to cover my hand with his own, stopping my hopeful rambling. "No." His tone leaves no room for arguments. "I will contact them myself."

I swallow my disappointment. "What are you going to tell them?"

"That you are alive and well." His large thumb is gently massaging the inside of my palm, his touch distracting me, turning my bones to jelly.

"But—" I almost moan when he presses on one particularly sensitive spot, "—but they wouldn't believe you—"

"They would." He withdraws his hand, leaving me feeling strangely bereft. "You can trust me on that."

Trust him? Yeah, right. "Why are you doing this to me?" I ask in frustration. "Is it because I talked to you in the club?"

He shakes his head. "No, Nora. It's because you're you. You're everything I've been looking for. Everything I've always wanted."

"You know that's crazy, right?" I'm so upset I forget to be afraid for a moment. "You don't even know me!"

"That's true," he says softly. "But I don't need to know you. I just need to know what I feel."

"Are you saying you're in love with me?" For some reason, that idea frightens me more than when I thought he just had weird sexual preferences.

He laughs, throwing his head back. I stare at him, irrationally offended. I don't want him to be in love with me, but does he have to find the idea so funny?

"Of course not," he says after he's finally done laughing. He's still grinning, though.

"Then what are you talking about?" I ask in frustration.

His smile slowly fades. "It doesn't matter, Nora," he says quietly. "All you need to know is that you're special to me."

"So why didn't you just ask me out on a date?" I'm struggling to comprehend the incomprehensible. "Why did you have to kidnap me?"

"Because you went on a date with that boy." There is sudden rage in Julian's voice, and icy terror spreads through my veins. "You kissed him when you were already mine."

I swallow. "But I didn't even know you wanted me." My voice shakes a little. "I only saw you at the club—"

"And at your graduation."

"And at my graduation," I agree, my heart hammering in my chest. "But I thought you might've been there for someone else. Like a younger brother or sister..."

He takes a deep breath, and I can see that he's much more calm now. "It doesn't matter now, Nora. I wanted you here, with me, not out there. It's much safer for you —and for that boy."

"Safer for Jake?"

Julian nods. "If you had gone out with him again, I would've killed him. It's best for everyone that you're here, away from him and others who might want you."

He's completely serious about killing Jake. It's not an idle threat. I can see it on his face.

My lips feel dry, so I lick them. His eyes follow my tongue, and I can see his breathing changing. My simple action clearly turned him on.

Suddenly, a crazy and desperate idea occurs to me. He obviously wants me. He's even willing to do things to make me happy—like letting my family know I'm alive. What if I use that fact to my advantage? I'm inexperienced, but I'm not completely naive. I know how to flirt with guys. Could I do this? Could I somehow seduce Julian into letting me go?

I'm going to have to be careful about it. I can't have a sudden about-face. I can't act like I despise him one minute and love him the next. He needs to believe that he can take me off the island and that I would willingly remain with him for as long as he wants me. That I would never look at Jake or another man again.

I'm going to have to take my time and convince Julian of my devotion.

or the rest of the dinner, I continue acting scared and intimidated. It's not really an act because I do feel that way. I'm in the presence of a man who casually talks about killing innocent people. How else am I supposed to feel?

However, I also try to be seductive. It's small things, like the way I brush my hair back while looking at him. The way I bite into a piece of papaya that Beth cut up for our dessert and lick the juice off my lips.

I know my eyes are pretty, so I look at him shyly, through half-closed eyelids. I've practiced that look in front of the mirror, and I know my eyelashes look impossibly long when I tilt my head at exactly the right angle.

I don't go overboard because he wouldn't find that believable. I just do little things that he might find arousing and appealing.

I also try to avoid any other confrontational topics.

Instead, I ask him about the island and how he came to own it.

"I came across this island five years ago," Julian explains, his lips curving into a charming smile. "My Cessna was having a mechanical problem, and I needed a place to land. Luckily, there's a flat, grassy area right on the other side, near the beach. I was able to bring down the plane without crashing it completely and make the necessary repairs. It took me a couple of days, so I got a chance to explore the island. By the time I was able to fly away, I knew this place was exactly what I wanted. So I purchased it."

I widen my eyes and look impressed. "Just like that? Isn't that expensive?"

He shrugs. "I can afford it."

"Do you come from a wealthy family?" I'm genuinely curious. My captor is a huge mystery to me. I stand a much better chance of manipulating him if I understand him at least a little bit.

His expression cools a little. "Something like that. My father had a successful business, which I took over after his death. I changed its direction and expanded it."

"What kind of business?"

Julian's mouth twists slightly. "Import-export."

"Of what?"

"Electronics and other things," he says, and I realize that he's not going to reveal more than that for now. I strongly suspect that 'other things' is a euphemism for something illegal. I don't know much about business, but I somehow doubt that selling TVs and MP3 players results in this kind of wealth.

I steer the conversation toward a more innocuous topic. "Does the rest of your family also use the island?"

His gaze goes flat and hard. "No. They're all dead."

"Oh, I'm sorry..." I don't really know what to say. What can you say that will make something like that better? Yes, he kidnapped me, but he's still a human being. I can't even imagine suffering that kind of loss.

"It's all right." His tone is unemotional, but I can sense the pain underneath. "It happened a long time ago."

I nod sympathetically. I genuinely feel bad for him, and I don't try to hide the glimmer of tears in my eyes. I'm too soft—Leah says that every time I cry at a depressing movie—and I can't help the sadness I feel at Julian's suffering.

It ends up working in my favor, because his expression warms slightly. "Don't pity me, my pet," he says softly. "I've gotten over it. Why don't you tell me about yourself instead?"

I blink at him slowly, knowing that the gesture draws attention to my eyes. "What would you like to know?" Didn't he find out everything about me in the process of stalking me?

He smiles. It makes him look so beautiful that I feel a tiny squeezing sensation in my chest. Stop it, Nora. You're the one seducing him, not the other way around.

"What do you like to read?" he asks. "What kind of movies do you like to watch?"

And for the next thirty minutes, he learns all about my enjoyment of romance novels and detective thrillers, my hatred of romantic comedies, and my love of epic movies with lots of special effects. Then he asks me about my favorite food and music, and listens attentively as I talk about my preference for eighties' bands and deep-dish pizza.

In a weird way, it's almost flattering, the way he's so utterly focused on me, hanging on to my every word. The way his blue eyes are glued to my face. It's as though he wants to really understand me, as though he truly cares. Even with Jake, I didn't get the sense that I was anything more than a pretty girl whose company he enjoyed.

With Julian, I feel like I'm the most important thing in the world to him. I feel like I truly matter.

After dinner, he leads me upstairs to his bedroom. My heart begins to pound in fear and anticipation.

Like the other two nights, I know I won't fight him. In fact, tonight I will go even further as part of my escape-by-seduction plan.

I will pretend to make love to him of my own free will.

As we walk into the room, I decide to brave a topic that has been nagging at the back of my mind. "Julian..." I ask, purposefully keeping my voice soft and uncertain. "What about protection? What if I get pregnant or something?"

He stops and turns toward me. There's a small smile on his lips. "You won't, my pet. You have that implant, don't you?"

My eyes widen in shock. "How do you know about that?" The implant is a tiny plastic rod underneath my skin, completely invisible except for a small mark where it was inserted.

"I accessed your medical history before bringing you here. I wanted to make sure you don't have any life-threatening medical conditions, like diabetes."

I stare at him. I should feel furious at this invasion of my privacy, but I feel relieved instead. It seems that my kidnapper is quite considerate—and more importantly, not trying to impregnate me.

"And you don't have to worry about any diseases," he adds, understanding my unspoken concern. "I've been recently tested, and I have always used condoms in the past."

I don't know if I believe that. "Why aren't you using them with me, then? Is it because I was a virgin?"

He nods, and there is a possessive gleam in his eyes. He lifts his hand and strokes the side of my face, making my heart beat even faster. "Yes, exactly. You're completely mine. I'm the only one who's ever been inside your pretty little pussy."

My breath catches in my throat, and I feel a gush of liquid warmth between my thighs.

I can't believe the strength of my physical response to him. Is this normal, that I get so aroused by someone

I fear and despise? Is this why Julian was drawn to me at the club? Because he sensed this about me? Because he somehow knew about my weakness?

Of course, given my plan, it's not necessarily a bad thing that he turns me on so much. It would be far worse if he disgusted me, if I couldn't bear to have him touch me.

No, this is for the best. I can be the perfect little captive, obedient and responsive, slowly falling in love with my captor.

So instead of standing stiff and scared, I give in to my desire and lean a little into his hand, as though involuntarily responding to his touch.

Something like triumph briefly flashes in his eyes, and then he lowers his head, touching his lips to mine. His strong arms wrap around me, molding me against his powerful body. He's fully aroused; I can feel the hard ridge of his erection against the softness of my belly. He's stroking my mouth with his lips, his tongue. He tastes sweet, from the papaya we just had.

Fire surges through my veins, and I close my eyes, losing myself in the overwhelming pleasure of his kiss. My hands creep up to his chest, touch it shyly. I can feel the heat of his body, smell the scent of his skin— male and musky, strangely appealing. His chest muscles flex under my fingers, and I can feel his heart beating faster.

He backs me toward the bed, and we fall on it. Somehow my hands are buried in his thick, silky hair, and I'm kissing him back, passionately, desperately. I'm not thinking about my grand seduction plan—I'm not thinking at all.

He bites my lower lip, sucks it into his mouth. His hand closes around my right breast, kneads it, squeezes the nipple through the dual barrier of the bra and the dress. His roughness is perversely arousing, even though I should be frightened by it.

I moan, and he flips me over, onto my stomach. One of his hands presses me down, pushing me into the mattress, while the other one lifts my skirt, exposing my underwear.

And then he pauses for a second, looking at my butt, lightly stroking it with his large palm. "Such curvy little cheeks," he murmurs. "So pretty in white."

His fingers reach between my legs, feel the wetness there. I can't help squirming at the light touch. I'm so turned on I just need a little bit more before I come.

He pulls down my underwear, leaving it hanging around my knees. His hand caresses my buttocks again, soothing me, arousing me. I'm trembling with anticipation.

Suddenly, I hear a loud smack and feel a sharp, stinging slap on my butt. I cry out, startled, more from the unexpected nature of the attack than from any real pain.

He pauses, rubs the area soothingly, and then does it again, slapping my right cheek with his open palm. Twenty slaps in quick succession, each one harder than the rest. It hurts; this is not a light, playful spanking.

He means to cause me pain.

Forgetting all about my resolution to play along, I begin to struggle, frightened. He holds me down easily, then transfers his attention to my other butt cheek, slapping it twenty times with equal force.

By the time he pauses, I'm sobbing into the mattress, begging him to stop. My backside feels like it's burning, throbbing in agony.

Even worse than the pain is the irrational sense of betrayal. To my horror, I realize that I had begun to trust my captor, to feel like I knew him a bit.

He'd caused me pain before, but I didn't think it was on purpose. I thought it was just because I was so new to sex. I hoped my body would adjust and there would be only pleasure in the future.

I was obviously a fool.

My entire body is shaking, and I can't stop crying. He's still holding me down, and I'm terrified of what he'll do next.

What he does next is as shocking as what he did before.

He turns me over and lifts me into his arms. Then he sits down, holding me on his lap, and rocks me back and forth. Gently, sweetly, like I'm a child that he's trying to console.

And despite everything, I bury my face against his shoulder and sob, desperately needing that illusion of tenderness, craving comfort from the one who made me hurt.

After I'm a bit more calm, he stands up and places me on my feet. My legs feel weak and shaky, and I sway a little as he carefully undresses me.

I wait for him to say something. Maybe to apologize or to explain why he hurt me. Was he punishing me? If so, I want to know what I did, so I can avoid doing it in the future.

But he doesn't speak—he simply takes off my clothes. When I'm naked, he begins to undress himself.

I watch him with a strange mixture of distress and curiosity. His body is still a mystery to me because I've kept my eyes closed for the last two nights. I haven't even seen his sex yet, even though I've felt it inside me.

So now I look at him.

His figure is magnificent. Completely male. Wide shoulders, a narrow waist, lean hips. He's powerfully muscled all over, but not in a steroid-enhanced body-builder way. Instead, he looks like a warrior. For some reason, I can easily picture him swinging a sword, cutting down his enemies. I notice a long scar on his thigh and another one on his shoulder. They only add to the warrior impression.

His skin is tan all over, with just the right amount of hair on his chest. There's more dark hair around his navel and trailing down to his groin area. His skin color makes me think he either goes around naked, or he's naturally darker, like me. Perhaps he has some Latino ancestry, too.

He's also fully aroused. I can see his cock jutting out at me. It's long and thick, similar to the ones I've seen in porn. No wonder I'm sore. I can't believe he's even able to fit inside me.

After we're both naked, he guides me to the bed. "I want you on all fours," he says quietly, giving me a light push.

My heart jumps in panic, and I resist for a second, turning to look at him instead. "Are you—" I swallow hard. "Are you going to hurt me again?"

"I haven't decided," he murmurs, lifting his hand to cup my breast. His thumb rubs my nipple, makes it harden. "I think it's probably enough for now."

Enough for now? I want to scream.

"Are you a sadist?" The question escapes me before I can think, and I freeze in place waiting for his answer.

He smiles at me. It's his beautiful Lucifer smile. "Yes, my pet," he says softly. "Sometimes I am. Now be a good girl and do as I asked. You might not like what happens otherwise…"

Before he even finishes speaking, I scramble to obey, getting on my hands and knees on the bed. Despite the warmth in the room, I'm shivering, trembling from head to toe.

Violent, gruesome images fill my mind, making me feel ill. I don't know much about S&M. Fifty Shades and a few other books of its ilk are the extent of my experience with the subject, but none of those romances depicted anything like my situation now. Even in my darkest, most secret fantasies, I've never imagined being held captive by a self-admitted sadist.

What is he going to do? Whip me? Torture me?

Chain me in a dungeon? Is there even a dungeon on this island? I picture a stone chamber filled with torture instruments, like in a movie about the Spanish Inquisition, and I want to puke. I'm sure normal BDSM is nothing like that, but there's nothing normal about my situation with Julian. He can literally do anything he wants to me.

He gets on the bed behind me and strokes my back. His touch is slow, gentle. It would be soothing, except I'm cringing, expecting a blow at any moment.

He probably realizes it because he leans over me and whispers in my ear, "Relax, Nora. I won't do anything else tonight."

I almost collapse on the bed in relief. Tears run down my face again. This time, they're tears of relief and gratitude. I'm pathetically grateful that he won't hurt me again. At least, not tonight.

And then I'm horrified. Horrified and disgusted— because when he starts kissing my neck, my body begins to respond to him as though nothing had happened. As though it's never known a moment of pain at his hands.

My stupid body doesn't care that he's a depraved bastard. That he's going to hurt me again and again. No, my body wants pleasure, and it doesn't care about anything else.

His warm mouth moves from my neck to my shoulders, then over my back. My breathing is shallow, erratic. Despite his reassurance, I'm still afraid of him, and the fear somehow makes me wetter.

His lips move to my buttocks, kiss the area that he

hurt just a few minutes earlier. His hand pushes on my lower back, and I arch slightly under his touch, understanding his unspoken command. His fingers slip between my legs, and one long finger finds its way into my slippery channel, entering deeply.

He curves that finger inside me, and I gasp as he presses on some sensitive spot deep inside. It makes me tense and tremble—but this time, not from fear.

As he pushes that curved finger in and out, I feel a pressure gathering inside me. My heartbeat skyrockets, and I suddenly feel hot, as though I'm burning from within. And then a powerful orgasm tears through my body, originating at my core and spreading outward. It's so strong that my vision blurs for a moment and I almost collapse on the bed.

Before my pulsations even stop, he gets on his knees behind me and begins to push in.

I'm wet and his entry is relatively easy, though he still feels huge inside me. My inner tissues feel tender and sore from last night's hard use, and I can't help a slight gasp of pain at the invasion. When he's in fully, his groin presses against my burning bottom, adding to the discomfort.

Grasping my hips, he begins to move in and out, slowly and rhythmically. Despite the initial pain, my body appears to like the feeling of fullness, of being stretched, and responds by producing even more lubrication. As his pace picks up, my breathing accelerates and helpless moans escape my throat each time he pushes deeply into me.

Suddenly, with no warning, my muscles tighten as my senses reach fever-pitch. The release ripples through me, the pleasure stunning in its intensity. Behind me, I can hear his groan as my climax provokes his own—and feel the warm spurt of his seed inside me.

And then we both collapse on the bed, his body heavy and slick with perspiration on top of mine.

9

I wake up slowly, in stages. First, I feel the tickling sensation of my hair on my face. Then the warmth of the sun on my uncovered arm. For a moment, my mind is floating in that soft, comfortable limbo between sleep and wakefulness, between dreams and reality.

I keep my eyes closed, not wanting to wake fully, because this is so nice.

Then I realize I can smell pancakes cooking in the kitchen.

My lips curl in a smile. It's the weekend, and my mom decided to spoil us again. She makes pancakes on special occasions and sometimes just because.

The hair tickles me again, and I reluctantly move my arm to push it off my face.

I'm more awake now, and the warm feeling inside me dissipates, replaced by harsh, gnawing fear.

No, please let it all be a dream. Please let it all be a bad dream.

I open my eyes.

It's not a dream. I can still smell the pancakes, but there's no way it could be my mom cooking them.

I'm on an island in the middle of the Pacific Ocean, held captive by a man who derives pleasure from hurting me.

I stretch carefully, taking stock of my body. Other than a slight tenderness in my bottom, I seem to be mostly fine. He had only taken me once last night, for which I am grateful.

Getting up, I walk naked to the mirror and look at my back. There are faint bruises on my buttocks, but nothing major. That's one of the benefits of my golden-tinted skin—I don't bruise easily. By tomorrow, it should look completely normal.

All in all, I seem to have survived another night in my captor's bed.

As I brush my teeth, I think back to last evening. The dinner, my silly plan to seduce him, my feeling of betrayal at his actions…

I can't believe I had begun to trust him even a tiny bit. Normal men don't kidnap girls from the park. They don't drug them and bring them to a private island. Men who like normal, consensual sex don't keep women captive.

No, Julian is not normal. He's a sadistic control freak, and I can never forget it. The fact that he hasn't hurt me badly yet doesn't mean anything. It's just a matter of time before he does something truly awful to me.

I need to escape before that happens, and I can't take my sweet time seducing Julian. He's far too dangerous and unpredictable.

I need to find a way off this island.

After I take a quick shower and brush my teeth, I go downstairs for breakfast. Beth must've already been in my room because there is another fresh set of clothes laid out. A swimsuit, flip-flops, and another sundress.

Beth herself is in the kitchen, and so are the pancakes I'd smelled earlier.

At my entrance, she smiles at me, yesterday's tension apparently forgotten. "Good morning," she says cheerfully. "How are you feeling?"

I give her an incredulous look. Does she know what Julian did to me? "Oh, just great," I say sarcastically.

"That's good." She seems oblivious to my tone. "Julian was afraid you might be a bit sore this morning, so he left me a special cream to give you just in case."

She does know.

"How do you live with yourself?" I ask, genuinely curious. How can a woman stand by and watch another woman being abused like this? How can she work for this cruel man?

Instead of answering, Beth places a large, fluffy pancake on a plate and brings it to me. There is also sliced mango on the table, right next to a bottle of maple syrup.

"Eat, Nora," she says, not unkindly.

I give her a bitter look and dig into the pancake. It's delicious. I think she added bananas to the batter because I can taste their sweetness. I don't even need the maple syrup, although I do add a few slices of mango for additional flavor.

Beth smiles again, and goes back to doing various kitchen chores.

After breakfast, I leave the house and explore the island on my own. Beth doesn't stop me. I still find it shocking that they're letting me wander around like this. They must be completely confident there is no way off the island.

Well, I intend to find a way.

I walk tirelessly for hours in the hot sun, until the flip-flops I'm wearing give me a blister. I stick close to the beach, hoping to find a boat tied somewhere, maybe in a cave or a lagoon.

But I find nothing.

How did I get here? Was it by plane or helicopter? Julian did mention yesterday that he had originally discovered this place while flying a plane. Maybe that's how he brought me here, via a private plane?

That would not be good. Even if I found the plane sitting somewhere, how would I fly it? I imagine it must be at least somewhat complicated.

Then again, with sufficient incentive, I might be able

to figure it out. I'm not stupid, and flying a plane is not rocket science.

But I don't find the plane either. There is a flat grassy area on the other side of the island with a structure at the end of it, but there's nothing inside the structure. It's completely empty.

Tired, thirsty, and with the blister beginning to bother me more with each step, I head back to the house.

~

"Julian left a couple of hours ago," Beth tells me as soon as I walk in.

Stunned, I stare at her. "What do you mean, he left?"

"He had some urgent business to take care of. If all goes well, he should be back within a week."

I nod, trying to keep a neutral expression, and go upstairs to my room.

He's gone! My tormentor is gone!

It's just Beth and me on this island. No one else.

My mind is whirling with possibilities. I can steal one of the kitchen knives and threaten Beth until she shows me a way off the island. There's probably internet here, and I might be able to reach out to the outside world.

I'm so excited I could scream.

Do they truly think I'm that harmless? Did my meek behavior thus far lull them into thinking I would continue to be a nice, obedient captive?

Well, they couldn't be more mistaken.

Julian is the one I'm afraid of, not Beth. With the two of them on this island, attacking Beth would've been pointless and dangerous.

Now, however, she's fair game.

An hour later, I quietly sneak into the kitchen. As I had expected, Beth is not there. It's too early to prepare dinner and too late for lunch.

My feet are bare, to minimize any sound. Cautiously looking around, I slide open one of the drawers and take out a large butcher knife. Testing it with my finger, I determine that it's sharp.

A weapon. Perfect.

The sundress that I'm wearing has a slim belt at the waist, and I use it to tie the knife to myself at the back. It's a very crude holster, but it holds the knife in place. I hope I don't cut my butt with the naked blade, but even if I do, it's a risk worth taking.

A large ceramic vase is my next acquisition. It's heavy enough that I can barely lift it over my head with two arms. I can't imagine a human skull would be a match for something like this.

Once I have those two things, I go look for Beth.

I find her on the porch, curled up with a book on a long, comfy-looking outdoor couch, enjoying the fresh air and the beautiful ocean view. She doesn't look when I poke my head outside through the open door, and I quickly go back in, trying to figure out what to do next.

My plan is simple. I need to catch Beth off-guard and bash her over the head with the vase. Maybe tie her up with something. Then I could use the knife to threaten her into letting me contact the outside world. This way, by the time Julian returns, I could already be rescued and pressing charges.

All I need now is a good spot for my ambush.

Looking around, I notice a little nook near the kitchen entrance. If you're coming in off the porch—like I think Beth will be—then you don't really see anything in that nook. It's not the best place to conceal oneself, but it's better than attacking her openly. I go there and press myself flat against the wall, the vase standing on the floor next to me where I can easily grab it.

Taking a deep breath, I try to still the fine trembling in my hands. I'm not a violent person, yet here I am, about to smash this vase into Beth's head. I don't want to think about it, but I can't help picturing her skull split open, blood and gore everywhere, like in some horror movie. The image makes me ill. I tell myself that it won't be like that, that she'll most likely end up with a nasty bruise or a mild concussion.

The wait seems interminable. It goes on and on, each second stretching like an hour. My heart is pounding and I'm sweating, even though the temperature in the house is much cooler than the heat outside.

Finally, after what feels like several hours, I hear Beth's footsteps. Grabbing the vase, I carefully lift it over my head and hold my breath as Beth steps through the open door leading from the porch.

As she walks by me, I grip the vase tightly and bring it down on her head.

And somehow I miss. At the last moment, Beth must've heard me move because the vase hits her on the shoulder instead.

She cries out in pain, clutching her shoulder. "You fucking bitch!"

I gasp and try to lift the vase again, but it's too late. She grabs for the vase, and it falls down, breaking into a dozen pieces between us.

I jump back, my right hand frantically scrambling for the knife. Shit, shit, shit. I manage to grab the handle and pull it out, but before I can do anything, she grabs my arm, moving as quickly as a snake. Her grip is like a steel band around my right wrist.

Her face is flushed and her eyes are glittering as she twists my arm painfully backward. "Drop the knife, Nora," she orders harshly, her voice filled with fury.

Panicking, I try to hit her in the face with my other hand, but she catches that arm too. She clearly knows how to fight—and she's also obviously stronger than me.

My right arm is screaming in pain, but I try to kick at her. I can't lose this fight. This is my best chance at escape.

My feet make contact with her legs, but I'm not wearing shoes and I do more damage to my toes than to her shins.

"Drop the knife, Nora, or I will break your arm," she

hisses, and I know that she's telling the truth. My shoulder feels like it's about to pop out of its socket, and my vision darkens as waves of pain radiate down my arm.

I hold out for one more second, and then my fingers release the knife. It falls to the floor with a loud thunk.

Beth immediately lets me go and bends down to pick it up.

I back away, breathing harshly, tears of pain and frustration burning in my eyes. I don't know what she's going to do to me now, and I don't want to find out.

So I run.

~

I am fast on my feet and in good shape. I can hear Beth chasing after me, calling my name, but I doubt she's ever done track before.

I run out of the house and down to the beach. Rocks, twigs, and gravel dig into my feet, but I barely feel them.

I don't know where I'm running, but I can't let Beth catch me. I can't be locked up in the room or worse.

"Nora!"

Fuck, she's a good runner too. I put on a burst of speed, ignoring the pain in my feet.

"Nora, don't be an idiot! There's nowhere to go!"

I know that's true, but I can't be a passive victim any longer. I can't sit meekly in that house, eat Beth's food, and wait for Julian to return.

I can't allow him to hurt me again and then make my body crave him.

My leg muscles are screaming, and my lungs are straining for air. I divorce myself from the discomfort, pretend I'm in a race with the finish line only a hundred yards away.

It feels like I'm running forever. When I glance back, I see that Beth is falling further and further behind.

My pace eases a little bit. I can't sustain that speed much longer. Without thinking too much, I head for the rocky side of the island, where I can clamber up the rocks and disappear in the heavily wooded area above them.

It takes me another ten minutes to get there. By then, I can no longer see Beth behind me.

I slow down and climb up the rocks. Now that I'm out of immediate danger, I can feel the cuts and bruises on my bare feet.

It's a slow and torturous climb. My legs are quivering from unaccustomed exertion, and I can feel a post-adrenaline slump coming on. Nevertheless, I manage to get myself up the rocky hill and into the woods.

Tropical vegetation, lush and thick, is all around me, hiding me from view. I go deeper into the brush, seeking a good spot to collapse in exhaustion. It wouldn't be easy to find me here. From what I remember during my earlier exploration, this forest covers a large portion of this side of the island.

I should be safe here for now.

As the darkness begins to fall, I take shelter under a large tree, where the underbrush is particularly impenetrable. I clear a little patch of ground for myself, making sure I'm not near any ant hills or anything else that could bite me. Then I lie down, ignoring the throbbing pain in my lacerated feet.

Not for the first time in my life, I'm grateful to my dad for taking me camping when I was a child. Thanks to his tutelage, I'm comfortable with nature in all its glory. Bugs, snakes, lizards—none of these bother me. I know I should be careful around certain species, but I don't fear them as a whole.

I'm far more scared of the snakes who brought me to this island.

Now that I'm away from Beth, I can think a little more clearly.

That lean, toned body of hers is clearly not from doing light cardio and yoga in the gym. She's strong—probably as strong as some men—and definitely much stronger than me.

She also seems to have had some kind of special training. Martial arts, maybe? I clearly made a mistake trying to take her prisoner. I should've slipped that knife into her back when she wasn't looking.

It's not too late, though. I can still sneak back into the house and surprise her there. I need access to that internet, and I need it now, before Julian returns.

I don't know what he'll do to me for attacking Beth —and I certainly don't want to find out.

a strange sensation wakes me up the next morning. It feels almost like—

"Oh shit!"

I jump up, trying to shake off the long-legged spider that's leisurely strolling up my arm.

The spider flies off, and I frantically brush at my face, hair, and body, trying to get rid of any other potential creepy-crawlies.

Okay, so I'm not exactly afraid of spiders, but I really, really don't like them on me.

This is definitely not the most pleasant way to wake up.

My heart rate gradually returns to normal, and I take stock of my situation. I'm thirsty, and my entire body aches from sleeping on the hard ground. I also feel grimy, and my feet hurt. Lifting up one leg, I peer at the sole of the foot. I'm pretty sure there's dried blood on there.

My stomach is rumbling with hunger. I didn't have dinner last night, and I'm absolutely starving.

On the plus side, Beth hasn't found me yet.

I'm not really sure what I'm going to do next. Perhaps make my way back to the house and try to ambush Beth there again?

I think about it and decide it's probably the best course of action at this point. Sooner or later, Beth or Julian will find me. The island is not that big, and I would not be able to hide from them for long. And I can't risk procrastinating, in case Julian returns sooner than expected. Two against one are terrible odds.

I'm also getting hungrier by the minute, and I tend to get light-headed if I don't eat regularly. I could probably find fresh water to drink, but food is more iffy. I don't know where Beth gets those mangos from. If I try to hide for another couple of days, I might be too weak to attack anyone, much less a woman who could be a freaking warrior princess.

Besides, she might not be expecting me quite yet, and I could really use an element of surprise.

So I take a deep breath and start walking—or rather, limping—back toward the house. I know this might not end well for me, but I have no choice. I either fight now, or I will forever be a victim.

It takes me about two hours to get back. I end up having to stop and take breaks when I can no longer tolerate the agony in my feet.

It's kind of ironic that I escaped because I'm afraid of pain, and I ended up hurting myself so badly in the process. Julian would probably love to see me like this. That perverted bastard.

Finally, I reach the house and crouch behind some large bushes near the front door. I don't know if it's locked or not, but I don't think I can just stroll in through the main entrance. For all I know, Beth is right there in the living room.

No, I need to be more strategic about it.

After a few minutes, I carefully make my way to the back of the house, toward the large screened porch where I had attacked Beth yesterday.

To my relief, no one is there.

Taking care not to make a sound, I open the screen door and slip inside. In my hand I'm holding a large rock. I would much rather have a knife or a gun, but a rock will have to do for now.

Crab-walking to one of the windows, I glance inside and am gratified to find the living room empty.

Straightening, I walk up to the glass door that leads to the living room, quietly slide it open, and step inside.

The house is completely silent. There's no one cooking in the kitchen or setting the table.

The digital clock in the living room reads 7:12. I'm hoping that Beth is still asleep.

Still clutching the rock, I sneak into the kitchen and find another knife. Holding both, I carefully head upstairs.

Beth's bedroom is the first one on the left. I know because she showed it to me during the house tour.

Holding my breath, I quietly push open the door...
and freeze.

Sitting there on the bed is the person I fear
most.

Julian.

He's back early.

~

"Hello, Nora."

His voice is deceptively soft, his perfect face expressionless. Yet I can feel the rage burning quietly
underneath.

For a second, I just stare at him, paralyzed by terror.
I can't hear anything but the roaring of my own heartbeat in my ears. And then I start to back away, still
keeping my eyes trained on his face. My hands are
raised defensively in front of me, rock and knife
clutched tightly in each.

At that moment, steely hands grip my arms from
behind, painfully squeezing my wrists. I scream, struggling, but Beth is too strong. The knife twists backward
in my hand, nearly reaching my shoulder.

In a flash, Julian is on me, and both the knife and the
rock are wrenched out of my hands. Beth releases me
and Julian grabs me, holding me tightly as I scream and
writhe hysterically in his arms.

The harder I fight, the tighter his arms become
around me, until I go limp, almost fainting from lack
of air.

Then he picks me up and carries me out of Beth's room.

To my surprise, he brings me downstairs and stops in front of the door that leads to his office. A tiny panel opens on the side, and I can see a red light moving over Julian's face, like a laser at a supermarket checkout.

Then the door slides open.

I stifle a gasp of surprise. His office door opens via a retina scan—something I've only seen before in spy movies.

As he carries me inside, I try to struggle again, but it's futile. His arms are completely immovable, holding me securely in his grip.

I'm once again helpless in his embrace.

Tears of bitter frustration slide down my face. I hate being so weak, so easily handled. He's not even winded from our struggle.

I'm not sure what I'm expecting him to do. Perhaps beat me, or brutally take me.

But he simply places me on my feet when we're inside his office.

As soon as he releases me, I take a few steps back, needing to put at least some distance between us.

He smiles at me, and there's something disturbing in the beauty of that smile. "Relax, my pet. I won't hurt you. Not now, at least."

And as I watch, he walks over to a large desk and slides open the drawer, taking out a remote control. Then he points it at a wall behind me.

I turn around warily and stare at two large flat-panel

TV screens. They look very high-tech, not at all like the ones I'm used to seeing at home.

The left screen lights up. The image is strange because it's so unexpected.

It looks like a regular bedroom in someone's house. The bed is unmade, sheets bunched up carelessly on the mattress. Posters of various football players line the walls, and there is a laptop sitting on the desk.

"Do you recognize it?" Julian asks.

I shake my head.

"Good," he says. "I'm glad about that."

"Whose bedroom is it?" I ask, a sick feeling appearing in my stomach.

"Can't you guess?"

I stare at him, feeling colder by the minute. "Jake's?"

"Yes, Nora. Jake's."

I begin to shake inside. "Why is it on your TV?"

"Do you remember when I told you that Jake is safe as long as you behave?"

I stop breathing for a second. "Yes…" My whisper is barely audible.

Truthfully, I had forgotten about his initial threat to Jake, too consumed with the experience of my own captivity. I don't think I took the threat seriously to begin with, certainly not after I learned we were on an island thousands of miles away from my hometown. Somewhere in the back of my mind, I had been convinced Julian can't really harm Jake. Not from a distance, at least.

"Good," Julian says. "Then you'll understand why I'm

doing this. I don't want to keep you locked up, unable to go anywhere or do anything. This island is your new home, and I want you to be happy here—"

Happy here? I'm more than ever convinced that he's crazy.

"—but I can't have you trying to hurt Beth in pointless escape attempts. You need to learn that there are consequences to your actions—"

The sick feeling inside me spreads throughout my body. "I'm sorry! I won't do it anymore! I won't, I promise!" My words are hurried and jumbled. I don't know if I can prevent what's about to happen, but I have to try. "I won't hurt Beth, and I won't try to escape. Please, Julian, I learned my lesson..."

Julian looks at me almost sadly. "No, Nora. You haven't. I had to come back today, cutting short my business trip because of what you did. Beth is not here to be your jailer. That's not her role. She's here to take care of you, to make sure you're comfortable and content. I can't have you repaying her kindness by trying to kill her—"

"I wasn't trying to kill her! I just wanted..." I stop, not wanting to reveal my plan to him.

"You thought you could take her hostage?" Julian looks amused now. "To do what? Get her to take you off the island? Help you reach the outside world?"

I look at him, neither denying nor admitting it.

"Well, Nora, let me explain something to you. Even if your attack had succeeded—which it wouldn't have, because Beth is more than capable of handling one small girl—she wouldn't have been able to help you. When I leave, the plane leaves with me. There's no boat or any other way off the island."

His words confirm what I had already suspected from my explorations. But I'm still hoping that—

"And I'm the only one who has access to my office. There's no computer or communication equipment anywhere else in the house. All Beth can do is send me a direct message on a special line that we have set up. So you see, my pet, she would've been quite useless as a hostage."

So much for that hope. Each sentence feels like a nail getting pounded deeper into my coffin. If he's not lying to me, then my situation is far, far worse than I feared.

Unless Julian chooses to let me go, I'll be stuck on his island forever.

I want to scream, cry, and throw things, but I can't let myself fall apart right now. Instead, I nod and pretend to be calm and rational. "I understand. I'm sorry, Julian. I didn't know any of this before. I won't try to escape again, and I won't hurt Beth. Please believe me…"

"I'd like to, Nora." He looks almost regretful. "But I can't. You don't know me yet, so you're not sure if you can believe me. I need to show you that I'm a man of my word. The sooner you accept the inevitable, the happier you'll be."

And with that, he reaches into his pocket and pulls out something that looks like a phone. Pressing a button, he waits a couple of seconds, then says curtly, "You can proceed."

Then he turns his attention to the screen.

I do the same, a hollow sense of dread in my stomach.

The TV still shows an empty room, but a few seconds later, the door opens and Jake walks in.

He looks terrified. One of his eyes is swollen shut, and his nose is off-center, like it's broken. He's followed by a large masked figure toting a gun.

A horrified gasp escapes my lips. "Please, no..." I'm not even cognizant of moving, but my hands are somehow on Julian's arm, tugging at him in desperation.

"Watch, Nora." There's no emotion on Julian's face as he pulls me into his arms, holding me so that I'm facing the TV. "I want you to learn once and for all that actions have consequences."

On the screen, the masked henchman suddenly reaches for Jake—

"No!"

—and hits him hard across the face with the handle of the gun. Jake stumbles backward, blood trickling out of the corner of his mouth.

"Please, no!" I'm sobbing and struggling in Julian's iron grip, my eyes glued to the violent scene taking place thousands of miles away.

Jake's attacker is relentless, hitting him over and over. I scream, feeling each blow inside my heart. Every brutal strike against Jake's body is killing something inside me, some belief in a brighter future that has held me together thus far.

When Jake falls to his knees, the man kicks him in the ribs, and I can hear Jake's pained groan.

"Please, Julian," I whisper in defeat, slumping in his arms. "Please, stop..." I know I'm begging for mercy from a man who has none. He's murdering Jake in front of my eyes, and there's absolutely nothing I can do about it.

My captor lets the beating proceed for another minute before he releases me and pulls out his phone. I stare at him, trembling from head to toe. I don't even dare hope.

Julian quickly types in a text. On the screen, I see Jake's assailant pausing and reaching into his pocket.

Then he stops completely and leaves Jake's room.

Jake is left lying on the floor, covered in blood. I remain glued to the screen, needing to know that he is alive. After a minute, I hear his groan and see him getting up. He hobbles toward the house phone, moving like an old man instead of an athletic young guy.

And then I hear him calling 911.

I sink to the floor and bury my face in my hands.

Julian has won.

I know that my life will never be my own again.

11

*W*hen I wake up the next morning, Julian is gone again.

I don't really remember what happened after I collapsed in Julian's office yesterday. The rest of the day is fuzzy in my memory. It's like my brain had switched off, unable to process the violence I had witnessed. I think I vaguely recall Julian picking me up off the floor and bringing me to the shower. He must've washed me and bandaged my feet because they're wrapped in gauze this morning and hurting a lot less when I walk.

I'm not sure if he had sex with me last night. If he did, then he must've been unusually gentle because I don't have any soreness this morning. I do remember sleeping with him in my bed, with his large body curved around mine.

In some ways, what happened simplifies things. When there's no hope, when there's no choice, everything becomes remarkably clear. The fact of the matter is that Julian holds all the cards. I'm his for as long as he wishes to keep me. There's no escape for me, no way out.

And once I accept that fact, my life becomes easier. Before I know it, I have been on the island for nine days.

Beth tells me so over breakfast this morning.

I've grown to tolerate her presence. I have no choice —without Julian there, she's my only source of human interaction. She feeds me, clothes me, and cleans after me. She's almost like my nanny, except she's young and sometimes bitchy. I don't think she's forgiven me fully for trying to bash her head in. It hurt her pride or something.

I try not to bug her too much. I leave the house during the day, spending most of my time on the beach or exploring the woods. I come back to the house for meals and to pick up a new book to read. Beth told me Julian will bring me more books when I'm done with the hundred or so that are currently in my room.

I should be depressed. I know that. I should be bitter and raging all the time, hating Julian and the island. And sometimes I do. But it takes so much energy, constantly being a victim. When I'm lying in the hot sun, absorbed in a book, I don't hate anything. I just let myself get carried away by some author's imagination.

I try not to think about Jake. The guilt is almost unbearable. Rationally, I know Julian is the one who did this, but I can't help feeling responsible. If I had never gone out with Jake, this would've never happened to him. If I hadn't approached him during that party, he wouldn't have been savagely beaten.

I still don't know what Julian is or how he's able to have such a long reach. He's as much of a mystery to me today as he's ever been.

Maybe he's in the Mafia. That would explain the thugs he has in his employ. Of course, he could simply be a wealthy eccentric with sociopathic tendencies. I truly don't know.

Sometimes I cry myself to sleep at night. I miss my family, my friends. I miss going out and dancing at a club. I miss human contact. I'm not a loner by nature. Back home, I was always in touch with people—Facebook, Twitter, just hanging out with friends at the mall. I like to read, but it's not enough for me. I need more.

It gets so bad that I try talking to Beth about it.

"I'm bored," I tell her over dinner. It's fish again. I learned that Beth catches it herself near the cove on the other side of the island. This time, it's with mango salsa. It's a good thing I'm a seafood fan because I get a lot of it here.

"You are?" She seems amused. "Why? Don't you have enough books to read?"

I roll my eyes. "Yes, I still have seventy or so left. But there's nothing else to do…"

"Want to help me fish tomorrow?" she asks, giving me a mocking look. She knows she's not my favorite person, and she fully expects me to turn her down immediately. However, she doesn't realize the extent to which I need human interaction.

"Okay," I say, obviously surprising her. I've never been fishing, and I can't imagine it's a particularly fun activity, especially if Beth is going to be snarky the entire time. Still, I'd do just about anything to break the routine at this point.

"Okay, then," she says. "The best time to catch these fuckers is right around dawn. Think you're up for it?"

"Sure," I say. I normally hate waking up early, but I get so much sleep here that I'm sure it won't be too bad. I probably sleep close to ten hours at night and also catch an occasional nap in the afternoon sun. It's kind of ridiculous, really. My body seems to think I'm on vacation at some relaxing retreat. There are apparently perks to not having internet or other distractions; I don't think I've felt so well-rested in my entire life.

"Then you better go to sleep soon because I'll come by your room early," she warns.

I nod, finishing up my dinner. Then I head upstairs to my room and cry myself to sleep again.

"When is Julian coming back?" I ask, watching Beth as she carefully arranges the bait at the end of the hook. What she's doing looks disgusting, and I'm glad she's not making me help her.

"I don't know," Beth says. "He'll come back when he's done taking care of business."

"What kind of business?" I've asked this before, but I'm hoping one of these days Beth will answer me.

She sighs. "Nora, stop prying."

"What's the big deal if I know?" I give her a frustrated look. "It's not like I'm going anywhere anytime soon. I just want to know what he is, that's all. Don't you think it's normal to be curious in my situation?"

She sighs again and casts the lure into the ocean with a smooth, practiced motion. "Of course it is. But Julian will tell you everything himself if he wants you to know."

I take a deep breath. I'm obviously not going to get anywhere with that line of questioning. "You're really loyal to him, huh?"

"Yes," Beth says simply, sitting down beside me. "I am."

Because he saved her life. I'm curious about that too, but I know she's touchy on that subject. So instead I ask, "How long have you known him?"

"About ten years," she says.

"Since he was nineteen?"

"Yes, exactly."

"How did you two meet?"

Her jaw hardens. "That's none of your business."

Uh-huh. I sense I'm again approaching the difficult subject. I decide to proceed anyway. "Was that when he saved your life? Is that how you met him?"

She gives me a narrow-eyed look. "Nora, what did I tell you about prying?"

"Okay, fine…" Her non-answer is answer enough for me. I move on to another topic of interest. "So why did

Julian bring me here? To this island, I mean? He's not even here himself."

"He'll come back soon enough." She gives me an ironic look. "Why, do you miss him?"

"No, of course not!" I give her an offended glare.

She raises her eyebrows. "Really? Not even a little bit?"

"Why would I miss that monster?" I hiss at her, uncontrollable anger suddenly boiling up from the pit of my stomach. "After what he did to me? To Jake?"

She laughs softly. "Methinks the lady doth protest too much…"

I jump to my feet, unable to bear the mockery in her voice any longer. In this moment, I hate her so much I would've gladly stabbed her with a knife if I had it handy. I've never had much of a temper, but something about Beth brings out the worst in me.

Thankfully, I regain control over myself before I storm off and make a complete fool of myself. Taking a deep breath, I pretend that I intended to get up all along. Walking to the water, I test the temperature with my toe and then walk back toward Beth, sitting down again.

"Really warm water on this side of the island," I say calmly, as though I'm not still burning with anger inside.

"Yeah, the fish seem to like it here," she replies in the same even tone. "I always catch some nice ones in this area."

I nod and look out over the water. The sound of the waves is soothing, helping me control whatever it was that came over me. I don't fully understand why I reacted so strongly to her teasing. Surely I should've just given her a contemptuous look and coldly dismissed her ridiculous suggestion. Instead I'd risen to her bait.

Could there be some truth to her words? Is that why they irritated me so much? Am I actually missing Julian?

The idea is so sickening that I want to throw up.

I try to think about it rationally for a bit, to sort through the confusing jumble of feelings in my chest.

Okay, yes, a small part of me does resent the fact that he left me here on this island, with only Beth for company. For someone who supposedly wanted me enough to steal me, Julian is certainly not being very attentive.

Not that I want his attentions. I want him to stay as far away from me as possible. But at the same time, I am oddly insulted that he's staying away. It's like I'm not desirable enough for him to want to be here.

As soon as I analyze it all logically, I see the absurdity of my contradictory emotions. The whole thing is so silly, I have to mentally kick myself.

I'm not going to be one of those girls who falls in love with their kidnapper. I refuse to be. I know being here on this island is screwing with my head, and I'm determined not to let it.

Perhaps I can't escape from Julian, but I can keep him from getting under my skin.

Two days later, Julian returns.

I learn about it when he wakes me up from my nap on the beach.

At first, I think I'm having a dream. In my dream, I'm warm and safe in my bed. Gentle hands start stroking my body, soothing me, caressing me. I arch toward them, loving their touch on my skin, reveling in the pleasure they're giving me.

And then I feel hot lips on my face, my neck, my collarbone. I moan softly, and the hands become more demanding, pulling at the straps of my bikini top, tugging the bikini bottoms off my legs…

The realization of what's happening filters through to my half-conscious brain, and I wake up with a sudden gasp, adrenaline rushing through my veins.

Julian is crouched over me, looking down at me with that darkly angelic smile of his. I'm already naked, lying on top of the large beach towel that Beth gave me this morning. He's naked too—and fully aroused.

I stare up at him, my heart racing with a mixture of excitement and dread. "You're back," I say, stating the obvious.

"I am," he murmurs, leaning down and kissing my neck again. Before I can gather my scattered thoughts, he's already lying on top of me, his knee parting my thighs and his erection prodding at my tender opening.

I squeeze my eyes shut as he begins to push inside me. I'm wet, but I still feel uncomfortably stretched as he slides in all the way. He pauses for a second, letting me adjust, and then he begins to move, slowly at first and then with increasing pace.

His thrusts press me into the towel, and I can feel the sand shifting under my back. I clutch at his hard shoulders, needing something to hold on to as the familiar tension starts to gather low in my belly. The head of his cock brushes against that sensitive spot somewhere inside me, and I gasp, arching to take him deeper, needing more of that intense sensation, wanting him to bring me over the edge.

"Did you miss me?" he breathes into my ear, slowing down just enough to prevent me from reaching my peak.

I'm coherent enough to shake my head.

"Liar," he whispers, and his thrusts become harder, more punishing. He's ruthlessly driving me higher and higher until I'm screaming, my nails raking down his back in frustration as the elusive release hovers just beyond my reach.

And then I'm finally there, my body flying apart as a powerful orgasm sweeps through me, leaving me weak and panting in its wake.

With a suddenness that startles me, he pulls out and flips me over, onto my stomach.

I cry out, frightened, but he merely pushes inside me again and resumes fucking me from behind, his body large and heavy on top of mine. I am surrounded by him; my face is pressed into the towel and I can hardly breathe. All I can feel is him: the back-and-forth movement of his thick cock inside my body, the heat emanating from his skin. In this position, he goes deep, even deeper than usual, and I can't help the pained gasps that escape my throat as the head of his cock bumps against my cervix with each thrust of his hips. Yet the discomfort doesn't seem to prevent the pressure growing inside me again, and I climax again, my inner muscles clenching helplessly around his shaft.

He groans harshly, and then I can feel him coming too, his cock pulsing and jerking within me, his pelvis grinding into my buttocks. It enhances my own orgasm, draws out my pleasure. It's like we're linked together, because my contractions don't stop until his are fully over.

Afterwards, he rolls over onto his back, releasing me, and I draw in a shaky breath. With limbs that feel weak and heavy, I get up on all fours and find my bikini, then pull it on while he watches me, a lazy smile on his beautiful lips. He doesn't seem to be in a rush to get dressed himself, but I can't stand to be naked around him. It makes me feel too vulnerable.

The irony of that doesn't escape me. Of course I'm vulnerable. I'm as vulnerable as a woman can be: completely at the mercy of a ruthless madman. A couple of tiny patches of material aren't going to protect me from him.

Nothing will, if he decides to really hurt me.

I decide not to think about that. Instead I ask, "Where were you?"

Julian's smile widens. "You did miss me after all."

I give him a sardonic look, trying to ignore the fact that he's naked and sprawled out only a couple of feet away from me. "Yeah, I missed you."

He laughs, not the least bit put off by my snarky attitude. "I knew you would," he says. Then he gets up and pulls on a pair of swimming trunks that were lying on the sand next to us. Turning toward me, he offers me his hand. "A swim?"

I stare at him. Is he serious? He expects me to go for a swim with him like we're friends or something?

"No, thanks," I say, taking a step back.

He frowns a little. "Why not, Nora? You can't swim?"

"Of course I can swim," I say indignantly. "I just don't want to swim with you."

He raises his eyebrows. "Why not?"

"Um... maybe because I hate you?" I don't know why I'm being so brave today, but it seems like the time apart made me less afraid of him. Or maybe it's because he appears to be in a light, playful mood, and is thus just a bit less scary.

He smiles again. "You don't know what hatred is, my pet. You might not like my actions, but you don't hate me. You can't. It's not in your nature."

"What do you know about my nature?" For some reason, I find his words offensive. How dare he say that I can't hate my kidnapper? Who does he think he is, telling me what I can and cannot feel?

He looks at me, his lips still curved in that smile. "I know you've had what they call a normal upbringing, Nora," he says softly. "I know that you were raised in a loving family, that you had good friends, decent boyfriends. How could you possibly know what real hatred is?"

I stare at him. "And you know? You know what real hatred is?"

His expression hardens. "Unfortunately, yes," he says, and I can hear the truth in his voice.

A sick feeling floods my stomach. "Am I the one you hate?" I whisper. "Is that why you're doing this to me?"

To my huge relief, he looks surprised. "Hate you? No, of course I don't hate you, my pet."

"Then why?" I ask again, determined to get some answers. "Why did you kidnap me and bring me here?"

He looks at me, his eyes impossibly blue against his tan skin. "Because I wanted you, Nora. I already told you that. And because I'm not a very nice man. But you already figured that out, didn't you?"

I swallow and look down at the sand. He's not even the least bit ashamed of his actions. Julian knows what he's doing is wrong, and he simply doesn't care.

"Are you a psychopath?" I don't know what prompts me to ask this. I don't want to make him angry, but I can't help wanting to understand. Holding my breath, I look up at him again.

Thankfully, he doesn't seem offended by the question. Instead, he looks thoughtful as he sits down on the towel next to me. "Perhaps," he says after a couple of seconds. "One doctor thought I might be a borderline sociopath. I don't check all the boxes, so there's no definitive diagnosis."

"You saw a doctor?" I don't know why I'm so shocked. Maybe because he doesn't seem like the type to go to a shrink.

He grins at me. "Yeah, for a bit."

"Why?"

He shrugs. "Because I thought it might help."

"Help you be less of a psychopath?"

"No, Nora." He gives me an ironic look. "If I were a true psychopath, nothing could help that."

"So then what?" I know I'm prying into some very personal matters, but I feel like he owes me some answers. Besides, if you can't get personal with a man who just fucked you on the beach, then when can you?

"You're a curious little kitten, aren't you?" he says softly, putting his hand on my thigh. "Are you sure you really want to know, my pet?"

I nod, trying to ignore the fact that his fingers are only inches away from my bikini line. His touch is both arousing and disturbing, playing havoc with my equilibrium.

"I went to a therapist after I killed the men who murdered my family," he says quietly, looking at me. "I thought it might help me come to terms with it."

I stare at him blankly. "Come to terms with the fact that you killed them?"

"No," he says. "With the fact that I wanted to kill more."

My stomach turns over, and my skin feels like it's crawling where Julian is touching me. He has just admitted to something so horrible that I don't even know how to react.

As if from a distance, I hear my own voice asking, "So did it help you come to terms with it?" I sound calm, like we're discussing nothing more tragic than the weather.

He laughs. "No, my pet, it didn't. Doctors are useless."

"You've killed more?" The numbness encasing me is fading, and I can feel myself beginning to shake.

"I have," he says, a dark smile playing on his lips. "Now aren't you glad you asked?"

My blood turns to ice. I know I should stop talking now, but I can't. "Are you going to kill me?"

"No, Nora." He sounds exasperated for a moment. "I've already told you that."

I lick my dry lips. "Right. You're just going to hurt me whenever you feel like it."

He doesn't deny it. Instead he gets up again and looks at me. "I'm going for a swim. You can join me if you like."

"No, thanks," I say dully. "I don't feel like swimming right now."

"Suit yourself," he says, and then walks away, striding into the water.

Still in a state of shock, I watch his tall, broad-shouldered frame as he goes deeper into the ocean, his dark hair shining in the sun.

The devil does indeed wear a beautiful mask.

*A*fter Julian's revelations on the beach, I don't feel like asking any more questions for a while. I already knew I was being held by a monster, and what I learned today just solidifies that fact. I don't know why he was so open with me, and that scares me.

At dinner, I mostly keep quiet, only answering questions posed directly to me. Beth is eating with us today, and the two of them are carrying on a lively conversation, mostly about the island and how she and I have been spending our time.

"So you're bored?" Julian asks me after Beth tells him about my lack of interest in reading all the time.

I lift my shoulders in a shrug, not wanting to make a big deal of it. After what I learned earlier, I'd take boredom over Julian's company any time.

He smiles. "Okay, I'll have to remedy that. I'll bring you a TV and a bunch of movies the next time I make a trip."

"Thanks," I say automatically, staring down into my plate. I feel so miserable that I want to cry, but I have too much pride to do it in front of them.

"What's the matter?" Beth asks, finally noticing my uncharacteristic behavior. "Are you feeling okay?"

"Not really," I say, gladly latching on to the excuse she gave me. "I think I got too much sun."

Beth sighs. "I told you not to sleep on the beach midday. It's ninety-five degrees out."

It's true; she had warned me about that. But my misery today has nothing to do with the heat and everything with the man sitting across the table from me. I know that when the dinner is over, he's going to take me upstairs and fuck me again. Maybe hurt me.

And I will respond to him, like I always do.

That last part is the worst. He beat up Jake in front of my eyes. He admitted to being a murdering sociopath. I should be disgusted. I should look at him with nothing but fear and contempt. The fact that I can feel even a smidgen of desire for him is beyond sick.

It's downright twisted.

So I sit there, picking at my food, my stomach filled with lead. I would get up and go to my room, but I'm afraid it will just speed up the inevitable.

Finally, the meal is over. Julian takes my hand and leads me upstairs. I feel like I'm going to my execution, though that's probably too dramatic. He said he wouldn't kill me.

When we're in the room, he sits down on the bed and pulls me between his legs. I want to resist, to put up at least some kind of fight, but my brain and my body don't seem to be on speaking terms these days. Instead, I stand there mutely, trembling from head to toe, while he looks at me. His eyes trace over my facial features, lingering on my mouth, then drop down to my neckline, where my nipples are visible through the thin fabric of my sundress. They're peaked, as though from arousal, but I think it's because I'm chilled. Beth must've turned on air-conditioning for the night.

"Very pretty," he says finally, lifting his hand and stroking the edge of my jaw with his fingers. "Such soft golden skin."

I close my eyes, not wanting to look at the monster in front of me. I wanted to kill more... I wanted to kill more... His words repeat over and over in my mind, like a song that's stuck on replay. I don't know how to turn it off, how to go back in time and scrub the memories of this afternoon from my mind. Why did I insist on knowing this about him? Why did I probe and pry until I got these kind of answers? Now I can't think about anything but the fact that the man touching me is a ruthless killer.

He leans closer to me, and I can feel his hot breath on my neck. "Are you sorry you asked me all those questions today?" he whispers in my ear. "Are you, Nora?"

I flinch, my eyes flying open. Does he also read minds?

At my reaction, he pulls back and smiles. There's something in that smile that makes my chill ten times worse. I don't know what's going on with him tonight, but whatever it is, it frightens me more than anything he's done before.

"You're scared of me, aren't you, my pet?" he says softly, still holding me prisoner between his legs. "I can feel you shaking like a leaf."

I want to deny it, to be brave, but I can't. I am scared, and I am shaking. "Please," I whisper, not even knowing why I'm begging. He hasn't done anything to me yet.

He gives me a light push then, releasing me from his hold. I take a few steps back, glad to put some distance between us.

He gets up off the bed and walks out of the room.

I stare after him, unable to believe he just left me alone. Could it be that he doesn't want sex right now? He did already have me once on the beach earlier today.

And just as I'm about to let myself feel relief, Julian returns, a black gym bag in his hands.

All blood drains from my face. Horrifying thoughts run through my mind. What does he have in there—knives, guns, some kind of torture devices?

When he takes out a blindfold and a small dildo, I'm almost grateful. Sex toys. He just has some sex toys in that bag. I would take sex over torture any day of the week.

Of course, with Julian the two are not necessarily separate, as I learn this night.

"Strip, Nora," he tells me, walking over to sit down on the bed again. He lays the blindfold and the dildo on the mattress. "Take off your clothes, slowly."

I freeze. He wants me to disrobe while he watches?

For a moment, I think about refusing, but then I start to undress with clumsy fingers. He has already seen me naked today. What would I achieve by being modest now? Besides, I'm still sensing that strange vibe from him. His eyes are glittering with excitement that goes beyond simple lust.

It's an excitement that makes my blood run cold.

He watches as the dress falls off my body and I kick off my flip-flops. My movements are wooden, stiff with fear. I doubt a normal man would find this striptease arousing, but I can see that it turns Julian on. Under the dress, I'm wearing only a pair of cream-colored lacy panties. The cold air washes over my skin, making my nipples harden even more.

"Now the underwear," he says.

I swallow and push the panties down my legs. Then I step out of them.

"Good girl," he says approvingly. "Now come here."

This time I'm unable to obey him. My self-preservation instinct is screaming that I need to run, but there's nowhere to run to. Julian would catch me if I tried to make it out the door right now—and it's not like I can get off this island anyway.

So I just stand there, naked and shivering, frozen in place.

Julian gets up himself. Contrary to my expectations, he doesn't look angry. Instead he seems almost... pleased. "I see that I was right to begin training you tonight," he says as he comes up to me. "I've been too soft with you because of your inexperience. I didn't want to break you, to damage you beyond repair—"

My shaking intensifies as he circles around me like a shark.

"—but I need to start molding you into what I want you to be, Nora. You're already so close to perfection, but there are these occasional lapses..." He traces his fingers down my body, ignoring the way I'm cringing from his touch.

"Please," I whisper, "please, Julian, I'm sorry." I don't know what I'm sorry for, but I will say anything right now to avoid this training, whatever it may be.

He smiles at me. "It's not a punishment, my pet. I just have certain needs, that's all—and I want you to be able to satisfy them."

"What needs?" My words are barely audible. I don't want to know, I truly don't, yet I can't seem to stop myself from asking.

"You'll see," he says, wrapping his fingers around my upper arm and leading me toward the bed. When we get there, he reaches for the blindfold and ties it around my eyes. My hands automatically try to go to my face, but he pulls them down, so that they're hanging by my sides.

I hear rustling sounds, as though he's searching for something in that bag. Terror rips through me again, and I make a convulsive movement to free my eyes, but he catches my wrists. Then I feel him binding them behind my back.

At this point I start to cry. I don't make a sound, but I can feel the blindfold getting wet from the moisture escaping my eyes. I know I was helpless before, even without being blindfolded and tied up, but the sense of vulnerability is a thousand times worse now. I know there are women who are into this, who play these types of games with their partners, but Julian is not my partner. I've read enough books that I know the rules—and I know that he's not following them. There's nothing safe, sane, or consensual about what's going on here.

And yet, when Julian reaches between my legs and strokes me there, I'm horrified to realize that I'm wet.

That pleases him. He doesn't say anything, but I can feel the satisfaction emanating from him as he begins to play with my clit, occasionally dipping the tip of one finger inside me to monitor my physical response to his stimulation. His movements are sure, not the least bit hesitant. He knows exactly what to do to enhance my arousal, how to touch me to make me come.

I hate that, his expertise in bringing me pleasure. How many women has he done this to? Surely it takes practice to get so good at making a woman orgasm despite her fear and reluctance.

None of this matters to my body, of course. With each stroke of his skilled fingers, the tension inside me builds and intensifies, the insidious pressure starting to gather low in my belly. I moan, my hips involuntarily pushing toward him as he continues to play with my sex. He's not touching me anywhere else, just there, but it seems to be enough to drive me insane.

"Oh yes," he murmurs, bending down to kiss my neck. "Come for me, my pet."

As though obeying his command, my inner muscles contract... and then the climax rushes through me with the force of a freight train. I forget to be afraid; I forget everything in that moment except the pleasure exploding through my nerve endings.

Before I can recover, he pushes me onto the bed, face down. I hear him moving, doing something, and then he lifts me and arranges me on top of a mound of pillows, elevating my hips. Now I'm lying on my stomach with my ass sticking out and my hands tied behind my back, even more exposed and vulnerable than before. I turn my head sideways, so I don't suffocate in the mattress.

My tears, which had almost stopped before, begin again. I have a terrible suspicion I know what he's going to do to me now.

When I feel something cool and wet between my butt cheeks, my suspicion is confirmed. He's spreading lube on me, preparing me for what's to come.

My shaking intensifies, and he strokes the curve of my buttocks with his large palm.

"Hush, baby." His tone is soft and soothing. "I'll teach you to enjoy this too."

I hear more sounds, and then I feel something pushing into me, into that other opening. I tense, clenching my muscles with all my might, but the pressure is too much to resist and the thing begins to penetrate me.

"Please," I moan as a burning pain begins, and Julian actually listens this time, pausing for a second.

"Relax, my pet," he says softly, caressing my leg with

one of his hands. "It's nothing but a small toy. It won't hurt you if you relax."

"Isn't hurting me the whole point?" I ask bitterly. "Isn't that what gets your rocks off?"

"Do you want me to hurt you?" His voice is soft, almost hypnotic. "It would get my rocks off, you're right... Is that what you want, my pet? For me to hurt you?"

No, I don't. I don't want that at all. I give an almost imperceptible shake of my head and do my best to relax. I don't think I'm successful at it. It's just too wrong, the feeling of something pushing in there from the outside.

Nonetheless, Julian seems pleased with my efforts. "Good," he croons. "Good girl, there we go..." He applies steady pressure, and the thing goes deeper into me, past the resistance of my sphincter, inch by slow inch. When it's all the way in, he pauses, letting me get used to the sensation.

The burning pain is still there, as is the almost nauseating feeling of fullness. I focus on taking small, even breaths and not moving. After about a minute, the pain begins to subside, leaving only the disorienting sensation of a foreign object lodged inside my body.

Julian leaves the toy in place and starts stroking me all over, his touch oddly gentle. He starts with my feet, rubbing them, finding all the kinks and massaging them away. Then he moves up my calves and thighs, which are almost vibrating with tension. His hands are skilled and sure on my body; what he's doing is better than any massage I've ever had. Despite everything, I feel myself melting into his touch, my muscles turning to mush under his fingers. By the time he gets to my neck and shoulders, I'm as relaxed as I've been since waking up on this island. If I hadn't been blindfolded, bound, and sodomized, I would've thought I was in a spa.

When he removes the toy some twenty minutes later, it slides right out, without even a hint of discomfort. He pushes it back in again, and this time, the pain is minimal. If anything, it feels... interesting... particularly when his fingers find my clit and begin stimulating it again.

I don't resist the pleasure those fingers bring me. Why bother? I would take pleasure over pain any day of the week. Julian is going to do whatever he wants, and I might as well enjoy some parts of it.

So I divorce my mind from the wrongness of it all and let myself simply feel. I can't see anything with the blindfold, and I can't put up much of a fight with my hands tied behind my back. I'm completely helpless—and there's something peculiarly liberating in that. There's no point in worrying, no point in thinking. I'm simply drifting in the darkness, high on post-massage endorphins.

He fucks me with the toy, pushing it in and out of me at the same time as his fingers press on my clit. His movements are rhythmic, coordinated, and I moan as my sex starts to throb, the pressure inside me growing with each thrust. Abruptly, the tension gets to be too much, and there's a sudden, intense burst of pleasure, starting at my core and radiating outward. My muscles clamp down on the toy, and the unusual sensation only intensifies my orgasm. Unable to control myself, I cry out, grinding against Julian's fingers. I want the ecstasy to last forever.

All too soon, though, it's over, and I'm left limp and shaking in the aftermath. Julian is not done with me, of course, not by a long shot. Just as I'm starting to recover, he withdraws the toy and presses a different, larger object to my back opening. It's his cock, I realize, tensing again as he begins to push in.

"Nora..." There is a warning note in his voice, and I know what he wants from me, but I don't know if I can do it. I don't know if I can relax enough to let him in. It's too much; he's too thick, too long. I don't understand how something that big can enter me there without ripping me apart.

But he's relentless, and I feel my muscles slowly giving in, unable to resist the pressure he's applying. The head of his cock pushes past the tight ring of my sphincter, and I cry out at the burning, stretching sensation. "Shh," he says soothingly, stroking my back as he slowly goes deeper. "Shh... it's all good..."

By the time he's in all the way, I'm a trembling, sweating mess. There's pain, yes, but there's also the novelty of having something so large invading my body in this weird, unnatural way. I know people do this—and supposedly even derive pleasure from this act—but I can't imagine ever doing this willingly.

He pauses, letting me adjust to the sensations, and I sob softly into the mattress, wanting nothing more than for this to be over. He's patient, though, his strong hands caressing me, relaxing me, until my tears subside and I no longer feel like passing out.

He senses it when my discomfort begins to ease, and starts to move inside me, slowly, carefully. I can hear his harsh breathing, and I know that he's exerting a lot of control over himself, that he probably wants to fuck me harder but is trying not to 'damage me beyond repair.' Nevertheless, his movements cause my insides to twist and churn, causing me to cry out with every stroke.

And just when I think I can't bear it anymore, he slides one hand under my hips and finds my swollen clit again. His fingers are gentle, his touch butterfly-soft, and I begin to feel a familiar warmth in my belly, my body responding to him despite the painful invasion. What he's doing isn't taking away the pain, but it's distracting me from it, allowing me to focus on the pleasure. I never knew pleasure and pain could co-exist like that, but there's something strangely addictive in that combination, something dark and forbidden that resonates with a part of myself I never knew existed.

His pace picks up, and somehow that makes it better. Maybe some nerve endings are desensitized by now—or maybe I'm simply getting used to having him inside me —but the pain lessens, almost disappears. All that's left is a host of other sensations—strange, unfamiliar sensations that are intriguing in their own way. That, and the pleasure from his clever fingers playing with my sex, arousing me until I'm crying out for a different reason, until I'm begging Julian to do it, to send me over the edge again.

And he does. My entire body tightens and explodes, shuddering with the force of my release. He groans as my muscles clamp down on his shaft, and I feel the liquid warmth from his seed bathing my insides, the saltiness of it stinging my raw flesh.

"Good girl," he whispers in my ear, his cock softening within me. He kisses my earlobe, and the tender gesture is such a contrast to what he'd just done that I feel disoriented. Is this normal kidnapper behavior? When he withdraws from me, I feel empty and cold, almost as if I'm missing the heat from his body pressing me down.

He doesn't leave me alone for long, though. He unties my hands first and rubs them lightly, then he takes off my blindfold. I blink, letting my eyes adjust to the soft light in the room, and move my arms, bracing myself on my elbows.

"Come," he says softly, wrapping his fingers around my upper arm. "Let's get you into the shower."

I let him tug me to my feet and lead me into the bathroom. My legs feel shaky, and I'm glad he's holding me. I don't know if I could've walked there by myself.

He turns on the shower, waits for the water to heat up for a few seconds, and leads us into the large stall. Then he thoroughly washes every part of my body, rinsing away all traces of lube and semen. He even shampoos and conditions my hair, his fingers massaging my skull and relaxing me again. By the time he's done, I feel clean and cared for.

"Now it's your turn," he says, turning up my palm and pouring some body wash into it.

"You want me to wash you?" I say incredulously, and he nods, a small smile curving his lips. With the water running down his muscular body, he's even more gorgeous than usual, like some kind of a sea god.

A sea monster, I correct myself. A beautiful sea monster.

He continues looking at me expectantly, waiting to see if I will do as he asked, and I mentally shrug. Why not wash him, really? It won't hurt me in the least. And besides, as much as I hate him, I can't deny that I am curious about his body—that touching him is something I find exciting.

So I rub my hands together and run them over his chest, spreading the soap all over his bronzed skin. He raises his arms, and I wash his sides and underarms, then his back.

His skin is mostly smooth, roughened in just a few places by dark, masculine hair. I can feel the powerful muscles bunching under my fingers, and I find myself enjoying this experience. In this moment, I can almost pretend that I want to be here, that this stunning creature is my lover instead of my captor.

I wash him as thoroughly as he washed me, my soapy hands gliding over his legs, his feet. By the time I get to his sex, his cock begins to harden again, and I freeze, realizing that my ministrations unintentionally aroused him.

He correctly interprets my reaction as fear. "Relax, my pet," he murmurs, his voice filled with amusement. "I'm only human, you know. As delicious as you are, I need more than a few minutes to recover fully."

I swallow and turn away, rinsing my hands under the water spray. What the hell am I doing? He hadn't forced me to touch him. I had done it of my own accord. He'd asked, but I am pretty sure I could've refused and he would've let it slide. The dark undercurrent I'd sensed in him earlier this evening is not there now. In fact, Julian seems to be in a good mood, his manner almost playful.

I want to get out of the shower now, so I make a move to slide past him. He stops me, his arm blocking my way.

"Wait," he says softly, tilting my chin up with his fingers. Then he bends his head and kisses me, his lips sweet and gentle on mine. A now-familiar response warms my body, making me want to rub myself against him like a cat in heat. He doesn't let it go far, though. After about a minute, he lifts his head and smiles down at me, his blue eyes gleaming with satisfaction. "Now you can go."

Utterly confused, I step out of the shower, dry myself off, and escape into my room as quickly as I can.

13

That night I learn about Julian's nightmares.

After the shower, he joins me in my bed, his muscular body curving around me from the back, one heavy arm draping over my torso. I stiffen at first, unsure of what to expect, but all he does is go to sleep while holding me close to him. I can hear the even rhythm of his breathing as I stare into the darkness, and then I gradually fall asleep too.

I wake up to a strange noise. It startles me out of deep sleep, and my eyes fly open, my heart pounding from an adrenaline surge.

What was that? For a moment, I don't dare breathe, but then I realize that the sounds are coming from the other side of the bed—from the man sleeping beside me.

I sit up in bed and peer at him. It looks like he rolled away from me in the night, gathering all the blankets to himself. I'm completely naked and uncovered, and I actually feel a little chilly with the air-conditioning running at full blast.

The sounds escaping his throat are muffled, but there is a raw quality to them that gives me goose-bumps. They remind me of an animal in pain. He's breathing hard, almost gasping for air.

"Julian?" I say uncertainly. I don't really know what to do in this situation. Should I wake him up? He's clearly having a bad dream. I recall him telling me about his family, that they were all murdered, and I can't help feeling pity for this beautiful, twisted man.

He cries out, his voice low and hoarse, and flops over onto his back, one arm hitting the pillow only a few inches away from me.

"Um, Julian?" I reach out cautiously and touch his hand.

He mumbles and turns his head, still deeply asleep. If we were anywhere but on this island, this would be the perfect moment for me to try to escape. As it stands, however, there's really no point in going anywhere, so I just watch Julian warily, wondering if he's going to wake up on his own or if I should try harder to wake him.

For a few moments, it seems like he's settling down, his breathing calming a bit. Then he suddenly cries out again.

It's a name this time.

"Maria," he rasps out. "Maria…"

For one shocking second, I feel a hot tide of jealousy sweeping over me. Maria… He's dreaming of another woman.

Then my rational side reasserts itself. Maria could easily be his mother or his sister—and even if she's not, why should I care that he's dreaming of her? It's not like he's my boyfriend or anything.

So I swallow and reach for him again, suppressing the residual pangs of jealousy. "Julian?"

As soon as my fingers touch his arm, he grabs me, his motions so fast and startling that only a small gasp escapes me as he pulls me toward him. His arms around me are inescapable, his embrace almost suffocating, and I can feel him shaking as he holds me tightly against him, my face pressed into his shoulder. His skin is cold and clammy with sweat, and I can hear his heart galloping in his chest.

"Maria," he mumbles into my hair, his fingers digging into my back with such force that I'm sure there will be bruises there tomorrow. Yet somehow I don't mind because I know he's not doing this on purpose. He's in the grip of his nightmare and he's seeking comfort—and I'm the only one who can provide it right now.

After a while, I can hear his breathing easing. His arms relax a little, no longer squeezing me with such desperation, and his frantic heartbeat begins to slow. "Maria," he whispers again, but there's less pain in his voice now, as though he's reliving happier times with her, whatever those may be.

I let him hold me, not moving lest I wake him from his now-peaceful rest. He's not the only one receiving comfort here. Despite everything he's done to me, I can't deny that a part of me wants this from him, this feeling of closeness, of safety. He's the only thing I have to fear; logically, I know that. It doesn't matter, though, because right now I feel like he's holding the darkness at bay, keeping me safe from whatever other monsters may be lurking out there.

Just as I'm keeping him safe from his nightmares.

When I wake up the next morning, Julian is gone again.

"Where is he?" I ask Beth at breakfast, watching as she cuts up a mango for me. I still feel an occasional twinge of discomfort when I move, a reminder of my captor's more exotic proclivities.

"A work emergency," she says, her hands moving with a graceful efficiency that I can't help but admire. "He should be back in a couple of days."

"What kind of work emergency?"

Beth shrugs. "I don't know. You can ask Julian that when he returns."

I look at her, trying to understand what motivates her... and Julian. "You said I'm the first girl he brought here, to this island," I say, keeping my tone casual. "So what did he do with the others?"

"There were no others." She's done with the mango, and she's placing the plate in front of me before sitting down to eat her own breakfast.

"So why is he doing this to me? I know he's got peculiar tastes, but surely there are women who are into that—"

Beth grins at me, showing even white teeth. "Of course. But he wants you."

"Why? What's so special about me?"

"You'll have to ask Julian that."

Again that non-answer. Her evasiveness makes me want to scream. I spear a piece of mango with my fork and chew it slowly, thinking this over.

"Is it because of Maria?" I'm not sure what makes me ask this, except that I can't get that name out of my head.

It's apparently the right question, though, because it stops Beth in her tracks. "Julian told you about Maria?" She sounds shocked.

"He mentioned her." It's not really a lie. Her name did come up, even though Julian doesn't know it. "Why does that surprise you?"

She shrugs again, no longer looking so shocked. "I guess it doesn't, now that I think about it. If he's going to tell anyone, it would probably be you."

Me? Why? I'm burning with curiosity, but I try to keep my expression impassive, like none of this is news to me. "Of course," I say calmly, eating my mango.

"Then you understand, Nora," she says, looking at me. "You have to understand at least a little bit. Your resemblance to her is uncanny. I saw the photo, and she could've been your younger sister."

"That similar?" I struggle to keep the shock out of my voice. My heart is pounding in my chest. This is so much more than I could've hoped for, and Beth just handed me this information on a silver platter.

She frowns. "He didn't tell you that?"

"No," I say. "He didn't tell me much. Just a little bit." Just her name, uttered in the throes of a nightmare.

Beth's eyes widen as she realizes that she probably revealed more than she should have. She looks unhappy for a moment, but then her expression smooths out. "Oh well," she says. "I guess now you know. I'll have to tell Julian about this, of course."

I swallow, and the piece of mango slides down my throat like a rock. I don't want her to tell Julian anything. I don't know what he'll do to me when he finds out that I know about Maria—that I saw him when he was at his most vulnerable.

My stupid curiosity.

"Why?" I say, trying not to sound anxious. "You're the one he's going to be upset with, not me."

"I wouldn't be too sure of that, Nora," Beth says, giving me a slightly malicious smile. "And besides, I don't ever keep secrets from Julian. He's very good at prying them out of people."

And getting up, she starts washing the dishes.

I spend the next two days alternating between speculating about Maria and worrying about Julian's return.

Who is she? Someone who looks a lot like me, apparently. So similar that she could be my younger sister,

Beth said. How old is this girl? Who is she to Julian? The questions gnaw at me, interfering with my sleep. He took me because of my resemblance to her—that much is obvious to me. But why? What happened to her? Why is she in his nightmares?

I want to know, I want to understand, yet I'm afraid of Julian's reaction when he returns and finds out that I snooped. I could try to explain that I learned all of this accidentally, that I didn't mean to invade his privacy, but I strongly suspect my captor is not the understanding type.

Beth doesn't tell me anything else about Maria. In fact, she doesn't talk to me much at all. She's one of those rare individuals who seems happy being by herself. If I were her, I would go crazy being stuck here on this island, doing nothing but cooking, cleaning, and looking after Julian's sex toy, but she seems perfectly fine with it.

I, on the other hand, am far from fine. I am constantly thinking about my old life, missing my family and friends. They probably think I'm dead at this point. I'm guessing there was a big search for me, but I doubt it yielded any results.

I also think about Jake, wondering if he recovered from his beating. It had looked so brutal, what Julian's thug had done to him. Does Jake know that it was my fault? That he got attacked in his house because of me?

Taking a deep breath, I tell myself that it doesn't matter if he knows or not. Whatever Jake and I could've had together is over. I belong to Julian now, and there's no point in thinking about any other man.

In a way, I am lucky. I know that. I'm sure many girls end up in far worse circumstances than me. I once saw a documentary about sexual slavery, and the images of those hollow-eyed women had haunted me for days. They'd seemed broken, completely and utterly crushed by whatever had been done to them, and even the fact that they'd been rescued didn't seem to dispel the suffering etched into their faces.

My captivity is different. It's much nicer, much more comfortable. Julian is not trying to break me, and I'm grateful for that. I may be his sex slave, but at least he's my only master. Things could definitely be much worse.

Or so I tell myself as I wait for his return, desperately hoping that Julian's reaction to my prying won't be as bad as I fear.

14

*J*ulian comes back in the middle of the night. I must've been sleeping lightly because I wake up as soon as I hear the quiet murmur of conversation downstairs. My captor's deeper tones are interspersed with Beth's more feminine ones, and I have a strong suspicion I know what they're talking about.

I sit up in bed, my heart galloping in my chest. Getting up, I quickly pull on yesterday's clothes and run to the bathroom to freshen up. I don't know why I care about brushing teeth right now, but I do. I want to be as awake and prepared as possible for whatever Julian decides to do to me.

Then I just sit on the bed and wait.

Finally, the door to my room opens and Julian walks in. He looks unusually tired, with dark shadows under his eyes and a hint of stubble on his normally clean-shaven face. These flaws should've diminished his beauty, but they only humanize him a bit, somehow enhancing his attractiveness.

"You're awake." He sounds surprised.

"I heard voices," I explain, watching him warily.

"And you decided to greet me. How nice of you, my pet."

I know he's mocking me, so I don't say anything, just continue looking at him. My palms are sweating, but I'm doing my best to project a calm demeanor.

He sits down on the bed next to me and lifts his hand to touch my hair. "Such a sweet pet," he murmurs, lifting a thick strand and playfully tickling my cheek with it. "Such a curious little kitten…"

I swallow, my breathing fast and shallow. What is he going to do to me?

He gets up and starts to undress while I watch him, frozen in place by a mixture of fear and strange anticipation. His clothes come off, revealing the powerfully masculine body underneath, and I feel a wave of desire rolling through me, heating up my core.

I want him. Despite everything, I want him, and that's the most screwed-up thing of all. He's probably going to do something awful to me, but I still want him more than I could've ever imagined wanting anyone.

In for a penny, in for a pound. "Did you do this to Maria?" I ask quietly. "Did you also keep her as your pet?"

He looks at me, his eyes as blue and mysterious as the ocean. "Are you sure you want to go there, Nora?" His voice is soft, deceptively calm.

I stare at him, feeling uncharacteristically reckless. "Why, yes, Julian, I do." My tone is bitterly sarcastic, and I realize that part of my boldness stems from jealousy, that I hate the idea of this Maria being special to Julian. But even that realization is not enough to stop me. "Who is she? Some other girl you abused?"

His expression darkens, and I hold my breath, waiting to see what he would do now. In a way, I want to provoke him. I want him to punish me, to hurt me. I want it because I need him to be nothing more than a monster—because I need to hate him for the sake of my sanity.

He walks over and sits down on the bed next to me. I fight the urge to flinch when he reaches for me and wraps his strong fingers around my neck. Gripping my throat, he leans over and brushes his cheek against mine, back and forth, as though enjoying the soft texture of my skin against the roughness of his stubble-covered jaw. His fingers don't squeeze, but the threat is there, and I can feel myself shaking, my breathing speeding up in terrified anticipation.

He chuckles softly, and I feel the gust of air against my ear. Despite his weary appearance, his breath is fresh and sweet, as though he had just been chewing gum. I close my eyes, trying to convince myself that Julian wouldn't really kill me, that he's just toying with me right now.

He kisses my ear, nibbling lightly on my earlobe. His touch in that sensitive area sends pleasurable chills down my spine, and my breathing changes again, becomes slower and deeper as I get more aroused. I can smell the warm, musky scent of his skin, and my nipples tighten, reacting to his nearness. The ache between my thighs is growing, and I squirm a little, trying to relieve the pressure building inside me.

"You want me, don't you?" he whispers in my ear, slipping his hand under the skirt of my dress and lightly stroking my sex. I know he can feel the moisture there, and I suppress a moan as one long finger pushes inside me, rubbing against my slick inner wall. "Don't you, Nora?"

"Yes." I gasp as he touches a particularly sensitive spot.

"Yes, what?" His voice is harsh, demanding. He wants my complete surrender.

"Yes, I want you," I admit in a broken whisper. I can't deny it. I want Julian. I want the man who kidnapped me, who hurt me. I want him, and I hate myself for it.

He withdraws his finger then and lets go of my throat. Startled, I open my eyes and meet his gaze. He lifts his hand to my face, pressing his finger against my lips. It's the same finger that was just inside me. "Suck it," he orders, and I obediently open my mouth, sucking the finger in. I can taste myself, my own desire, and it makes me even more turned on.

When he's satisfied that the finger is clean, he removes it from my mouth, grasping my chin with his hand instead, forcing me to meet his gaze. I stare up at him, mesmerized by the dark blue striations in his irises. My body is throbbing with need, desperately craving his possession. I want him to take me, to fill the aching emptiness within.

But all he does is look at me, a mocking half-smile playing on his beautiful lips. "You think I'm going to punish you tonight, Nora?" he asks softly. "Is that what you're expecting me to do?"

I blink, startled by the question. Of course I expect him to do that. I did something that upset him, and he's not shy about hurting me when I'm on my best behavior.

Apparently reading the answer on my face, he smiles wider. "Well, sorry to disappoint you, my pet, but I'm far too exhausted to do your punishment justice tonight. All I want right now is your mouth." And with that, he fists his hand in my hair and pushes me down, so that I'm kneeling between his legs, his erection at my eye level.

"Suck it," he murmurs, looking down at me. "Just like you did my finger."

I'm no stranger to blow-jobs, having given quite a few to my ex-boyfriend, so I know what to do. I close my lips around the thick column of his shaft and swirl my tongue around the tip. He tastes a little salty, a little musky, and I look up, watching his face as I cup his balls in my hand and squeeze them lightly. He groans, his eyes closing and his hand tightening in my hair, and I continue, moving my mouth up and down on his cock, swallowing him deeper every time.

For some reason, I don't mind pleasuring him this way. In fact, I find it strangely enjoyable. Even though it's an illusion, I feel like he's at my mercy at the moment, that I am the one who has the power right now. I love the helpless groans that escape his throat as I use my hands, my lips, and my tongue to bring him to the very brink of orgasm before slowing down. I love the agonized expression on his face when I take his balls into my mouth and suck on them, feeling them tightening in my mouth. I love the way he shudders when I lightly scrape my fingernails on the underside of his balls, and when he finally explodes, I love the way he grabs my head, holding me in place as he comes, his cock pulsing and throbbing in my mouth.

When he releases me, I lick my lips, cleaning off the traces of semen while looking up at him the whole time.

He stares down at me, still breathing heavily. "That was good, Nora." His voice is low and raspy. "Very good. Who taught you to do that?"

I shrug. "It's not like I was a nun before I met you," I say without thinking.

His eyes narrow, and I realize that I just made a mistake. This is a man who seems to revel in the fact that he was my first, who likes the idea that I belong to him and only to him. Any references to ex-boyfriends are best kept to myself.

To my relief, he doesn't seem inclined to punish me for this transgression either. Instead, he pulls me up, back onto the bed. Then he undresses me, turns off the light, and puts his arm around me, holding me close as he drifts off to sleep.

~

My punishment doesn't take place until the following night. Julian again spends the day in his office, and I don't see him until dinnertime.

For some reason, I'm not as frightened as I was before. The little interlude last night—and sleeping in Julian's arms afterwards—soothed my anxiety, making me think the punishment won't be as bad as I'd initially feared. He didn't seem particularly angry that I'd found out about Maria, which is a big relief. I hope he'll forgo punishing me altogether, particularly if I do my best to behave today.

The three of us have dinner again, and I listen to Julian and Beth discussing the latest developments in the Middle East. It surprises me how well informed both of them seem to be about the topic. Before my kidnapping, I was pretty good about following current events, but I've never heard most of the politicians' names they're mentioning. Then again, if Julian really does run an international import-export company, then it makes sense for him to have his finger on the pulse of world politics.

My curiosity gets the best of me again, and I ask if Julian's company does a lot of business in the Middle East.

He smiles at me as he spears a piece of shrimp with his fork. "Yes, my pet, it does."

"Is that where you went on this trip?"

"No," he says, biting into the juicy shrimp. "I was in Hong Kong this time."

I make a mental note of that. Hong Kong had to be

close enough to the island for him to fly there, conduct his business, and fly back—all within two days. I picture a map of the Pacific Ocean in my head. It's a bit fuzzy, as geography is not my strong point, but I think this island must not be that far from the Philippines.

Beth offers me some curried potatoes to go with my shrimp, and I take them, thanking her with a smile. I've noticed that we get more food variety shortly after Julian comes back from the mainland. I'm guessing he brings us food supplies from wherever he goes to.

Beth smiles back at me, and I see that she's in a good mood. In general, she seems happier when Julian is here, more lighthearted. I'm sure it's not fun for her, dealing with my attitude all the time. One could almost feel bad for her—'almost' being the key word.

"I've never been to Asia," I tell Julian. "Is Hong Kong really how they show it in movies?"

Julian grins at me. "Pretty much. It's amazing. Probably one of my favorite cities. The architecture is fascinating, and the food…" He makes a show of licking his lips. "The food is just to die for." He rubs his belly, and I laugh, charmed despite myself.

The rest of the dinner passes in the same pleasant manner. Julian tells me amusing stories about the different places he's been to in Asia, and I listen in fascination, occasionally gasping and laughing at some of the more outrageous tales. Beth sometimes chimes in, but for the most part, it's as though it's just Julian and me, having fun on a date.

Like that time when we had dinner alone, I find myself

falling under Julian's spell. He's more than charming; he's simply mesmerizing. His allure goes beyond his looks, although I can't deny the physical attraction between us. When he laughs or gives me one of his genuine smiles, I feel a warm glow, like he's the sun and I'm basking in his rays. Everything about him appeals to me—the way he talks, how he gestures to emphasize a point, the way his eyes crinkle at the corners when he grins at me. He's also an excellent storyteller, and three hours simply fly by as he entertains me with tales of his adventures in Japan, where he once lived for a year as a teenager.

I don't want this dinner to end, so I try to stretch it out as much as I can, helping myself to second, third, and fourth helpings of the fruit Beth prepared as dessert. I'm sure Julian is aware of my delaying tactics, but he doesn't seem to mind.

Finally, everything has been eaten, and Beth gets up to wash the dishes. Julian smiles at me, and for the first time this evening, I feel a flicker of fear. I can again sense that dark undercurrent in his smile, and I realize that it's been present all along—that it's always there with Julian. The charming man that I've just spent three hours with is about as real as a figment of my imagination.

Still smiling, he offers me his hand. It's a courtly gesture, but I can't help the chill that runs down my spine as I see a familiar gleam in his blue eyes. He again looks like a dark angel, his sublime beauty tinted with a faint shadow of evil.

Swallowing to get rid of the sudden knot in my throat, I place my hand in his and let him lead me upstairs. It's better this way, more civilized. It allows me to pretend for a few moments longer—to hold on to the illusion of having a choice.

When we enter my room, he has me undress and lie down on the bed, on my stomach. Then he ties me up again, binding my wrists tightly behind my back. A blindfold goes over my eyes, and pillows under my hips. It's the exact same position in which he took me last time, and I can't help tensing as I remember the agony—and the ecstasy—of his possession.

Is that what he's going to do? Have anal sex with me again? If so, it's not that bad. I survived the last time, and I'm sure I'll be fine again.

So when I feel the coolness of lube between my cheeks, I try to relax, to let him do whatever he wants. A toy slides in, the invasion startling but not particularly painful. I can definitely tolerate it. As before, he leaves the toy inside me as he gives me a massage, relaxing me, arousing me with his touch. He kisses the back of my neck, nibbles on the sensitive spot near my shoulder, and then his mouth travels down my spine, kissing each vertebrae. At the same time, his finger slips into my vaginal opening, adding to the tension coiling low in my belly.

My release, when it comes, is so powerful that I buck against the mattress, my entire body shuddering and convulsing. While I'm recovering from the aftershocks,

Julian withdraws his finger, and I feel cool air on my back as he leans away from me for a second.

The lick of fire along my buttocks is as sharp as it is sudden. Startled, I cry out, trying to twist away, but I don't get far, and the second hit is even more painful than the first, landing on my thighs. He's whipping me with something, I realize. I don't know what it is, but I can hear the swish in the air as he brings it down on my defenseless ass, again and again while I sob and try to roll away.

Apparently tired of chasing me all over the bed, he unties my hands and then ties them above my head, securing my wrists to the wooden headboard.

"Julian, please, I'm sorry!" I plead, desperate to make him stop. "Please, I'm sorry I was prying. Please, I won't do it again, I won't—"

"Of course you will, my pet," he whispers in my ear, his breath warm on my neck. "You're as curious as a little cat. But sometimes you should let things slide. For your own good, you understand?"

"Yes! Yes, I do. Please, Julian—"

"Shh," he soothes, kissing my neck again. "You need to accept your punishment like a good girl." And with that, he pulls back again, leaving my back and buttocks exposed to him.

I try to scramble away, but he catches my legs, holding my ankles together with one hand. He's strong, far stronger than I could've imagined, because he's able to hold my flailing legs with just one arm while whipping me with the other.

I can hear the swishing sound his prop makes, and I can't help the screams that escape my throat each time it lands on my ass. My butt and thighs feel like they're on fire, and the blindfold is soaked with my tears. I want it to stop, I'm begging him to stop, but Julian is immune to my pleas.

It seems to go on forever, until I'm too hoarse to scream and too exhausted to struggle. I can't even gather enough energy to keep my muscles tense, and somehow that seems to help the pain. I relax further, make my body go limp, and the pain becomes more manageable, each lash feeling less like a bite and more like a stroke.

As the whipping proceeds, my world seems to narrow until nothing exists outside of the present moment. I'm not thinking anymore; I'm simply feeling, simply being. There's something surreal, yet incredibly addictive in the experience. Each swish brings with it a sharp sensation that pulls me deeper into this strange state, making me feel like I'm floating. The pain is no longer unbearable; instead it's comforting in some perverse way. It's grounding me, providing me with what I need at that moment. A warm glow spreads throughout my body, and all my worries, all my fears disappear. It's a high unlike anything I've ever experienced before.

When Julian finally stops and unties me, I cling to him, trembling all over. Without the blindfold and the restraints, I feel lost, overwhelmed. As though knowing what I need, he pulls me onto his lap and cradles me gently in his arms, letting me cry against his shoulder until I no longer feel like I'm going to fall apart.

After a while, I become cognizant of the hard length of his erection pressing into my buttocks, which are sore and throbbing from the whipping. The little toy he put in my ass before is still there, lodged securely inside me, and I realize that the warm glow within me is different now, more sexual in nature.

Apparently sensing the shift in my mood, Julian carefully lifts me and positions me so that I'm facing him while straddling his lap. My hands are on his shoulders, and I can feel the powerful muscles playing under his skin. With my thighs spread wide, the tip of his cock presses against my sex. The smooth head slides between my folds and rubs against my clit, intensifying my arousal. I moan, my head arching back, and he slowly enters me, penetrating me inch by slow inch. With the toy in my ass, he feels even bigger than usual, and I gasp as he goes deeper, filling me with his thickness.

It feels good, so unbelievably good, and I moan again, tightening my inner muscles around his shaft. He groans, closing his eyes, and I do it again, wanting more of the sensation.

He opens his eyes and stares at me, his face taut with lust and his eyes glittering. I hold his gaze, fascinated by the fierce need I see there. He's as much in my thrall right now as I am in his, and the realization adds to my desire, further heating up my core.

Raising his hand, he curves his palm around my cheek, wiping away the remnants of tears with his thumb. Then he bends his head and kisses me, as tenderly as I've ever been kissed. I revel in that kiss; his affection is like a drug to me right now—I need it with a desperation I don't fully understand.

I close my eyes, and my hands slide up his shoulders, finding their way into his hair. It's thick and soft to the touch, like dark satin. Pressing closer to him, I rub my naked breasts against his powerfully muscled chest, delighting in the feel of his hair-roughened skin against my sensitive nipples. His lips are firm and warm on mine, and the cock inside me is unbelievably hard, stretching me, filling me to the brim.

Still kissing me, he begins to rock back and forth, causing his shaft to move within me ever so slightly, sending waves of heat throughout my body. However, each movement also serves as a reminder of the earlier beating, and a pained moan escapes my throat as my sore buttocks rub against his hard thighs. He swallows the sound, his mouth now consuming mine with unrestrained hunger.

His hand slides into my hair, holding it tightly as he devours me with his kiss, his hips rocking harder, adding to the pressure building within my core. His other hand moves down my body, and then he presses on the toy, pushing it deeper inside my rear passage.

I fly apart. My orgasm is so strong, I can't even make a sound. For a few blissful seconds, I'm completely swamped by pleasure, by ecstasy so intense that it's almost agonizing. My body shudders and undulates on top of Julian's, and my movements trigger his own release.

In the aftermath, he holds me, stroking my sweat-dampened hair. I can feel his shaft softening within me, and then he reaches between my butt cheeks and tugs on the toy, carefully pulling it out.

Then he makes me get up and leads me into the shower.

15

*H*e takes care of me in the shower again, washing me, soothing me with his touch. He's especially careful around the tender area of my thighs and buttocks, making sure not to add to my discomfort. To my relief, it doesn't look like the skin is broken anywhere. My ass is pink with some reddish welts, and I'm sure there will be bruising, but there is no trace of blood anywhere.

When I'm clean and dry, he guides me back to bed. He's silent and so am I. I'm still not fully out of that strange state I was in earlier. It's as though my mind is partially disconnected from my body. The only thing holding me together is Julian and his oddly gentle touch.

We lie down together, and Julian turns off the lights, wrapping us in darkness. I lie on my stomach, because any other position is too painful. He pulls me closer to him, so that my head is pillowed on his chest and my arm is draped over his ribcage, and I close my eyes, wanting nothing more than the oblivion of sleep.

"My father was one of the most powerful drug lords in Colombia." Julian's voice is barely audible, his breath ruffling the fine hair near my forehead. I had already begun to fall asleep, but I'm suddenly wide awake, my heart hammering in my chest.

"He started grooming me to be his successor when I was four years old. I held my first gun when I was six." Julian pauses, his hand lightly stroking my hair. "I killed my first man when I was eight."

I'm so horrified that I just lie there, frozen in place by shock.

"Maria was the daughter of one of the men in my father's organization," Julian continues, his voice low and emotionless. "I met her when I was thirteen, and she was twelve. She was everything that I was not. Beautiful, sweet… innocent. You see, unlike my father, her parents sheltered her from the reality of their lives. They wanted her to be a child, to know nothing about the ugliness of our world.

"But she was bright, like you. And curious. So very, very curious…" His voice trails off for a second, as though he's lost in some memory. Then he shakes it off and resumes his story. "She followed her father one day to see what he was doing. Hid in the back of his car. I found her there because it was my job to be a lookout, to guard the meeting spot."

I can barely breathe, unable to believe that Julian is telling me all this. Why now? Why tonight?

"I could've told her father, gotten her in trouble, but she begged so prettily, looked at me so sweetly with her big brown eyes that I couldn't do it. I made one of my father's guards take her home instead.

"After that, she came to see me on purpose. She wanted to get to know me better, she said. To be friends with me." There is a note of remembered disbelief in Julian's voice, as though nobody in their right mind could've wanted something like that.

I swallow, my heart stupidly aching for the young boy he had been once. Had he even had friends, or had his father stolen that from him too, just as he had destroyed Julian's childhood?

"I tried to tell her that it wasn't a good idea, that I wasn't somebody she should be around, but she wouldn't listen to me. She'd find me somewhere almost every week, until I had no choice but to give in and start spending time with her. We went fishing together, and she showed me how to draw." He pauses for a second, his hand still stroking my hair. "She was very good at drawing."

"What happened to her?" I ask when he doesn't say anything else for a minute. My voice is strangely hoarse. I clear my throat and try again. "What happened to Maria?"

"One of my father's rivals learned that she was seeing me. We had just raided his warehouse, and he was pissed. So he decided to teach my father a lesson... through me."

Every little hair on my body is standing on end, and I

feel a chill roughening my skin with goosebumps. I can already see where this story is heading, and I want to tell Julian to stop, to go no further, but I can't get a single word past the constriction in my throat.

"They found her body in an alley near one of my father's buildings." His voice is steady, but I can sense the agony buried deeply within. "She had been raped, then mutilated. It was meant to be a message to me and my father. Back the fuck off, it said."

I squeeze my eyelids together, trying to keep the tears burning my eyes from leaking out, but it's a futile effort. I know Julian can probably feel the wetness on his chest. "A message? To a thirteen-year-old boy?"

"By that time, I was already fourteen." I can't see Julian's bitter smile, but I can sense it. "And age didn't matter. Not to my father... and certainly not to his rival."

"I'm sorry." I don't know what else to say. I want to cry—for him, for Maria, for that young boy who'd lost his friend in such a brutal manner. And I want to cry for myself, because I now understand my captor better—and I realize that the darkness in his soul is worse than anything I could've imagined.

Julian shifts underneath me, and I become aware of the fact that my hand is now on his shoulder and my nails are digging into his skin. I force myself to unclench my fingers and take a deep breath. I need to get a hold on myself, or I'm going to burst out sobbing.

"I killed those men." His tone is casual now, almost conversational, though I can feel the tension in his body.

"The ones who raped her. I tracked them down and killed them, one by one. There were seven of them. After that, my father sent me away, first to America, then to Asia and Europe. He was afraid all that killing would be bad for business. I didn't come back until years later, when he and my mother were killed by yet another rival."

I focus on controlling my breathing and keeping the bile in my throat down. "Is that why you don't have a Spanish accent?" My question comes totally out of the left field. I don't even know what makes me ask something so trivial at a moment like this.

But it's apparently the right thing to do because Julian relaxes slightly, some of the tension leaving his muscles. "Yes. That's partially why, my pet. Also, my mother was an American, and she taught me English from a young age."

"An American?"

"Yes. She was a model in her youth, a tall, beautiful blond. They met in New York, when my father was there on a business trip. He swept her off her feet, and they were married before he told her anything about his business."

"What did she do when she found out?" I know I'm probably focusing on the wrong things here, but I need to distract myself from the gruesome images filling my mind—images of a dead girl who's a younger version of me...

"There was nothing she could do," Julian says. "She was already married to him, and living in Colombia."

He doesn't explain further, but he doesn't need to. It's clear to me that his mother was as much of a prisoner as I am—except that she'd chosen her captivity, at least initially.

For a few minutes, we just lie there quietly, without talking. I'm no longer drowsy. I don't know if I'll be able to sleep tonight at all. The ache in my body is nothing compared to the despair in my heart.

"So is that what you do now? Drugs?" I ask, finally breaking the silence. It's not far from my original supposition that he's part of the Mafia or some other criminal organization.

"No," he says, to my surprise. "That part of my life ended when my parents were killed. I took the family business in a different direction."

"Which direction?" I remember him telling me something about an import-export organization, but I can't imagine Julian doing something as innocuous as selling electronics. Not after what I've just learned about his upbringing.

He chuckles, as though amused at my persistence. "Weapons," he says. "I'm an arms dealer, Nora."

I blink, surprised. I know a little—or at least, I think I know—about drug dealers, thanks to some popular TV shows. Arms dealers, however, are a complete mystery to me. I strongly suspect Julian isn't talking about a few guns here or there.

I have a million questions about his profession, but there's something I need to know first, while Julian seems to be in a sharing mood. "Why did you steal me? Is it because I remind you of Maria?"

"Yes," he says softly, his voice wrapping around me like a cashmere scarf. "When I first saw you in that club, you looked so much like her, it was uncanny. Except you were older—and even more beautiful. And I wanted you. I needed you. For the first time in years, I was truly feeling. Of course, the emotions you evoked in me were nothing like what I'd once felt for her. She was my friend, but you..." He inhales deeply, his chest moving under my head. "I just needed you to be mine, Nora. When I touched you that day, when I felt the silkiness of your skin, I so badly wanted to take you, to strip off those tight clothes you were wearing and fuck you senseless right then and there, on the floor of that club. And I wanted to hurt you... the way I sometimes like to hurt women, the way they ask me to hurt them... I wanted to hear you scream—in pain and in pleasure."

His hand continues playing with my hair, and the caressing touch keeps me calm enough to listen. In the darkness, none of this is real. There's only Julian and his voice, telling me things that a normal person would find frightening—things that somehow make me wet instead.

"I brought you here, to my island, because it's the safest place for you. My business associates are always looking for signs of weakness, and you, my pet, are a weakness of mine. I've never felt this way about another woman. I've never been so—" he pauses for a moment, as though searching for the right word, "—so fucking obsessed. Just the thought of another man touching you, kissing you, drove me crazy. I tried to stay away, to put you out of my mind, but I couldn't resist seeing you one more time at your graduation. And when I saw you there, I knew you felt it too, this connection between us —and I knew then that it was inevitable... that I would take you, and you would always be mine."

His words wash over me like a warm ocean wave, bringing with it trepidation and a kind of unhealthy excitement. Some twisted part of me revels in the fact that I'm special to Julian, that he's as helplessly drawn to me as I am to him.

For some strange reason, I feel compelled to reciprocate his openness. "I was afraid of you," I tell him quietly. "In the club, and then when I saw you at my graduation, I was afraid."

"Only afraid?" He sounds amused and mildly disbelieving.

"Afraid and attracted," I admit. This seems to be the night for revelations. Besides, he already knows the truth. Despite my fear, I desire him. I've wanted him from the very beginning, and nothing he's done since changes that fact.

"Good." He runs his hand lightly down my back. "That's very good, my pet. It'll make things easier for both of us."

Easier? I consider that statement. Easier for him, certainly. But for me? I'm not so sure.

"Did you ever contact my family?" I ask, thinking of

his promise all those days ago. "Do they know that I'm alive?"

"Yes." His hand pauses at the curve of my spine. "They know."

I wonder what he told them and how they reacted. I wonder if it made it better for them or worse.

"Will you ever let me go?" I already know the answer, but I need to hear him say it anyway.

"No, Nora," he replies, and I can feel his smile in the darkness. "Never."

And bringing me closer, he holds me until we both eventually fall asleep.

16

Over the next few months, my life on the island falls into a routine of sorts. When Julian is there, my world revolves around him. His moods, his needs and desires, rule my days and nights.

He's an unpredictable lover—gentle one day, cruel the next. And sometimes he's a mix of both, a combination that I find particularly devastating. I understand what he's doing to me, but understanding doesn't make it any less effective. He's training me to associate pain with pleasure, to enjoy whatever he does to me, no matter how shocking and perverted it is. And always afterwards, there's that unsettling tenderness. He turns me inside out, takes me apart, and puts me back together—all in the span of one night.

And his training is working. I go into his arms willingly now, craving that high I often get from a particularly brutal session. Julian tells me that I'm a natural submissive with latent masochistic tendencies. I don't know if I believe him—I know that I certainly don't want to believe him—but I can't deny that his peculiar brand of lovemaking resonates with me on some level. Toys, whips, canes—he's used them all, and I have invariably found pleasure in some part of what he was doing.

Of course, he's not always sadistic. Sometimes he's almost sweet, massaging me all over, kissing me until I melt, and then making love to me when I'm nearly out of my mind with need. On days like that, I don't want to leave the island. All I want is for Julian to keep holding me, caressing me... loving me, in whichever way he can.

Perhaps that is the most disturbing part of it all—the fact that I now crave my captor's love. I don't even know if he's capable of that emotion, but I can't help needing it from him. He wants me, I know that, but it's not enough. Somewhere along the way, I've lost my hatred for him, and I don't even know how or when it happened. I still resent my captivity, but those feelings are now separate from the way I feel about Julian.

Instead of dreading his visits to the island, I now eagerly await them. His business keeps him away more than I like, and I begin to understand how pets feel, waiting for their owner to come home from work.

"Why can't you conduct more of your business from here?" I ask him one day, after we wake up together in the morning. He always sleeps with me now. He likes holding me during the night; it helps him with his nightmares.

"I do as much remotely as I can. Why, do you want

me here, my pet?" His gaze is coolly mocking as he turns his head to look at me. He doesn't like it when I question him about his business. It's a part of his life that he seems to want to keep separate. In general, I get the sense that he's sheltering me and Beth from some of the uglier parts of his world. Beth is fully aware of what Julian does, of course, but I don't know if she knows much more about arms dealing than I do.

"Yes," I tell him honestly. "I want you here." It's pointless to pretend otherwise; Julian knows exactly how I feel. He's very good at reading me—and manipulating me. I have no doubt that he's enjoying my growing attachment to him and likely doing his best to facilitate it.

Sure enough, at my admission, his lips curve in a sensual smile. "All right, baby," he says softly, "I'll try to be here more." And reaching for me, he brings me toward him for a kiss that makes me dissolve in his embrace.

With each day that passes, my old life seems further and further away, fading into that nebulous time known as the past. When Julian is gone, I occupy myself by reading, swimming, hiking all around the island, and the occasional fishing expeditions with Beth. Julian brought us a large-screen TV with a DVD player and hundreds of movies, so Beth and I have something to do during rainy weather, too.

We're still not exactly friends, Beth and I, but we've definitely grown closer. Partially, I think she likes the fact that I no longer try to escape. After my one failed attempt to bash her over the head—and the horrible incident with Jake that followed—I've been a model prisoner.

Of course, it would be foolish to be anything else. Even during Julian's visits, when his plane is here, it's locked inside the hangar I found on the other side of the island. I'm pretty sure Julian keeps the keys to the hangar in his office, where only he can access them. And even if I somehow got my hands on the keys, I sincerely doubt there would be an operating manual conveniently stored inside the plane, teaching me how to fly it.

No, my captor knew exactly what he was doing when he brought me to this island. It's as secure a prison as any I could imagine.

As days turn into weeks and then into months, I try to find more activities to fill up my free time—and to prevent myself from pining after Julian when he's not there.

The first thing I do is start running again.

I begin with short distances at first, to make sure I don't strain my knee, and then I slowly increase both speed and distance. I run either in the mornings or at night, when it's cooler, and it's not long before I am in as good of a shape as I'd been during my days on the track team. I can do a three-mile run in under seventeen minutes—an accomplishment that makes me ridiculously happy.

I also take up painting. Not because I remember Julian saying that Maria was good at drawing, but because I find it both entertaining and relaxing. I had enjoyed art classes in school, but I was always too busy with friends and other activities to give painting a serious attempt. Now, however, I have plenty of time on my hands, so I start learning how to properly draw and paint. Julian brings me a ton of art supplies and several instructional videos, and I soon find myself absorbed in trying to capture the beauty of the island on canvas.

"You know, you're very good at this," Beth says thoughtfully one day, coming up to me on the porch as I'm finishing a painting of the sunset over the ocean. "You've got the colors down exactly—that glowing orange shaded with the deep pink."

I turn and give her a big smile. "You really think so?"

"I do," Beth says seriously. "You're doing well, Nora."

I get the sense that she's talking about more than just the painting. "Thanks," I say dryly. Should I add that to my list of achievements—the fact that I'm able to thrive in captivity?

She grins in response, and for the first time, I feel like we truly understand each other. "You're welcome."

Walking over to the outdoor couch, she curls up on it, pulling out her book. I watch her for a few seconds, then go back to painting, trying to replicate the multidimensional shimmer of the water—and thinking about the puzzle that is Beth.

She still hasn't told me much about her past, but I get the sense that for her, this island is a retreat of sorts, a sanctuary. She sees Julian as her rescuer, and the outside world as an unpleasant and hostile place. "Don't you miss going to the mall?" I asked her once. "Having dinner with your friends? Going dancing? You're not a prisoner here; you could leave at any time. Why don't you have Julian take you with him on one of his trips? Do something fun before you come back here again?"

Her response was to laugh at me. "Dancing? Fun? Letting men put their hands all over my body—that's supposed to be fun?" Her voice turned mocking. "Should I also shop for sexy clothes and make-up, so I look all pretty for them? And what about pollution, drive-by shootings, and muggings—should I miss those, too?" Laughing again, she shook her head. "No, thanks. I'm perfectly happy right here."

And that's as much as she would say on that topic.

I don't know what happened to make her so bitter, but I strongly suspect Beth hasn't had an easy life. When we were watching Pretty Woman, she kept making snide comments about how real prostitution is nothing like the fairy tale they were showing. I didn't ask her about it then, but I've been curious ever since. Could she have been a prostitute in the past?

Putting down my brush, I turn and look at Beth. "Can I paint you?"

She looks up from her book, startled. "You want to paint me?"

"Yes, I do." It would be a nice change of pace from all those landscapes I've been focusing on lately—and it might also give me a chance to get to know her better.

She stares at me for a few seconds, then shrugs. "All right. I guess."

She seems uncertain about this, so I give her an encouraging smile. "You don't have to do anything—just sit there like that, with your book. It makes for a nice visual."

And it's true. The rays of the setting sun turn her red curls into a blazing flame, and with her legs tucked under, she looks young and vulnerable. Much more approachable than usual.

I set aside the painting I was working on and put up a blank canvas. Then I begin to sketch, trying to capture the symmetric angles of her face, the lean lines and curves of her body. It's an absorbing task, and I don't stop until it gets too dark for me to see anything.

"Are you done for today?" Beth asks, and I realize that she's been sitting in the same position for the past hour.

"Oh, yeah, sure," I say. "Thanks for being such a good model."

"No problem." She gives me a genuine smile as she gets up. "Ready for dinner?"

For the next three days, I work on Beth's portrait. She patiently models for me, and I find myself so busy that I hardly think about Julian at all. It's only at night that I have a chance to miss him—to feel the cold emptiness of my king-sized bed as I lie there aching for his embrace.

174

He's gotten me so addicted that a week without him feels like a cruel punishment—one that I find infinitely worse than any sexual torture my captor has doled out thus far.

"Did Julian say when he's going to be back?" I ask Beth as I'm putting the final touches on the painting. "He's already been gone for seven days."

She shakes her head. "No, but he'll be here as soon as he can manage. He can't stay away from you, Nora, you know that."

"Really? Has he said something to you?" I can hear the eagerness in my voice, and I mentally kick myself. How pathetic can one get? I might as well put a stamp on my forehead: another stupid girl who fell for her kidnapper. Of course, I doubt many kidnappers have Julian's lethal charm, so maybe I should cut myself some slack.

Thankfully, Beth doesn't tease me about my obvious infatuation. "He doesn't need to say it," she says instead. "It's perfectly obvious."

I put down my brush for a second. "Obvious how?" This conversation is fulfilling a need I didn't even know I had—that for a real girl-to-girl gossip session about men and their inexplicable emotions.

"Oh, please." Beth is starting to sound exasperated. "You know Julian is fucking crazy about you. Whenever I talk to him, it's Nora this, Nora that... Does Nora need anything? Has Nora been eating well?" She lowers her voice comically, mimicking Julian's deeper tones.

I grin at her. "Really? I didn't know this." And I

didn't. I mean, I knew that Julian is crazy about fucking me—and he definitely admitted to a certain obsession with me because of my resemblance to Maria—but I didn't know I was this much on his mind outside of the bedroom.

Beth rolls her eyes. "Yeah, right. You're not nearly as naive as you pretend to be. I've seen you batting those long lashes at him over dinner, trying to wrap him around your little finger."

I give her my best wide-eyed-innocent look. "What? No!"

"Uh-huh." Beth doesn't seem fooled in the least.

She's right, of course; I do flirt with Julian. Now that I'm no longer quite so afraid of my captor, I am again doing my best to get into his good graces. Somewhere in the back of my mind, there is a persistent hope that if he trusts me enough—if he cares for me enough—he might take me off the island.

When this plan had first occurred to me—in those terrifying first few days of my captivity—I had been playacting. As soon as I found myself off the island, I would've done my best to escape, regardless of any promises I might've made. Now, however, I don't even know what I would do if Julian took me with him. Would I try to leave him? Do I even want to leave him? I honestly have no idea.

"Have you ever been in love?" I ask Beth, picking up my brush again.

To my surprise, a dark shadow passes over her face. "No," she says curtly. "Never."

"But you have loved… someone, right?" I don't know what makes me ask that, but I've apparently touched a nerve, because Beth's entire body tightens, like I just struck her a blow.

To my surprise, however, instead of snapping at me, she just nods. "Yes," she says quietly. "Yes, Nora, I have loved." Her eyes are unnaturally bright, as though glittering with unspilled moisture.

And I realize then that she's suffering—that whatever happened to her had left deep, indelible scars on her psyche. Her thorny exterior is just a mask, a way to protect herself from further hurt. And right now, for whatever reason, that mask has slipped, exposing the real woman underneath.

"What happened to this person?" I ask, my voice soft and gentle. "What happened to the one you loved?"

"She died." Beth's tone is expressionless, but I can sense the bottomless well of agony in that simple statement. "My daughter died when she was two."

I inhale sharply. "I'm sorry, Beth. Oh God, I'm so sorry…" Setting down my brush again, I walk over to Beth's couch and sit down, putting my arms around her.

At first, she's stiff and rigid, as though not used to human contact, but she doesn't push me away. She needs this right now; I know better than anyone how soothing a warm embrace can be when your emotions are all over the place. Julian delights in making me fall apart, so he can then be the one to mend me and put me back together.

"I am sorry," I repeat softly, rubbing her back in a slow circular motion. "I am so sorry."

Gradually, some of the tension drains out of Beth's body. She lets herself be soothed by my touch. After a while, she seems to regain her equilibrium, and I let her go, not wanting her to feel awkward about the hug.

Scooting back a bit, she gives me a small, embarrassed smile. "I'm sorry, Nora. I didn't mean to—"

"No, it's all right," I interrupt. "I'm sorry I was prying. I didn't know—"

And then we both look at each other, realizing that we could apologize until the end of time and it wouldn't change anything.

Beth closes her eyes for a second, and when she opens them, her mask is firmly back in place. She's my jailer again, as independent and self-contained as ever.

"Dinner?" she asks, getting up.

"Some of this morning's catch would be great," I say casually, walking over to put away my art supplies.

And we continue on, as though nothing had happened.

*a*fter that day, my relationship with Beth undergoes a subtle, but noticeable change. She's no longer quite so determined to keep me out, and I slowly get to know the person behind the prickly walls.

"I know you think you got a rough deal," she says one day as we're fishing together, "but believe me, Nora, Julian really does care about you. You're very lucky to have someone like him."

"Lucky? Why?"

"Because no matter what he's done, Julian is not really a monster," Beth says seriously. "He doesn't always act in a way that society deems acceptable, but he's not evil."

"No? Then what is evil?" I'm genuinely curious how Beth defines the word. To me, Julian's actions are the very epitome of something an evil man might do—my stupid feelings for him notwithstanding.

"Evil is someone who would murder a child," Beth

says, staring at the bright blue water. "Evil is someone who would sell his thirteen-year-old daughter to a Mexican brothel..." She pauses for a second, then adds, "Julian is not evil. You can trust me on that."

I don't know what to say, so I just watch the waves pounding against the shore. My chest feels as though it's being squeezed in a vise. "Did Julian save you from evil?" I ask after a while, when I'm certain that I can keep my voice reasonably steady.

She turns her head to look at me. "Yes," she says quietly. "He did. And he destroyed the evil for me. He handed me a gun and let me use it on those men—on the ones who killed my baby daughter. You see, Nora, he took a used-up, broken street whore and gave her her life back."

I hold Beth's gaze, feeling like I'm crumbling inside. My stomach is churning with nausea. She's right: I didn't know the real meaning of suffering. What she's been through is not something I can comprehend.

She smiles at me, apparently enjoying my shocked silence. "Life is nothing more than a fucked-up roulette," she says softly, "where the wheel keeps spinning and the wrong numbers keep coming up. You can cry about it all you want, but the truth of the matter is that this is as close to a winning ticket as it gets."

I swallow to get rid of the knot in my throat. "That's not true," I say, and my voice sounds a bit hoarse. "It's not always like this. There is a whole other world out there—the world where normal people live, where nobody tries to hurt you—"

"No," Beth says harshly. "You're dreaming. That world is about as real as a Disney fairy tale. You might have lived like a princess, but most people don't. Normal people suffer. They hurt, they die, and they lose their loved ones. And they hurt each other. They tear at each other like the savage predators they are. There is no light without darkness, Nora; the night ultimately catches up with us all."

"No." I don't believe it. I don't want to believe it. This island, Beth, Julian—it's all an anomaly, not the way things always are. "No, that's not—"

"It's true," Beth says. "You might not realize it yet, but it's true. You need Julian just as much as he needs you. He can protect you, Nora. He can keep you safe."

She seems utterly convinced of that fact.

"Good morning, my pet," a familiar voice whispers in my ear, waking me up, and I open my eyes to see Julian sitting there, leaning over me. He must've come here straight from some formal business meeting, because he's wearing a dress shirt instead of his usual more casual attire. A surge of happiness blazes through me. Smiling, I lift my arms and twine them around his neck, pulling him closer toward me.

He nuzzles my neck, his warm heavy weight pressing me into the mattress, and I arch against him, feeling the customary stirrings of desire. My nipples harden, and my core turns into a pool of liquid need, my entire body melting at his proximity.

"I missed you," he breathes in my ear, and I shiver with pleasure, barely suppressing a moan as his talented mouth moves down my neck and nibbles at a tender spot near my collarbone. "I love it when you're like this," he murmurs, raining gentle kisses on my upper chest and shoulders, "all warm, soft and sleepy... and mine..."

I do moan now, as his mouth closes around my right nipple and sucks on it strongly, applying just the right amount of pressure. His hand slips under the blanket and between my thighs, and my moans intensify as he begins to stroke my folds, his finger drawing teasing circles around my clit.

"Come for me, Nora," he orders softly, pressing down on my clit, and I shatter into a thousand pieces, my body tensing and peaking, as though on his command. "Good girl," he whispers, continuing to play with my sex, drawing out my orgasm. "Such a good, sweet girl..."

When my aftershocks are over, he steps back and begins undressing. I watch him hungrily, unable to tear my eyes away from the sight. He's beyond gorgeous, and I want him so badly. His shirt comes off first, exposing his broad shoulders and washboard stomach, and I can no longer contain myself. Sitting up, I reach for the zipper of his dress pants, my hands shaking with impatience.

He draws in a sharp breath as my palm brushes against his engorged cock. As soon as I succeed in freeing it, I wrap my fingers around the shaft and bend my head, taking him into my mouth.

"Fuck, Nora!" he groans, grasping my head and thrusting his hips at me. "Oh, fuck, baby, that's good..." His fingers slide through my hair, tangling in the unbrushed strands, and I slowly suck him in deeper, opening my throat to take in as much of his length as I can.

"Oh fuck..." His raspy moan fills me with delight, and I squeeze his balls lightly, reveling in the heavy feel of them in my palm. His cock gets even harder, and I know he's on the verge of coming, but, to my surprise, he pulls away, taking a step back.

He's breathing heavily, his eyes glittering like blue diamonds, but he manages to control himself long enough to get rid of his remaining clothing before he climbs on top of me. His strong hands wrap around my wrists, stretching them above my head, and his hips settle heavily between my open thighs, his thick shaft nudging against my vulnerable entrance. I stare up at him with a mixture of apprehension and excitement; he looks magnificent and savage, with his dark hair disheveled and his beautiful face drawn tight with lust. He's not going to be particularly gentle today—I can already see that.

And I'm right. He enters me with one powerful thrust, sliding so deep inside me that I gasp, feeling like he's splitting me in half. And yet my body responds to him, producing more lubrication, easing his way. He fucks me brutally, without mercy, but my screams are those of pleasure, the tension inside me spiraling out of control one more time before he finally comes.

~

At breakfast, I'm a little sore, but happy regardless. Julian is here, and all is right with my world. He seems to be in a good mood as well, teasing me about watching an entire season of Friends in one week and asking about my latest running times. He likes it that I'm so much into fitness lately—or rather, he likes the results of it.

Physically, I'm in the best shape I have ever been, and it shows. My body is lean and toned, and I'm a walking testament to the benefits of a healthy diet, lots of fresh air, and regular exercise. My thick brown hair is growing without any sign of split ends, and my skin is perfectly smooth and tan. I can't remember the last time I had so much as a pimple.

"My last three-mile run was 16:20," I tell Julian without false modesty. "I bet not many guys can beat that."

"That's true," he agrees, his blue eyes dancing with laughter. "I probably couldn't."

"Really?" I'm intrigued by the idea of beating Julian at something. "Want to try? I'd be glad to race you."

"Don't do it, Julian," Beth says, laughing. "She's fast. She was quick before, but now she's like a fucking rocket."

"Oh yeah?" He lifts one eyebrow at me. "A fucking rocket, huh?"

"That's right." I give him a challenging look. "Want to race, or are you too chicken?"

Beth begins to make clucking noises, and Julian grins, throwing a piece of bread at her. "Shut up, you traitor."

Laughing at their antics, I throw a piece of bread at Julian, and Beth scolds both of us. "I'm the one who has to clean up this whole mess," she grumbles, and Julian promises to help her with the bread crumbs, soothing her temper with one of his megawatt smiles.

When he's like this, his charm is like a living thing, drawing me in, making me forget the truth about my situation. On the back of my mind, I know that none of this is real—that this sense of connection, this camaraderie is nothing more than a mirage—but with each day that passes, it starts to matter less and less. In a strange way, I feel like I'm two people: the woman who's falling in love with the gorgeous, ruthless killer sitting at the breakfast table and the one who's observing the whole thing with a sense of horror and disbelief.

After breakfast, I change into my running clothes—a pair of shorts and a sports bra—and go read a book on the porch, so I can digest my food before the run. Julian goes into his office as usual. His business doesn't wait just because he's on the island; an illegal arms empire requires constant attention.

While Julian rarely talks about his work, I've managed to glean a few things over the past several months. From what I understand, my captor is the head of an international operation specializing in the manufacture and distribution of cutting-edge weapons and certain types of electronics. His clients are those organizations and individuals who cannot obtain weapons by legitimate means.

"He deals with some really dangerous motherfuckers," Beth told me once. "Psychopaths, many of them. I wouldn't trust them as far as I can throw them."

"So why does he do this?" I asked. "He's so rich. I'm sure he doesn't need the money…"

"It's not about the money," Beth explained. "It's about the thrill of it, the challenge. Men like Julian thrive on that."

I wonder sometimes if that's what Julian likes about me—the challenge of making me bend to his will, of shaping me to become whatever it is he thinks he needs. Does he find it thrilling, the knowledge that I'm his captive and that he can do whatever he wants with me? Does the illegal aspect of the whole thing excite him?

"Ready to go?" Julian's voice interrupts my thoughts, and I look up from my book to see him standing there, dressed in only a pair of black running shorts and sneakers. His naked torso ripples with thick, perfectly defined muscles, and his smooth golden skin gleams in the sunlight, making me want to touch him all over.

"Um, yeah." I get up, putting down my book and begin to stretch, watching Julian doing the same out of the corner of my eye. His body is incredible, and I wonder what he does to keep in shape. I've never seen him working out here on the island.

"Do you do some kind of exercise when you go on your trips?" I ask, shamelessly staring as he bends over and touches his toes with surprising flexibility. "How do you stay so fit?"

He straightens and grins at me. "I train with my men when I can. I guess you could call it exercise."

"Your men?" I immediately think of the thug who had beaten up Jake. The memory makes me sick, and I push it away, not wanting to think about such dark matters now. I have to do this sometimes, to separate this new life of mine into neat little sections, keeping the good times apart from the bad. It's my own patented coping mechanism.

"My bodyguards and certain other employees," Julian explains as we head out toward the beach, walking fast to warm up. "Some of them are former Navy SEALs, and training with them is no picnic, believe me."

"You train with Navy SEALs?" I stop and give Julian a hard look. "You were just kidding earlier, weren't you? About not being able to beat me in a race?"

His lips curve in a slightly mischievous—and utterly seductive—smile. "I don't know, my pet," he says softly. "Was I? Why don't you race me and see?"

"All right," I say, determined to give it my best shot. "Let's do this."

We start our race near a tree that I marked specifically for this purpose. On the other side of the island, there is another tree that serves as the finish line. If we run on the sand, along the ocean, it's exactly three miles from here to that point.

Julian counts to five, I set my stopwatch, and we're off, each starting at a reasonably fast pace that's not our top speed. As I run, I feel my muscles easing into the rhythm of the movement, and I gradually pick up the pace, pushing myself harder than I usually do at this point in the run. Julian runs beside me, his longer stride enabling him to keep up with me with ease.

We run silently, not talking, and I keep sneaking glances at Julian out of the corner of my eye. We're halfway through the course, and I'm sweating and breathing hard, but my gorgeous captor seems to be barely exerting himself. He's in phenomenal shape, his smooth muscles glistening with light drops of perspiration, bunching and releasing with every movement. He runs lightly, landing on the balls of his feet, and I envy his easy stride, wishing that I had even a quarter of his obvious strength and endurance.

As we get into the last half-mile, I put on a burst of speed, determined to try to beat him despite the obvious futility of the effort. He's not even winded yet, and I'm already gasping for breath. He picks up his speed too, and no matter how hard I run, I can't put any distance between us. He's practically glued to my side.

By the time we get within a hundred yards of the tree, I am dripping with sweat and every muscle in my body is screaming for oxygen. I'm on the verge of collapse and I know it, but I make one last heroic attempt and sprint for the finish line.

And just as my hand is about to touch the tree, marking me the race winner, Julian's palm slaps the bark, literally a second before mine.

Frustrated, I whirl around and find myself with my back pressed against the tree and Julian leaning over me. "Gotcha," he says, his eyes gleaming, and I see that he's breathing almost normally.

Gasping for air, I push at him, but he doesn't back away. Instead, he steps closer, and his knee wedges between my thighs. At the same time, his hands grab the backs of my knees, lifting me up against him, my thighs spread wide as he grinds his erection against my pelvis.

Our little race apparently turned him on.

Panting, I stare up at him, my hands grabbing at his shoulders. I can barely remain upright, and he wants to fuck?

The answer is obviously yes, because he sets me down on my feet for a second, pulls down my shorts and underwear, and then does the same thing to his own clothes. I sway on my feet, my legs shaking from the exertion. I can't believe this is happening. Who fucks right after a race? All I want to do is lie down and drink a gallon of water.

But Julian has other ideas. "Get on your knees," he orders hoarsely, pushing me down before I have a chance to comply.

I land on my knees heavily and brace myself with my

hands. The position actually helps me regain my breath somewhat, and I gratefully suck in air. My head is spinning from the heat outside—and from the aftermath of a hard run—and I hope I don't end up passing out.

A hard, muscular arm slides under my hips, holding me in place, and then I feel his cock pressing against my buttocks. Dizzy and trembling, I wait for the thrust that will join us together, my treacherous sex wet and throbbing with anticipation. My body's response to Julian is insane, ridiculous, given my overall physical state.

He brushes my sweat-soaked hair off my back and leans forward to kiss my neck, covering me with his heavy body. "You know," he whispers, "you're beautiful when you run. I've been wanting to do this since the first mile." And with that, he pushes deep inside me, his thickness stretching me, filling me all the way.

I cry out, my hands clutching at the dirt as he begins thrusting, both of his hands now holding my hips as he rams into me. My senses narrow, focusing only on this —the rhythmic movements of his hips, the pleasure-pain of his rough possession... I feel like I'm burning inside, dying from the violent brew of heat and lust. The pressure building inside me is too much, unbearable, and I throw my head back with a scream as my entire body explodes, the release rocketing through me with so much force that I literally pass out.

By the time I become conscious again, I am cradled on Julian's lap. He's got his back pressed against the finish-line tree, and he's feeding me small sips of water, making sure that I don't choke. "You okay, baby?" he asks, looking down at me with what appears to be genuine concern on his beautiful face.

"Um, yeah." My throat still feels dry, but I'm definitely feeling better—and more than a little embarrassed about my fainting spell.

"I didn't realize you'd gotten this dehydrated," he says, a small frown bisecting his brow. "Why did you push yourself so hard?"

"Because I wanted to win," I admit, closing my eyes and breathing in the scent of his skin. He smells like sex and sweat, an oddly appealing combination.

"Here, drink some more water," he says, and I open my eyes again, obediently drinking when he presses a bottle to my lips. The bottle is from the cooler I keep stashed on this side of the island to keep hydrated after my runs.

After a few minutes—and an entire bottle of water—I feel well enough to start walking back. Except Julian doesn't let me walk. Instead, as soon as I get to my feet, he bends down and lifts me into his arms as effortlessly as if I were a doll. "Hold on to my neck," he orders, and I wrap my arms around him, letting him carry me back home.

18

---

*T*he next morning I wake up to the luxurious sensation of having my feet massaged. It feels so incredible that, for a few seconds, I think I'm dreaming and try to avoid waking up. The feel of strong fingers kneading my foot is all too real, however, and I moan in bliss as each individual toe is rubbed and stroked with just the right amount of pressure.

Opening my eyes, I see Julian sitting on the bed, gloriously naked and holding a bottle of massage oil. Pouring some into his palm, he bends over me and starts massaging my ankles and calves next.

"Good morning," he purrs, looking at me. I stare back at him, mute with surprise. Julian has given me massages in the past, but usually only as a way to relax me before doing something that would make me scream. He's never woken me up in this pleasurable way before.

There is a half-smile on his sensuous lips, and I can't

help feeling nervous. "Um, Julian," I say uncertainly, "what… what are you doing?"

"Giving you a massage," he says, his eyes gleaming with amusement. "Why don't you relax and enjoy it?"

I blink, watching as his hands slowly move up my calves. He has large hands—strong and masculine. My legs look impossibly slender and feminine in his grasp, though I have well-defined muscles from all the running. I can feel the calluses on his palms scratching lightly against my skin, and I swallow, the unbidden thought that those hands belong to a killer entering my mind.

"Turn over," he says, tugging on my legs, and I plop over on my belly, still feeling nervous. What is he up to? I don't like surprises when it comes to Julian.

He starts kneading the back of my legs, unerringly finding the areas most sore from yesterday's race, and I groan as tight muscles begin to loosen up under his skilled fingers. Still, I can't relax completely; Julian is far too unpredictable for my peace of mind.

Apparently sensing my unease, he bends over me and whispers in my ear, "It's just a massage, my pet. No need to be so worried about it."

Somewhat reassured, I let myself relax, sinking into the comfort of my mattress. Julian's hands are magic; I've had professional massages that were nowhere near as good. He's completely attuned to me, paying attention to the slightest change in my breathing, to the most minute twitch in my muscles… After several minutes of this, I no longer care about his strange behavior; I'm simply wallowing in the bliss of this experience.

When my entire body has been thoroughly massaged and I'm lying there in limp contentment, Julian stops and shepherds me into the shower. Then he goes down on me, pleasuring me with his mouth until I explode in mind-blowing release.

At breakfast, I'm practically humming with contentment. This is the best morning I've had in months, maybe even years. By some strange coincidence, Beth made my favorite food—Eggs Benedict with crab cakes. I haven't had anything this decadent since my arrival on the island. The food Beth cooks for us is good, but it's usually on the healthy side. Fruits, vegetables, and fish seem to make up the majority of our diet. I can't remember the last time I had something as rich and satisfying as the Hollandaise sauce Beth made today.

"Mmm, this is so good," I moan around a mouthful. "Beth, this is amazing. These are probably the best eggs I've ever had."

She grins at me. "They did come out well, didn't they? I wasn't sure if I got the recipe right, but it seems like I might have."

"Oh, you did," I reassure her before I serve myself another portion. "This is great."

Julian smiles, his eyes gleaming with warm amusement. "Hungry, my pet?" He himself has already eaten a sizable serving, but I'm on the verge of catching up to him.

"Starving," I tell him, bringing another forkful to my mouth. "I guess I burned a lot of calories yesterday."

"I'm sure you did," he says, his smile widening, and then he tells Beth about how I almost won the race, leaving out the part about our fucking and my passing out afterwards.

When the breakfast is over, I'm so stuffed I can't eat another bite. Thanking Beth for the meal, I stand up, about to go get a book for a relaxing reading session on the porch, when Julian surprises me by wrapping his hand around my wrist. "Wait, Nora," he says softly, pulling me back down into my seat. "There's one more thing Beth prepared today." And he shoots Beth an indecipherable look—at which point she immediately gets up and goes into the kitchen.

"Um, okay." I'm beyond confused. She had prepared something, but didn't serve it during the actual meal?

At that moment, Beth comes back to the table, carrying a tray with a large chocolate cake—a cake with a bunch of burning candles.

"Happy birthday, Nora," Julian says with a smile as Beth places the cake in front of me. "Now make a wish and blow out those candles."

I blow out the candles on autopilot, barely registering the fact that it takes me three attempts to do this. Beth cheers, clapping her hands, and I hear the sounds as though they're coming from a distance. My mind is whirling, yet I feel oddly numb, as if nothing can touch me right now. All I can think about, all I can concentrate on is the fact that it's my birthday.

My birthday. It's my birthday. Today I turned nineteen.

The realization makes me want to scream.

I met Julian shortly before my last birthday—and he brought me to this island shortly thereafter. If it's my birthday today, then nearly a year has passed since my abduction—since I've been here, at Julian's mercy and entirely isolated from the rest of the world.

A year of my life has passed in captivity.

I feel like I'm suffocating, like all air had left the room, but I know it's just an illusion. There's plenty of oxygen here; I simply can't seem to breathe in any.

"Nora?" Beth's voice somehow penetrates the din in my ears. "Nora, are you all right?"

I finally manage to draw in some much-needed air, and I look up from the cake. Beth is staring at me with a puzzled frown on her face, and Julian is no longer smiling. Instead he looks like a dangerous stranger again, his gaze filled with something dark and disturbing.

Holding myself together with superhuman effort, I squeeze out a shaky smile. "Of course. Thank you for the cake, Beth."

"We wanted to surprise you," she says, her features smoothing out as she takes my words at face value. "I hope you have some room left for dessert. Chocolate cake is your favorite, right?"

The ringing in my ears intensifies. "Um, yes." Despite

my best attempts, my voice sounds choked. "And you definitely surprised me."

"Leave us, Beth," Julian says sharply, glancing at her. "Nora and I need to be alone right now."

Beth blinks, obviously taken aback by Julian's tone. I've never heard him speak like that to her before. Nevertheless, she obeys immediately, practically running up the stairs to her room.

I haven't seen Julian this angry in a while and I know I should be frightened, but at this moment, I can't seem to bring myself to care about what's to come. Every muscle in my body is trembling with the effort to contain the terrible storm I can feel brewing inside me, and it's a relief to have Beth away from here. A year. It's been a fucking year. The rage that's building inside me is unlike anything I've ever experienced before; it's like a dam has broken and would not be contained. A red mist descends on me, veiling my vision, and the ringing in my ears grows louder as my emotions spin out of control.

As soon as Beth is out of sight, I explode. I'm no longer rational or sane; instead I'm fury personified. I grab at the nearest thing I can reach—the chocolate cake —and throw it across the room, the dark-colored icing splattering everywhere. My plate and cup follow, hitting the wall and shattering into a million pieces, and all the while, I hear screaming, coming at me from far away. Some still-functioning part of my brain realizes that it's me—that it's my own screams and curses I'm hearing— but I can't stop it any more than I can contain a typhoon. All the anger, terror, and frustration of the past year has boiled to the surface, erupting in a lava of fierce rage.

I don't know how long I exist in that mindless state before steely arms wrap around me from the back, imprisoning me in a familiar embrace. I kick and scream until my voice grows hoarse, but my struggles are futile. Julian is far, far stronger than me, and he uses that strength now to subdue me, to hold me tight until I completely exhaust myself and slump against him in defeat, tears running down my face.

"Are you done?" he whispers in my ear, and I can hear the familiar dark note in his tone. As usual, I find it both sinister and arousing, my body now conditioned to crave the pain that's to come—and the mind-shattering bliss that inevitably accompanies it.

I shake my head in response to his question, but I know that I am done, that whatever it was that came over me has passed, leaving me drained and empty.

Julian turns me around in his arms, so that I'm facing him. I stare up at him, my tear-glazed gaze helplessly drawn to the perfect symmetry of his features. His high cheekbones are tinged with a hint of color, and there is something disquieting in the way he looks at me—as though he wants to devour me, to tear out my soul and swallow it whole. Our eyes meet, and I know that I'm standing on the edge of a precipice right now, that a sinkhole is opening up underneath my feet.

And in that moment, I see things clearly.

I am not angry because I've been imprisoned on the

island for an entire year. No, my rage goes far, far deeper. What burns me up inside is not the fact that I've been a captive this whole time—it's that I've grown to like my captivity.

Over the past few months, I have somehow come to terms with my new life. I've grown to enjoy the calm, relaxing rhythms of the island. The ocean, the sand, the sun—it's about as close to paradise as anything I can imagine. Freedom and all that it implies is now just a vague, impossible dream. I can barely picture the faces of those I left behind; they are just blurry, shadowy figures in my mind. The only thing that matters to me now is the man holding me in his hard embrace.

Julian—my captor, my lover.

"Why, Nora?" he asks, almost soundlessly. His arms tighten around me, his fingers digging into the soft skin of my back. When I don't reply, his expression darkens further. "Why?"

I remain silent, unwilling to take that last, irrevocable step. I can't bare myself to Julian like that. I just can't. He's already taken far too much from me; I can't let him have this too.

"Tell me," he orders, one hand sliding up to twist in my hair, forcing my neck to bend backwards. "Tell me now."

"I hate you," I croak, gathering the last shreds of my defiance. My voice is like sandpaper, hoarse from all the screaming. "I hate you—"

His eyes flash with blue fire. "Is that right?" he whispers, leaning over me, still holding me arched helplessly against him. "You hate me, my pet?"

I hold his gaze, refusing to blink. In for a penny, in for a pound. "Yes," I hiss, "I hate you!" I need to convince him of my hatred because the alternative is unthinkable. He can't know the truth. He just can't.

Julian's face hardens, turning to ice. In one swift motion, he sweeps the remaining dishes off the kitchen table onto the floor and pushes me onto the table, forcing me to bend over, my face sliding on the smooth wooden surface. I try to kick back with my legs, but it's useless. He's gripping the back of my neck with one strong hand, and then I hear the menacing sound of a belt being unbuckled.

I kick back harder, and actually manage to make contact with his leg. Of course, it gains me nothing. I can't escape from Julian. I will never be able to escape from Julian.

He leans over me, pressing me into the table, his hard fingers tightening around the back of my neck. "You're mine, Nora," he says harshly, his large body dominating me, arousing me. "You belong to me, do you understand? Each and every single part of you is mine." His erection presses against my buttocks, its uncompromising hardness both a threat and a promise.

He rears back, still holding me down with one hand on my neck, and I hear the sibilant whisper of a belt being pulled from its loops. A moment later, my dress is flipped up, exposing my lower body. I squeeze my eyes shut, bracing for what's to come.

Thwack. Thwack. The belt descends on my ass, over and over again, each strike like fire licking at my thighs and buttocks. I can hear my own cries, feel my body tensing with each blow, and then the pain propels me into that strange state where everything is turned upside down—where pain and pleasure collide, become indistinguishable from one another, and my tormentor is my only solace. My body softens, melts, each stroke of the belt starting to feel more like a caress, and I know that I somehow need this right now—that Julian has tapped into that dark, secret part of myself that is a mirror image of his own twisted desires. It's a part of me that longs to give up control, to lose myself completely and just be his.

By the time Julian stops and turns me over, there isn't an ounce of defiance left in my body. My head is swimming from an endorphin rush more powerful than anything I have ever experienced, and I'm clinging to him, desperate for comfort, for sex, for anything resembling love and affection. My arms twine around Julian's neck, pulling him down on the table with me, and I revel in the taste of him, in the deep, hungry kisses with which he consumes my mouth. My backside feels like it's on fire, but it doesn't diminish my lust one bit; if anything, it intensifies it. Julian has trained me well. My body is conditioned to crave the pleasure that I know comes next.

He fumbles with his jeans, opening the zipper, and then he's inside me, entering me with one powerful thrust. I shudder with relief, with ecstasy that borders on agony, and wrap my legs around his waist, taking him deeper, needing him to fuck me, to claim me in the most primitive way possible.

"Tell me, baby," he whispers in my ear, his lips brushing against my temple. His right hand slides into my hair, holding me immobile. "Tell me how much you hate me." His other hand finds the place where we're joined, rubs there, then moves down a couple of inches to my other opening. "Tell me…"

I gasp as his finger pushes into my anus, my senses overwhelmed by all the conflicting sensations. Dazed, I open my eyes and stare at Julian, seeing my own dark need reflected on his face. He wants to possess me, to break me so he could put me back together, and I can no longer fight him on this.

"I don't hate you." My words come out low and raspy, and I swallow to moisten my dry throat. "I don't hate you, Julian."

Something like triumph flashes on his face. His hips thrust forward, his shaft burrowing deeper inside me, and I suppress a moan, still holding his gaze.

"Tell me," he orders again, his voice deepening. His eyes are burning into mine, and I can no longer resist the demand I see there. He wants all of me, and I have no choice but to give it to him.

"I love you." My voice is barely audible, each word feeling like it's being wrenched out of my very soul. "I don't hate you, Julian… I can't… I can't because I love you."

I can see his pupils dilating, turning his eyes darker.

His cock swells within me, even thicker and harder than before, and then he pulls out and slams back inside, making me gasp from the savagery of his possession.

"Tell me again," he groans, and I repeat what I said, the words coming easier the second time around. There's no point in hiding from the truth anymore, no reason to lie. I have fallen head over heels for my sadistic captor, and nothing in the world can change that fact.

"I love you," I whisper, my hand moving up to cradle his cheek. "I love you, Julian."

His eyes darken further, and then he bends his head, taking my mouth in a deep, all-consuming kiss.

Now I am truly his, and he knows it.

19

The next three months fly by.

After that day—after what I think of as the Birthday Incident—my relationship with Julian undergoes a noticeable change, becoming more... romantic, for lack of a better word.

It's a fucked-up romance, I know that. I may be addicted to Julian, but I'm not so far gone that I don't realize how unhealthy this is. I am in love with the man who kidnapped me, the man who is still holding me prisoner.

The man who seems to need my love as much as he needs my body.

I don't know if he loves me back. I don't even know if he's capable of that emotion. How can you love someone whose freedom you stole without a second thought? And yet I can't help feeling that he must care for me, that his obsession with me is not only sexual in nature. It's there in the way I catch him looking at me sometimes, in the way he tries to anticipate my every need.

He constantly brings me my favorite foods, my favorite books and music. If I so much as mention needing a hand lotion, he buys it for me on his next trip. I am about as pampered as a girl can be. He even takes pride in my accomplishments, praising my artwork and going so far as to take several paintings with him off the island to hang in his office in Hong Kong.

He also misses me when we're not together. I know because he tells me so—and because every time he returns, he falls on me like a starving man just getting out of prison. That, more than anything, gives me hope that his feelings for me go beyond that of owner for his possession.

"Do you see other women? Out there, in the real world?" I ask him at breakfast after one night when he takes me three times in a row. The question had been eating at me for months, and I simply can't contain myself any longer. My captor is more than gorgeous; he's got that dangerous, magnetic appeal that probably draws women to him by the dozen. I can easily imagine him sleeping with a different beauty every night—a thought that makes me want to stab something. Even with his sadistic proclivities, I know he would have no trouble finding bed partners; there are probably plenty of women who, like me, derive pleasure from erotic pain.

He smiles at me with dark amusement, not the least bit put off by my obvious display of jealousy. "No, my pet," he says softly. Reaching over, he takes my hand, stroking the inside of my wrist with his thumb. "Why would I want to fuck someone else when I have you? I haven't been with another woman since the day we met."

"You haven't?" I can't conceal my shock. Julian had been faithful to me this whole time?

He looks at me, his lips curved in a sinfully delicious smile. "No, baby, I have not," he says—and in that moment, I feel like the happiest woman in the world.

I love it when he calls me 'baby.' It's a common endearment, I know, but somehow when Julian says it, it sounds different—like he's caressing me with that word. I much prefer 'baby' to being called 'my pet.'

Ultimately, though, I know that's what I am to him— his pet, his possession. He likes the idea that I belong to him, that he's the only man who gets to touch me, to see me. He likes dressing me in the clothes that he provides for me, feeding me the food that he brings. I am completely dependent on him, utterly at his mercy, and I think something about that appeals to him, appeasing the demons I frequently sense lurking beneath the surface.

Truthfully, I don't mind being possessed. It's a disturbing realization, but some part of me seems to like this kind of dynamic. I feel safe and cared for, even though logic tells me I'm far from safe with a man who deals in weapons for a living—a man who admitted to killing without any regret. The hands that touch me at night are those that brought death to others, but there is a certain piquancy in that. It makes everything more intense somehow, helps me feel more alive.

Besides, despite his need to hurt me, Julian has never truly harmed me—not physically, at least. When he's in one of his sadistic moods, I end up with marks and bruises on my skin, but those fade quickly. He's careful never to scar my body, even though I know that blood and tears—my tears—excite him, turn him on.

When I share some of my feelings with Beth, she doesn't seem surprised in the least.

"I knew the two of you were made for each other from the first moment I saw you together," she says, giving me a wry look. "When you and Julian are in the same room, the air practically sizzles. I've never seen such chemistry between two people before. What you have together is rare and special. Don't fight it, Nora. He's your destiny—and you are his."

She seems completely convinced of that.

On the night my life irrevocably changes, everything starts out as normal.

Julian is on the island, and we share a delicious meal together before he brings me upstairs for a lengthy love-making session. It's one of those times when he's gentle, worshipping me with his body like I'm a goddess, and I fall asleep relaxed and satisfied, held tightly in his embrace.

When I wake up in the middle of the night to use

ANNA ZAIRES

the restroom, I become aware of a dull pain near my navel. Relieving myself, I wash my hands and crawl back into bed, stretching out next to Julian's sleeping form. I feel slightly nauseous too, and I wonder if I'm having indigestion. Could I have gotten food poisoning somehow?

I try to fall asleep, but the pain seems to get worse with every minute that passes. It migrates down into my lower right abdomen, becoming sharp and agonizing. I don't want to wake up Julian, but I can't bear it anymore. I need a painkiller of some kind, any kind.

"Julian," I whisper, reaching for him. "Julian, I think I'm sick."

He wakes up immediately and sits up in bed, turning on the bedside lamp. There's no trace of confusion on his face; he's as alert as if it's the middle of the day instead of three o'clock in the morning. "What's wrong?"

I curl into a little ball as the pain intensifies. "I don't know," I manage to say. "My stomach hurts."

His eyebrows snap together. "Where does it hurt, baby?" he says softly, pushing me onto my back.

"My... my side," I gasp, tears of pain starting to roll down my face.

"Here?" he asks, pressing on one side, and I shake my head no.

"Here?"

"Yes!" Somehow he has unerringly found the exact area that's in agony.

He immediately gets up and starts getting dressed. "Beth!" he yells. "Beth, I need you here right now!"

She runs into the room thirty seconds later, pulling on a bathrobe over her pajamas. "What happened?"

She sounds scared, and I am terrified too. I've never seen Julian like this before. He seems almost... frightened.

"Get ready," he says tersely. "I'm taking her to the clinic, and you're coming with us. It might be her appendix."

Appendicitis! Now that he said it, I realize it's the most probable explanation, but it's beyond scary. I'm no doctor, but I know that if my appendix bursts before they cut it out, I'm pretty much toast. It would be frightening even if I were an hour away from medical attention, but I'm on a private island in the middle of the Pacific. What if I don't make it to the hospital in time?

Julian must be thinking the same thing because the expression on his face is grim as he wraps me in a robe and picks me up, carrying me out of the room.

"I can walk," I protest weakly, my stomach roiling as Julian swiftly walks down the stairs.

"Like hell you can." His tone is unnecessarily harsh, but I don't take offense. I know he's worried about me right now, and even with my insides in agony, I feel warmed by the thought.

By the time we reach the hangar, Beth has opened the gates for us and is already waiting in the back of the airplane. Julian straps me into the passenger seat, and I realize that my greatest wish is about to be granted.

I'm getting off the island.

My stomach lurches, and I grab for the brown paper

bag that's lying conveniently in front of me. Sudden hot nausea boils up in my throat, and I vomit into the bag, my entire body sweating and shaking.

I can hear Julian swearing as the plane begins to take off, and I'm so embarrassed I just want to die. "I'm sorry," I whisper, my eyes burning. I have never been so miserable in my entire life.

"It's all right," Julian says curtly. "Don't worry about it."

"Here." Beth hands me a wet wipe from the back. "This should make you feel a little better."

But it doesn't. Instead, as the plane climbs higher, I get nauseous again. Moaning, I clutch at my stomach, the pain in my right side intensifying.

"Fuck," Julian mutters. "Fuck, fuck, fuck." His knuckles are white where he's clutching the controls.

I vomit again.

"How long until we get there?" Beth's voice is unusually high-pitched.

"Two hours," Julian says grimly. "If the wind cooperates."

Those two hours turn out to be the longest ones of my life. By the time the plane begins its descent, I have thrown up five times and am long past the point of embarrassment. The pain in my stomach has long since morphed into agony, and I'm not cognizant of anything but my own bone-deep misery.

Strong hands reach for me, pulling me out of the airplane, and I am vaguely aware that Julian is carrying me somewhere, holding me cradled against his broad chest. There is a babble of voices speaking in a mixture of English and some foreign language, and then I'm placed on a gurney and wheeled through a long hallway into a white, sterile-looking room.

Several people in white coats bustle around me, one man barking out orders in that same strangely mixed language, and I feel a sharp prick in my arm as an IV needle is attached to my wrist. Dazed, I look up to see Julian standing in the corner, his face oddly pale and his eyes glittering... and then the darkness swallows me whole again.

20

When I regain consciousness, I am feeling only a little bit better. My head appears to be stuffed with wool, and the nagging pain in my side remains, though it feels different now, less sharp and more like an ache. For a second, I think that I fell asleep feeling sick and dreamed the whole thing, but the smell convinces me otherwise. It's that unmistakable antiseptic odor that you only encounter in doctor's offices and hospitals.

That odor means I'm alive... and off the island.

My heart starts racing at the thought.

"She's awake," an unfamiliar female voice says in accented English, apparently addressing someone else in the room.

I hear footsteps and feel someone sitting down on the side of my bed. Warm fingers reach out and stroke my cheek. "How are you feeling, baby?"

Opening my eyes with some effort, I gaze at Julian's

beautiful features. "Like I've been cut open and sewn back together," I manage to croak out. My throat is so dry and sore that it actually hurts to talk, and I can feel a dull, throbbing ache in my right side.

"Here." Julian is holding out a cup with a bent straw in it. "You must be thirsty."

He brings it toward my face, and I obediently close my lips around the straw, sucking down a little water. My mind is still hazy, and for a moment, the wall between the good and the bad memories crumbles. I remember that first day on the island, when Julian had offered me a bottle of water, and an involuntary shiver runs down my spine. In that moment, Julian is not the man I love; he is again my enemy, the one who stole me, the one who made me his against my will.

"Cold?" he asks, taking the cup away before leaning over to pull the blanket higher up, covering my shoulders.

"Um, yeah, a little." I'm off the island. Oh my God, I'm off the island. My mind is spinning. I feel torn, like I'm two different people—the terrified girl who insists this is her chance to escape and the woman who desperately craves Julian's touch.

"They took out your appendix," Julian says, brushing back a strand of hair that had been tickling my forehead. "The operation went smoothly, and there shouldn't be any complications. Isn't that right, Angela?" He looks up to the left.

"Yes, Mr. Esguerra."

Esguerra? Is that Julian's last name? Recognizing the

voice from before, I turn my head to see a petite young woman in white scrubs. Her smooth skin is a beautiful light brown color, and her hair and eyes are dark, nearly black. To me, she looks Filipino or maybe Thai—not that I can pretend to be an expert on either nationality.

What I do know is that she's the first person I've seen in fifteen months who is neither Beth nor Julian.

I'm off the island. Oh my God, I'm off the island. For the first time since my abduction, there is a real possibility of escape.

"Where am I?" I ask, staring at the young nurse. I can't believe Julian is letting someone else see me—me, the girl he kidnapped.

"You're in a private clinic in the Philippines," Julian replies when the woman merely smiles at me. "Angela is the nursing assistant who will be looking after you."

At that moment, the door opens and Beth walks in. "Oh, look who's awake," she exclaims, coming up to my bedside. "How are you feeling?"

"Okay, I think," I tell her cautiously. Holy shit, I'm off the fucking island.

"They said Julian got you here just in time," Beth tells me, pulling up a chair and sitting down next to my bed. "Your appendix was getting ready to go. They cut it out and sewed you right back up, so you should be right as rain."

I let out a nervous chuckle… and immediately groan, the movement tugging at the stitches in my side.

"Are you hurting?" Julian gives me a concerned look.

Turning to Angela, he orders, "Give her more painkillers."

"I'm okay, just a little sore," I try to reassure him. "Seriously, I don't need any drugs." The last thing I want is something clouding my mind right now. I'm off the island, and I need to figure out what to do. I'm doing my best to remain calm, but it's taking all of my willpower not to scream or do something stupid. Freedom is so close, I can practically taste it.

"Of course, Mr. Esguerra." Angela completely ignores my protests and comes up to the bed, fiddling with the clear bag that's feeding into my IV tube.

Julian leans over the bed and lightly kisses me on the lips. "You need to rest," he says softly. "I want you healthy. Do you understand me?"

I nod, my eyelids growing heavy as I feel the medicine beginning to work. For a moment, I feel like I'm floating, all pain gone, and then I'm not aware of anything else.

When I wake up again, I'm alone in the room. Bright sunlight is streaming through the clear large windows and several plants are blooming merrily on the windowsill. It's actually quite cozy. If it weren't for that hospital smell and the various machines and monitors, I would've thought I was in someone's bedroom. Whatever this private clinic is, it's quite luxurious—a fact that I didn't have a chance to really appreciate before.

The door opens and Angela walks into the room. Giving me a wide smile, she says in a cheerful voice, "How are you feeling, Nora?"

"Okay," I reply, a little warily. "Where is Julian?" Something about this woman rubs me the wrong way, and I can't quite figure out what. I know she's probably my best chance to escape, but I don't know if I can trust her. For one thing, she could easily be in Julian's employ, like Beth.

"Mr. Esguerra had to leave for a couple of hours," she says, still smiling at me. "Beth is here, however. She just went to the restroom."

"Oh, good." I stare at her, trying to gather my courage. I have to tell her that I've been kidnapped. I simply have to. This is my one opportunity to escape. She might be loyal to Julian, but I still have to try because I may never get a better shot at freedom.

Angela comes up to the bed and hands me the cup with the bent straw. "Here you go," she says in that same cheerful voice. "I'll bring you some food in a bit."

I lift my arm and take the cup from her, wincing a little as the movement pulls at the stitches. "Thanks," I say, greedily gulping down the water. I really, really need to tell her to call the police, or whatever the local law enforcement officials are called, but for some reason, I don't. Instead, I drink the water and watch as she walks out of the room, leaving me alone once again.

I groan mentally. What is wrong with me? Freedom is a real possibility for the first time in over a year, and here I am, waffling and procrastinating. I tell myself it's because I'm being cautious, because I don't want to risk anyone getting hurt—not Angela and certainly not anyone back home—but deep inside, I know the truth.

As alluring as freedom seems, it's also frightening. I've been a captive for so long that I actually long for the comfort of my cage; being here in this unfamiliar room makes me stressed, anxious, and there is a part of me that just wants to go back to the island, to my regular routine. Most importantly, however, freedom means leaving Julian, and I can't bring myself to do that.

I don't want to leave the man who kidnapped me.

I should be rejoicing at the thought of the police coming to arrest him, but I feel horrified instead. I don't want Julian behind bars. I don't want to be separated from him, not even for a minute.

Closing my eyes, I tell myself that I'm a fool, a brainwashed idiot, but it doesn't matter.

As I lie there in that hospital bed, I come to terms with the fact that I'm no longer an unwilling captive. Instead, I am simply a woman who belongs to Julian—just as he now belongs to me.

I recuperate in the clinic for the next week. Julian visits me every day, spending several hours by my side, and so does Beth. Angela takes care of me most of the time, although a couple of doctors have dropped by to view my charts and adjust my painkiller dosage.

I still have not told anyone about being a victim of

kidnapping, nor am I planning to do so anymore. For one thing, I get the sense that the clinic staff is paid to be discreet. Nobody seems the least bit curious about what an American girl is doing in the Philippines, nor are they inclined to question me in any way. The only thing Angela wants to know is whether I'm in pain, thirsty, hungry, or need to use the bathroom. I'm pretty sure that if I ask her to call the police for me, she would just smile and give me more painkillers.

I have also seen a number of guards stationed in the hallway outside the room. I catch glimpses of them when the door opens. They're armed to the teeth and look like scary sons of bitches, reminding me of the thug who beat up Jake.

When I ask Julian about them, he freely admits that they're his employees. "They're there for your protection," he explains, sitting down on the side of my bed. "I told you I have enemies, right?"

He did tell me, but I hadn't grasped the full extent of the danger before. According to Beth, there is a small army of bodyguards stationed at and around the clinic, all protecting us from whatever threat Julian is concerned about.

"What enemies?" I ask curiously, looking at him. "Who is after you?"

He smiles at me. "That's none of your concern, my pet," he says gently, but there is something cold and deadly lurking beneath the warmth of his smile. "I will deal with them soon."

I shudder a little, and hope that Julian doesn't notice. Sometimes my lover can be very, very scary.

"We're going home tomorrow," he says, changing the topic. "The doctors said you'll need to take it easy for the next few weeks, but there is no need for you to stay here. You can recover at home just as well."

I nod, my stomach tightening with a mixture of dread and anticipation. Home... Home on the island. This strange interlude at the clinic—so close to freedom —is almost over.

Tomorrow my real life begins again.

21

*P*op! Pop! The explosive sound of a car backfiring jerks me out of sound sleep. My heart hammering, I jackknife up to a sitting position, then clutch at the stitches in my side with a hiss of pain.

Pop! Pop! Pop! The sound continues, and I freeze. No car backfires like that.

I'm hearing gunshots. Gunshots and occasional screams.

It's dark, the only light coming from the monitors hooked up to me. I'm on the bed in the middle of the room —the first thing someone would see upon opening the door. It occurs to me that I might as well be sitting there with a bull's eye painted in the middle of my forehead.

Trying to control my ragged breathing, I pull the IV from my arm and get to my feet. It still hurts to walk, but I ignore the pain. I'm certain bullets would hurt a lot worse.

Padding barefoot toward the door, I open it just a tiny bit and peek out into the hallway. My stomach sinks. There isn't a single bodyguard in sight; the hallway in front of me is completely empty.

Shit. Shit, shit, shit.

Casting a frantic glance around, I look for a hiding spot, but the only cupboard in the room is too small for me to fit into. There is no other place to conceal myself. Staying here would be suicidal. I need to get out, and I need to do so now.

Pulling the hospital gown tighter around myself, I cautiously step out into the hallway. The floor is cold under my bare feet, adding to the icy chill inside me. Out here, I feel even more exposed and vulnerable, and the urge to hide grows stronger. Spotting a bunch of doors on the other end of the hallway, I choose one at random, opening it carefully. To my relief, there is no one inside, and I go in, closing the door quietly behind me.

The sound of gunfire continues at random intervals, coming closer each time. I step into the corner behind the door and plaster myself against the wall, trying to control my rising panic. I have no idea who the gunmen are, but the possibilities that occur to me are not reassuring.

Julian has enemies. What if it's them out there? What if he's fighting them right now alongside his body-guards? I imagine him injured, dead, and the coldness inside me spreads, penetrating deep into my bones.

Please, God, no. Please, anything but that. I would sooner die than lose him.

My entire body is trembling, and I feel cold sweat sliding down my back. The gunfire has stopped, and the silence is more ominous than the deafening noise from before. I can taste the fear; it's sharp and metallic on my tongue, and I realize that I'd bitten the inside of my cheek hard enough to draw blood.

Time moves at a painful crawl. Every minute seems to stretch into an hour, every second into eternity. Finally, I hear voices and heavy footsteps out in the hallway. It sounds like there are several men, and they're speaking in a language I don't understand—a language that sounds harsh and guttural to my ears.

I can hear doors opening, and I know they're looking for something... or someone. Hardly daring to breathe, I try to meld into the wall, to make myself so small I would be invisible to the gunmen prowling out in the hallway.

"Where is she?" a harsh male voice demands in strongly accented English. "She's supposed to be here, on this floor."

"No, she's not." The voice answering him is Beth's, and I stifle a terrified gasp, realizing that the men have somehow captured her. She sounds defiant, but I catch an undertone of fear in her voice. "I told you, Julian already took her away—"

"Don't fucking lie to me," the man roars, his accent getting thicker. The sound of a slap is followed by Beth's pained cry. "Where the fuck is she?"

"I don't know," Beth sobs hysterically. "She's gone, I told you, gone—"

The man barks out something in his own language, and I hear more doors opening. They're coming closer to the room where I'm hiding, and I know it's only a matter of time before they find me. I don't know why they're looking for me, but I know I'm the 'she' in question. They want to find me, and they're willing to hurt Beth to do it.

I hesitate for only a moment before stepping out of the room. On the other side of the hallway, I see Beth huddling on the floor, her arm held tightly by a black-garbed man. A dozen more men are standing around them, holding assault rifles and machine guns—which they point at me as soon as I come out.

"Are you looking for me?" I ask calmly. I've never been more terrified in my life, but my voice comes out steady, almost amused. I didn't know it was possible to be numb with fear, but that's how I feel right now—so terrified that I don't actually feel afraid anymore.

My mind is strangely clear, and I register several things at once. The men look Middle Eastern, with their olive-toned skin and dark hair. While a couple of them are clean-shaven, the majority seem to have thick black beards. At least two of them are wounded and bleeding. And for all their weapons, they seem quite anxious, as though they're expecting to be attacked any minute.

The man holding Beth barks out another order in a language I now realize is Arabic, and I recognize his voice as belonging to the man who'd spoken in English.

He seems to be their leader. At his command, two of the men walk up to me and grab my arms, dragging me toward him. I manage not to stumble, though my stitches ache with a renewed ferocity.

"Is this her?" he hisses at Beth, shaking her roughly. "Is this Julian's little whore?"

"That would be me," I tell him before Beth can answer. My voice is still unnaturally calm. I don't think it's fully hit me yet, the danger that I'm in. All I want to do right now is stop him from hurting Beth. At the same time, at the back of my mind I'm processing the fact that they want me because I'm Julian's lover. That could only mean one thing: Julian is alive and they mean to use me against him. I suppress a shudder of relief at the thought.

The leader stares at me, apparently as surprised by my uncharacteristic bravery as I am. Letting go of Beth, he comes up to me, grasping my jaw with hard, cruel fingers. Leaning in, he studies me, his dark eyes gleaming coldly. He's short for a man, only about five-seven at most, and his breath washes over my face, bringing with it the fetid odor of garlic and stale tobacco. I fight the urge to gag, holding his gaze defiantly with my own.

After a few seconds, he lets go of me and says something in Arabic to his troops. Two of the men hurry over and grab Beth again. She screams and starts fighting them, and one of them backhands her, stunning her into silence. At the same time, the leader's hand closes around my upper arm, squeezing it painfully. "Let's go," he says sharply, and I let myself be led toward the door at the end of the hallway.

The door opens to a staircase, and I realize that we're on the second floor. The gunmen form a circle around me, the leader, and Beth, and we all go down the stairs and out through a door that leads to an unpaved open area outside. We pass one man's dead body in the staircase, and there are several more lying outside. I avert my eyes, swallowing convulsively to keep the bile from rising up in my throat. The sun is bright, and the air is hot and humid, but I can barely feel the warmth on my frozen skin. The reality of my situation is beginning to sink in, and I start to shiver, small shudders wracking my frame.

There are several black SUVs waiting for us, and the men drag me and Beth to one of them, forcing us into the back seat. Two of them climb in with us, forcing us to huddle together. I can feel Beth shaking, and I reach over to squeeze her cold hand with my own, drawing comfort from the human touch. She looks at me, and the terror in her eyes chills my blood. Her freckled face is pale, and her right cheek is swollen, with a massive bruise starting to form there. Her lower lip is split in two places, and there is a smear of blood on her chin. Whoever these men are, they have no compunction about hurting women.

I desperately want to ask her what she knows, but I keep quiet. I don't want to draw any more attention to ourselves than necessary. My mind flashes back to the dead bodies we'd just passed, and I fight the urge to throw up. I don't know what these people intend for us, but I strongly suspect our chances of getting out alive are minimal. Every minute that we survive, every minute that they leave us alone, is precious, and we need to do whatever it takes to extend those minutes for as long as possible.

The car starts up and pulls away. Still holding Beth's hand, I look out the window, seeing the white building of the clinic disappearing behind us. The road we're on is unpaved and bumpy, and the atmosphere in the car is tense. The two men in the backseat with us are gripping their weapons tightly, and I again get the sense that they're afraid of something... or someone.

I wonder if it's Julian. Does he know what happened? Is he even now on his way to the clinic? I stare out the window, my eyes dry and burning. It wasn't supposed to be like this. I should be going back to the island today, back to the placid life I've had for the past year. It's a life I crave now with a desperate intensity. I want to lie in Julian's embrace, to feel his touch and smell the warm, clean scent of his skin. I want him to own me and protect me, to keep me safe from everything and everyone except himself.

But he's not here. Instead the car is bumping along the road, taking us further and further away from safety. It's hot inside, and I can smell the spicy odor of unwashed male bodies and sweat; it permeates the car, making me feel like I'm suffocating. Beth seems to be in shock, her face blank and withdrawn. I want to hug her, but we're pressed too tightly together, so I just gently squeeze her hand instead. Her fingers are limp and clammy in my palm.

The ride seems to last forever, but it must be only about an hour, because the sun is still not all the way up in the sky when we arrive at our destination. It's an airstrip in the middle of nowhere, and there is a sizable plane sitting there. It looks vaguely military to me. The men force us out of the car and drag us toward the plane. I do my best to walk where they're leading me, not wanting to tear my stitches open. Beth doesn't put up a fight either, though she seems too shellshocked to walk straight, forcing them to practically carry her in.

Inside, the plane is far from luxurious. As I had suspected, the body of the plane is military in style, with seats along the walls, instead of arranged into rows. It's the kind of plane I've seen in movies, usually with Navy SEALs jumping out of it with parachutes. The men strap Beth and me into two of the seats and handcuff our hands before sitting down themselves.

The engines rev up, the plane begins to roll, and then we're airborne, the sun shining brightly in my eyes.

22

*B*y the time we land a couple of hours later, I'm dying of thirst and desperately need to pee. Sneaking a glance at Beth, I see that she's in even worse discomfort, her eyes glazed and feverish-looking. The swelling on her face has turned into an ugly bruise, and her lips are crusted with blood. With my hands cuffed together, I can't even reach over to give her a comforting pat on the arm.

As soon as the plane touches down, they unbuckle us and drag us out of the plane with our hands still cuffed in front of us. The leader approaches us, giving us a quick once-over before pointing toward a black SUV parked a few yards away. He spits out some order at his men, and I understand it to mean that our journey is about to continue. Before they can force us into the vehicle, however, I speak up. "Hey," I say quietly, "I have to use the restroom."

Beth flashes me a panicked look, but I ignore her,

focusing my attention on the leader. I'm pretty sure I'd sooner die than piss my pants—or my hospital gown, as the matter may be. He hesitates for a second, staring at me, then jerks his thumb toward the bushes. "Go, bitch," he says harshly. "You have one minute."

I scramble toward the bushes, ignoring the man with a machine gun who follows me there. Thankfully, he looks away as I hike up my gown and squat to relieve myself, my face flaming with embarrassment. Out of the corner of my eye, I see Beth following my example a dozen yards away.

Once we're both done, we get into another hot, stuffy car. This time, the ride is even longer, the road winding through what appears to be some kind of jungle. By the time we get to a nondescript warehouse-like building—our final destination—I'm soaked with sweat and badly dehydrated. I'm hungry too, but that need is secondary to the thirst that's consuming me right now.

When we get into the building, we are led toward two metal chairs standing in the corner. My handcuffs are unlocked, but before I have a chance to rejoice, the same man who guarded me at the bushes binds my wrists together behind my back. Then he ties my ankles to the chair, one to each leg, before wrapping a rope all around my body to secure me to the chair. His touch on my skin is indifferent, impersonal; I'm just a thing to him, not a woman. Turning my head to the side, I see that the same thing is done to Beth, except that her handler seems to enjoy causing her pain, yanking her legs roughly apart to tie them to the chair. She doesn't make a sound, but her face gets even paler and her cracked lips tremble slightly.

I watch it all with helpless anger, then turn away once the man leaves her alone, focusing my attention on our surroundings instead.

It seems that my initial impression was correct. We're inside some warehouse, with tall boxes and metal shelves forming a maze in the middle. Now that we're securely tied to the chairs, the men leave us alone, gathering around a long table in the other corner.

Beth and I finally have some privacy to talk.

"Are you okay?" I ask her, taking care to keep my voice pitched low. "Did they hurt you? Before I came out, I mean…"

She shakes her head, her mouth tightening. "Just smacked me around a bit," she says quietly. "It's nothing. You shouldn't have come out, Nora. That was stupid."

"They would've found me anyway. It was just a matter of time." I'm convinced of that. "Do you know who they are or what they want from us?"

"I'm not sure, but I can guess," she says, her hands clenching tightly in her lap. "I think they're part of the Jihadist terrorist group that Julian told me about a couple of months ago. Apparently, they're upset that he wouldn't sell them some weapon that his company recently developed."

"Why not?" I ask curiously. "Why wouldn't he sell it to them?"

She shrugs. "I don't know. Julian is very selective

when it comes to his business partners, and it could be that he just didn't trust them enough."

"So they took us as leverage?"

"Yes, I think so," she says softly. "At least, that's what you're here for. Someone at the clinic must've been in their employ because they knew who you were and what you meant to Julian. I was sleeping in one of the rooms downstairs when they found me, and they immediately went up to the second floor, to the room where you were staying. I think they intend to use you to force Julian's hand when it comes to giving them this weapon."

I draw in a shaky breath. "I see." I can only imagine how men psychotic enough to kill innocent civilians would 'force Julian's hand.' Gruesome images of severed body parts dance through my mind, and I push them away with effort, not wanting to give in to the panic that threatens to swallow me whole.

"It's lucky that Julian wasn't at the clinic when they came," Beth says, interrupting my dark thoughts. "They killed everyone, all sixteen of Julian's men who were stationed there guarding us."

I swallow hard. "Sixteen men?"

Beth nods. "They had insane firepower, and they came with a good thirty or forty men of their own. You didn't see the worst of it, because they entered from the back. There were bodies piled six feet high in the other staircase, with many of the casualties coming from their side."

I stare at her, trying to control my breathing. Shit.

Shit, shit, shit. For them to sacrifice so many of their comrades, whatever they want from Julian must be a hell of a weapon. Would he give it to them to save us? Does he care for me and Beth enough? I know he wants me—and is concerned about my well-being on some level—but I have no idea if he would put me ahead of his business interests.

Of course, even if he gives them what they want, there is no guarantee that they will let us live. I remember what Julian told me about Maria's death... about how she was killed to punish him for some warehouse raid. In Julian's world, actions have consequences. Very brutal consequences.

"Do you think he'll come for us?" I ask Beth quietly. The irony of it all doesn't escape me. I now regard Julian as my potential savior, my knight in shining armor. He's not the one I need rescuing from anymore.

She looks at me, her eyes dark in her pale face. "He will," she answers softly. "He'll come for us. I just don't know if it will matter to us by then."

The next couple of hours drag by. The men largely ignore us, though I've seen a couple of them looking at my bare legs when their leader wasn't paying attention. Thankfully, the hospital gown is generally shapeless and made of thick material—about the least sexy outfit I can imagine. The thought of one—or several—of them touching me makes my skin crawl.

They also don't give us anything to eat or drink. That's not a good sign; it means they don't care if we live or die. My thirst is getting so bad that all I can think about is water, and there is an empty, gnawing feeling in my stomach. The worst thing of all, however, is the cold fear that comes at me in waves and the dark images that flicker through my mind like a bad horror movie.

I try to talk to Beth to keep myself from freaking out, but after our initial conversation, she's become quiet and withdrawn, responding in monosyllables at best. It's like mentally, she's not even there. I envy her. I'd like to be able to escape like that, but I can't. For my mind to let go, I need Julian and his particular brand of erotic torture.

When I'm just about ready to scream from frustration, two more men enter the warehouse. To my surprise, one of them looks like a businessman; his pinstriped suit is sharp and tailored, and a stylish Strotter bag hangs messenger-style across his body. He's also relatively young, probably only in his thirties, and appears to be in good shape. Smoothly shaven, with olive complexion and glossy dark hair, he could've been on the cover of GQ—if it weren't for the fact that he's most likely a terrorist.

He exchanges a few words with the men on the other side of the warehouse, then heads toward Beth and me. As he approaches us, I notice the cold gleam in his eyes and the way his nostrils flare slightly. There's something vaguely reptilian in his unblinking stare, and I suppress a shudder when he stops a couple of feet away and studies me, his head cocked to the side.

I stare back at him, my heart pounding heavily in my chest. Objectively, he could be considered handsome, but I don't feel even the slightest tug of attraction. The only thing I feel is fear. It's actually a relief; some part of me has always wondered if I'm simply wired wrong—if I'm destined to desire the men who scare me. Now I see that it's a Julian-specific phenomenon for me. I'm frightened and repulsed by the criminal standing in front of me now—a perfectly normal reaction that I embrace.

"How long have you known Esguerra?" the man asks, addressing me. He has a British accent, mixed with a hint of something foreign and exotic. At the sound of his voice, Beth looks up, startled, and I see that she's back with us for the moment.

I hesitate for a second before answering. "About fifteen months," I finally say. I don't see the harm in revealing that much.

He lifts his eyebrows. "And he kept you hidden this whole time? Impressive…"

I suppress the sudden urge to snicker. Julian quite literally kept me hidden on his island, so this guy is more right than he realizes. My lips twitch involuntarily, and I see a flicker of surprise cross the man's face.

"Well, you're a brave little whore, aren't you?" he says slowly, watching me with his dark gaze. "Or do you think this is all a joke?"

I don't say anything in response. What can I say? No,

I don't think it's a joke. I know you're going to torture me and probably kill me to get back at Julian. Somehow that just doesn't have the right ring to it.

His eyes narrow, and I realize I somehow managed to make him angry. He looks like a cobra about to strike. My heartbeat spikes, and I tense, bracing myself for a blow, but he simply reaches for his Strotter bag and opens it to reveal his iPad. Glancing down, he quickly types some email, then looks up at me. "Let's see if Esguerra thinks it's a joke," he says quietly, closing the bag. "For your sake, girl, I hope that's not the case."

Then he turns and walks away, heading back to where the other men are gathered.

Despite my terror and discomfort, I somehow manage to fall asleep in the chair. My body is still recovering from the operation, and I'm both physically and emotionally exhausted from the events of the past day.

I wake up to the sound of voices. The guy in the suit and the short one I had pegged as the leader are standing in front of me, setting up what looks like a large camera on a tall tripod.

I swallow, staring at them. My mouth feels as dry as the Sahara desert, and despite all the time that's passed, I don't have the least urge to pee. I'm guessing that means I'm badly dehydrated.

Seeing that I'm awake, the Suit—I decide to call him that in my mind—gives me a thin-lipped smile. "It's showtime. Let's see just how much Esguerra wants his little whore back."

Nausea roils my empty stomach, and I turn my head to look at Beth. She's staring straight ahead, her face white and her gaze vacant. I don't know if she slept at all, but she seems even more out of it than before.

They point the camera toward us, checking the angle a couple of times, and then the Suit comes over to stand next to me. As soon as the camera light goes on, he puts his hand on my head, roughly stroking my tangled hair. "You know what I want, Esguerra," he says evenly, looking at the camera. "You have until midnight tomorrow to get it to me. Do that, and your slut will remain unharmed. I'll even give her back to you. If not, well... you'll get her back anyway." He pauses, smiling cruelly. "Little by little."

I stare at the camera, bile rising in my throat. I haven't been harmed—yet—but I can sense the violence in these men. It's the same darkness that stains Julian's soul. Men like these are different. They don't abide by the social contract. They don't play by the same rules as everyone else.

The Suit's hand leaves my hair, and he takes a step toward Beth. "You may be doubting me, Esguerra," he says, still speaking to the camera. "You may be thinking that I lack resolve. Well, let me do a little demonstration of what will happen to your pretty whore if I don't get what I want. We'll start with the redhead and move on to that one—" he nods toward me, "—tomorrow after midnight."

"No!" I scream, realizing what he means to do. "Don't touch her!" I struggle to get free, but the ropes are holding me too tightly. There is nothing I can do but watch helplessly as he wraps his hand around Beth's throat and begins to squeeze. "Don't you fucking touch her! Julian will kill you for this! He'll fucking murder you—"

Ignoring my screams, the Suit barks out an order in Arabic, and a man steps forward, cutting Beth's ropes with a sharp knife. I catch a glimpse of her terrified eyes, and then they throw her on the ground, face down. The Suit presses his knee against her back and yanks on her hair, forcing her head to arch back. I can see her legs drumming uselessly against the ground, and my screams grow louder as the Suit takes out a short, thin knife and begins cutting Beth's cheek.

She yells, struggling, and I can see blood spraying everywhere as he slices open her face, leaving behind a deep bloody gash. I gag, my stomach heaving, but he's far from done. Beth's other cheek is next, and then he presses the knife into her upper arm, cutting off a strip of flesh. Her agonized screams echo throughout the warehouse, joined by my own hysterical cries. I feel her pain as though it's my own, and I can't bear it. "Leave her alone!" I shriek. "You fucking bastard! Leave her alone!"

He doesn't, of course. He continues cutting her, his dark eyes shining with excitement. He's enjoying this, I realize with sick horror; he's not doing it just for the camera. Beth's struggles grow weaker, her cries turning into sobbing moans. There is blood everywhere; Beth is practically drowning in it. I don't know how she's able to remain conscious through this. Black spots swim in front of my vision, and I feel like the walls are closing in on me, my ribcage squeezing my lungs and preventing me from drawing in air.

Suddenly, Beth's body jerks, and she lets out a strange gurgle before falling silent. All I can hear now is the sound of my own harsh, sobbing breaths. Beth is lying there unmoving, a pool of blood spreading out from her neck area. The Suit gets up, wiping the knife on his pants, and faces the camera. "That was an expedited show for you, Esguerra," he says, smiling widely. "I didn't want to drag it out too much, since I know you'll need the time to get me what I asked for. Of course, if I don't receive it, the next show will be much, much longer." Taking a step toward me, he runs one bloody finger down my cheek. "Your little whore is so pretty, I might even let my men play with her before I start…"

This time I can't control myself. Hot vomit rushes into my throat, and I barely manage to turn my head to the side before the contents of my stomach empty out onto the floor in a series of violent heaves.

*a*fter the camera is turned off, they leave me alone again. Beth's body is dragged away, and the floor is carelessly mopped, leaving behind several reddish-brown streaks. I stare at them, my thoughts slow and sluggish, as if I'm in a stupor. I'm no longer shaking, though an occasional shudder still wracks my body. My stitches ache dully, and I wonder if I tore any of them during my struggles earlier. I don't see any blood seeping through my hospital gown, so maybe I didn't.

A little while later, they bring me some water. I greedily gulp down the whole cup, causing some of the men to laugh and say something in Arabic while rubbing their crotches suggestively. I almost think they are hoping that Julian doesn't come through, so they get to 'play' with me before the Suit goes to work.

For now, though, they mercifully leave me alone. I am even allowed outside for a minute to use the restroom, and the same guy as before—the impassive one—guards me while I go into the bushes. I think he's now my official bathroom companion, and I mentally start calling him Toilet Guy.

I name some of the others, too. The one with the black beard down to the middle of his chest—I call him Blackbeard. The one with the receding hairline is Baldie. The short guy who led the raid on the clinic— he's Garlic Breath.

I do this to distract myself from thoughts of Beth. I can't allow myself to think about her yet—not if I want to remain sane. If I get out of this alive, then I will mourn the woman who had become my friend. If I survive, then I will allow myself to cry and grieve, to rage at the senseless violence of her death. But right now, I can only exist from moment to moment, focusing on the most inconsequential, ridiculous things to keep myself from being crushed under the weight of brutal reality.

Time ticks by slowly. As darkness descends, I stare at the floor, the walls, the ceiling. I think I even nod off a couple of times, although I jerk awake at the least hint of any sound, my heart racing. They still haven't fed me, and the hunger pangs in my stomach are a gnawing ache. It doesn't matter, though. I'm just grateful to still be alive—a state of affairs I know will not continue for long, unless Julian comes through with the weapon.

Closing my eyes, I try to pretend that I'm home on the island, reading a book on the beach. I try to imagine that at any moment, I can go back to the house and find Beth there, prepping dinner for us. I try to convince myself that Julian is simply away on one of his business trips and I will see him again soon. I picture his smile, the way his dark hair curls around his face, framing the hard masculine perfection of his features, and I ache for him, for the warmth and safety of his strong embrace, even as my mind gradually drifts toward an uneasy sleep.

A large hand clamps tightly over my mouth, jerking me awake. My eyes fly open, adrenaline surging through my veins. Terrified, I begin to struggle... and then I hear a familiar voice whispering in my ear, "Shh, Nora. It's me. I need you to be quiet now, okay?"

I nod slightly, my body shaking with relief, and the hand leaves my mouth. Turning my head, I stare at Julian in disbelief.

Crouching beside me, he's dressed all in black. A bulletproof vest is covering his chest and shoulders, and his face is painted with black diagonal stripes. There is a machine gun hanging across his shoulder, and an entire array of weapons is clipped to his belt. He looks like a deadly stranger. Only his eyes are familiar, startlingly bright in his paint-darkened face.

For a second, I'm convinced that I'm dreaming. He can't be standing here, in this warehouse in the middle of nowhere, talking to me. Not when his enemies are less than thirty yards away. My heart racing, I cast a quick, frantic glance around the warehouse.

The men in the other corner appear to be asleep, stretched out on blankets on the floor. I count eight of them—which means that several of them are probably outside, guarding the building. I don't see the Suit anywhere; he must also be outside.

Turning my attention back to Julian, I see him cutting through the ropes at my ankles with a wicked-looking knife. "How did you get in here?" I whisper, staring at him in dazed wonder.

He pauses for a second, looking up at me. "Be quiet," he says, his words almost inaudible. "I need to get you out before they wake up."

I nod, falling silent as he resumes cutting my ropes. Despite our perilous situation, I am almost dizzy with joy. Julian is here, with me. He came for me. The surge of love and gratitude is so strong, I can barely contain it. I want to jump up and hug him, but I remain still as he finishes his task, getting rid of the remaining ropes.

As soon as I'm free, he pulls me to my feet and wraps his arms around me, holding me tightly against him. I can feel the fine trembling in his powerful body, and then he releases me, taking half a step back. Framing my face with his palms, he looks down at me, his blue gaze hard and fiercely possessive. A moment of wordless communication passes between us, and I know. I know what he can't say right now.

I know he would always come for me.

I know he would kill for me.

I know he would die for me.

Lowering his arms, he takes my hand. "Let's go," he says quietly, still looking at me. "We don't have much time."

I grip his hand tightly, letting him lead me toward the darkened area near the wall on the opposite side of where the men are sleeping. The maze of shelves and boxes in the middle of the warehouse quickly hides us from their view, and Julian stops there, crouching down again and letting go of my palm. I hear a fumbling sound, like his hand is searching for something along the floor, and then there is a quiet creak as he lifts a board off the floor and places it to the side.

On the floor in front of us is a large square opening.

I kneel down beside it, peering into the darkness below.

"Climb down," Julian whispers in my ear, putting his hand on my knee and squeezing it lightly. The familiar touch calms me a bit. "There is a ladder."

I swallow, reaching out with my hand to find said ladder. How does he know this?

"I hacked into their computer and found the blueprints of this building," he explains quietly, as though reading my mind. "There is a storage area below that has a drainpipe leading outside. Find it and crawl through it." His hand leaves my knee, and I feel bereft without his touch, the danger of our situation hitting me again.

My fingers touch the metal ladder, and I grab it, maneuvering myself toward it. Julian holds my arm as I find my footing and cautiously begin to descend. It's pitch-black down there, and under normal circumstances, I would be hesitant to go into an unknown basement, but there's nothing more frightening to me right now than the men we're escaping from.

I climb down a few rungs, then look up, seeing Julian still sitting there. The expression on his face is tense and alert, like he's listening for something.

And then I hear it—a murmur of voices, followed by shouts in Arabic.

My absence had been discovered.

Julian rises to his feet with one smooth motion and looks down at me, his hands gripping the machine gun. "Go," he orders, his voice low and hard. "Now, Nora. Get to the drainpipe and outside. I'll hold them back."

"What? No!" I stare at him in horrified shock. "Come with me—"

He gives me a furious glare. "Go," he hisses. "Now, or we're both dead. I can't worry about you and fight them off."

I hesitate for a second, feeling torn. I don't want to leave him behind, but I don't want to stand in his way either. "I love you," I say quietly, looking up at him, and see a quick flash of white teeth in response.

"Go, baby," he says, his tone much softer now. "I'll be with you soon."

My heart aching, I do as he says, climbing down the ladder as quickly as I can. The shouts are growing louder, and I know the men are searching the warehouse, starting with the maze in the middle. It's only a matter of time before they get to the darkened area along this wall. My entire body is shaking with a combination of nerves and adrenaline, and I focus on not falling as I descend further into the darkness.

Rat-tat-tat! The burst of gunfire above startles me, and I climb down even faster, my breathing hard and erratic. As soon as my feet touch the floor, I stretch out my hands in front of me and begin to grope in the darkness, searching for the wall with the drain pipe.

More gunfire. Yells. Screams. My heart is pounding so hard, it sounds like a drum in my ears.

Something squeaks underneath my feet, and tiny paws run over my bare toes. I ignore it, frantically searching for that drainpipe. Rats are nothing to me right now. Somewhere up there, Julian is in mortal danger. I don't know if he's by himself or if he brought reinforcements, but the thought of him being hurt or killed is so agonizing that I can't focus on it now. Not if I want to survive.

My hands touch the wall, but I can't find an opening. It's too dark. Panting, I make my way along the wall, sweeping my hands up and down the smooth surface. My stitches ache, but I barely register the pain. I need to find a way out. If they catch me again, I will not survive for long.

Another burst of gunfire, followed by more yells.

I continue searching, my terror and frustration growing with every moment. Julian. Julian is up there. I try not to think about it, but I can't. There's nothing I can do to help him; logically, I know that. I'm barefoot and dressed in a hospital gown, without so much as a fork to defend myself with. In the meantime, he's armed to the teeth and wearing a bulletproof vest.

Of course, logic has nothing to do with the agonizing fear I feel at the thought of losing him.

He will survive, I tell myself as I continue looking for the drainpipe. Julian knows what he's doing. This is his world, his area of expertise. This is the part of his life he was shielding me from on the island.

My hands touch something hard on the wall near my knees and then sink into the opening.

The drainpipe. I found it.

There is another high-pitched squeak, and something scrambles out of the pipe toward me. I jump back, startled, but then I get on all fours and determinedly crawl inside, steeling myself for more potential rodent encounters.

The drainpipe is large enough that I can be on my hands and knees, and I crawl as fast as I can, ignoring the stale smell of sewage and rust. Thankfully, it's only a little bit wet in there, and I try not to dwell on what that wetness might be.

Finally, I reach the other opening. Compressing myself into a little ball, I manage to turn around and climb out feet first.

Stepping away from the pipe, I gaze at my surroundings. The sky above me is covered with stars, and the air is thick with the scent of warm earth and jungle vegetation. I can see the warehouse building on the small hill above me, less than fifty yards away.

I stare at it, sick with fear for Julian. There is another burst of gunfire, accompanied by flashes of bright light. The gunfight is still going on—which is a good sign, I tell myself. If Julian was dead—if the terrorists had won —there would be no more shooting. He must've come with reinforcements after all.

Wrapping my arms around myself, I press my back against a tree, my legs trembling from the combination of terror and adrenaline.

And in that moment, the sky lights up as the building explodes… and a blast of scorching-hot air sends me flying into the bushes several feet away.

24

*T*he next twenty-four hours are a blur in my memory.

After I get to my feet, I am dizzy and disoriented, my head throbbing and my body feeling like one giant bruise. There is a din in my ears, and everything seems to be coming at me as though from a distance.

I must've passed out from the blast, but I am not sure. By the time I recover enough to walk, the fire consuming the building is almost over.

Dazed, I stumble up the hill and start searching through the smoldering ruins of the warehouse. Occasionally, I find something that looks like a charred limb, and a couple of times, I come across a body that's very nearly whole, with only a head or a leg missing. I register these findings on some level, but I don't fully process them. I feel oddly detached, like I'm not really there. Nothing touches me. Nothing bothers me. Even the physical sensations are dulled by shock.

I search for him for hours. By the time I stop, the sun is high up in the sky, and I'm dripping with sweat.

I have no choice but to face the truth now.

There are no survivors. It's as simple as that.

I should cry. I should scream. I should feel something.

But I don't.

I just feel numb instead.

Leaving the warehouse, I begin walking. I don't know where I am going, and I don't care. All I'm capable of doing is putting one foot in front of the other.

By the time it starts getting dark, I come across a cluster of tiny houses made of wooden poles and cardboard. There is a shallow creek running through the middle of the settlement, and I see a couple of women doing laundry there by hand.

Their shocked faces are the last thing I remember before I collapse a few feet away from them.

"Miss Leston, do you feel up to answering a few questions for me? I'm Agent Wilson, FBI, and this is Agent Bosovsky."

I look up at the plump middle-aged man standing next to my bed. He's not at all like I imagined FBI agents to be. His face is round, almost cherubic-looking, with rosy cheeks and dancing blue eyes. If Agent Wilson wore a red hat and had a white beard, he would've made a great Santa Claus. In contrast, his partner—Agent

Bosovsky—is painfully thin, with deep frown lines etched into his narrow face.

For the past two days, I have been recuperating in a hospital in Bangkok. Apparently, one of the women at the creek had notified the local authorities about the girl that wandered into their village. I vaguely recall them questioning me, but I doubt I made any sense when I spoke to them. However, they understood enough to contact the American Embassy on my behalf, and the US officials took it from there.

"Your parents are on the way," Agent Bosovsky says when I continue to stare at them without saying a word. "Their flight lands in a few hours."

I blink, his words somehow penetrating the layer of ice that has kept me insulated from everyone and everything since the explosion. "My parents?" I croak, my throat feeling strangely swollen.

The thin agent nods. "Yes, Miss Leston. They were notified yesterday, and we got them on the earliest flight to Bangkok. They wanted to speak to you, but you were sedated at that point."

I process that information. The doctors already informed me that I have a mild concussion, along with first-degree burns and lacerations on my feet. Other than that, they were impressed by my overall good health—dehydration, recent surgery, and various bruises notwithstanding. Still, they must've sedated me to let me rest.

"Do you think you could answer some questions

before your parents arrive?" Agent Wilson asks gently when I continue to remain silent.

I nod, almost imperceptibly, and he pulls up a chair. Agent Bosovsky does the same thing.

"Miss Leston, you were abducted in June of last year," Agent Wilson says, the expression on his round face warm and understanding. "Can you tell us anything about your abduction?"

I hesitate for a moment. Do I want to tell them anything about Julian? And then I remember that he's dead and that none of it matters. For a second, the agony is so sharp, it steals my breath away, but then the numbing wall of ice encases me again. "Sure," I say evenly. "What do you want to know?"

"Do you know his name?"

"Julian Esguerra. He is—" I swallow hard, "—he was an arms dealer."

The FBI agent's eyes widen. "An arms dealer?"

I nod and tell them what I know about Julian's organization. Agent Bosovsky scribbles down notes as quickly as he can, while Agent Wilson continues asking me questions about Julian's activities and the terrorists who stole me from him. They seem disappointed that he's dead—and that I know so little—and I explain that I haven't been off the island since my abduction.

"He kept you there for the entire fifteen months?" Agent Bosovsky asks, the frown lines on his thin face deepening. "Just you and this woman, Beth?"

"Yes."

The agents exchange a look, and I stare at them, knowing what they're thinking. Poor girl, kept like an animal in a cage for a criminal's amusement. Once I felt that way too, but no longer. Now I would do anything to rewind the clock and go back to being Julian's captive.

Agent Wilson turns toward me and clears his throat. "Miss Leston, we'll have a sexual abuse counselor speak to you later this afternoon. She's very good—"

"There's no need," I interrupt. "I'm fine."

And I am. I don't feel victimized or abused. I just feel numb.

After a few more questions, they leave me alone. I don't tell them any details of my relationship with Julian, but I think they get the gist of it.

The FBI sketch artist comes to see me next, and I describe Julian to him. He keeps giving me funny looks as I correct his interpretation of my descriptions. "No, his eyebrows are a little thicker, a little straighter... His hair is a little wavier, yes, like that..."

He has particular trouble with Julian's mouth. It's hard to describe the beauty of that dark, angelic smile of his. "Make the upper lip a little fuller... No, that's too full—it should be more sensuous, almost pretty..."

Finally, we're done, and Julian's face stares at me from the white sheet of paper. A bolt of agony spears through me again, but the numbness comes to my rescue right away, as it did before.

"That's a handsome fellow," the artist comments, examining his handiwork. "You don't see men like that every day."

My hands clench tightly, my nails digging into my skin. "No, you don't."

The next person to visit my room is the sexual abuse counselor they mentioned to me before. She's a slightly overweight brunette who looks to be in her late forties, but something about her direct gaze reminds me of Beth.

"I'm Diane," she says, introducing herself to me as she pulls up a chair. "May I call you Nora?"

"That's fine," I say wearily. I don't particularly want to talk to this woman, but the determined look on her face tells me that she has no intention of leaving until I do.

"Nora, can you tell me about your time on the island?" she asks, looking at me.

"What do you want to know?"

"Whatever you feel comfortable telling me."

I think about it for a moment. The truth of the matter is that I'm not comfortable telling her anything. How can I describe the way Julian made me feel? How can I explain the highs and lows of our unorthodox relationship? I know what she's going to think—that I'm screwed up in the head for loving him. That my feelings aren't real, but a byproduct of my captivity.

And she would probably be right—but it doesn't matter to me anymore. There is right and wrong, and then there's what Julian and I had together. Nothing and no one will ever be able to fill the void left inside me. No amount of counseling would make the pain of losing him go away.

I give Diane a polite smile. "I'm sorry," I say quietly. "I'd rather not talk to you right now."

She nods, not the least bit surprised. "I understand. Often, as victims, we blame ourselves for what happened. We think we did something to cause this thing to happen to us."

"I don't think that," I say, frowning. Okay, maybe the thought did flit briefly through my mind when I was first taken, but getting to know Julian had quickly disabused me of that notion. He was a man who simply took what he wanted—and he had wanted me.

"I see," she says, looking slightly puzzled. Then her brow clears as she appears to solve the mystery in her mind. "He was a very good-looking man, wasn't he?" she guesses, staring at me.

I hold her gaze silently, not willing to admit anything. I can't talk about my feelings right now, not if I want to maintain that icy distance that keeps me sane.

She looks at me for a few seconds, then gets up, handing me her card. "If you're ever ready to talk, Nora, please call me," she says softly. "You can't keep it all bottled up inside. It will eventually consume you—"

"Okay, I will call you," I interrupt, taking the card and placing it on my bedside table. I'm lying through my teeth, and I'm sure she knows it.

The corners of her mouth tilt up in a faint smile, and then she exits the room, finally leaving me alone with my thoughts.

For my parents' arrival, I insist on getting up and putting on normal clothes. I don't want them to see me lying in a hospital bed. I'm sure they have already spent too much time worrying about me, and the last thing I want is to add to their anxiety.

One of the nurses gives me a pair of jeans and a T-shirt, and I gratefully put them on. They fit me well. The nurse is a petite Thai woman, and we're roughly the same size. It's strange to wear these types of clothes again. I had gotten so used to light summer dresses that jeans feel unusually rough and heavy against my skin. I don't put on any shoes, though, since my feet still have to heal from the burns I got wandering through the remnants of the warehouse.

When my parents finally enter the room, I am sitting in a chair, waiting for them. My mom comes in first. Her face crumples as soon as she sees me, and she rushes across the room, tears streaming down her face. My dad is right behind her, and soon they are both hugging me, chattering a mile a minute, and sobbing with joy.

I smile widely, hug them in return, and do my best to reassure them that I'm all right, that all of my injuries are minor and there's nothing to worry about. I don't cry, though. I can't. Everything feels dull and distant, and even my parents seem more like beloved memories than real people. Nonetheless, I make an effort to act normally; I already caused them far too much stress and anxiety.

After a little while, they calm down enough to sit and talk.

"He contacted you, right?" I ask, remembering Julian's promise. "He told you I was alive?"

My dad nods, his face drawn tight. "A couple of weeks after you disappeared, we got a deposit into our bank account," he says quietly. "A deposit in the amount of one million dollars from an untraceable offshore account. Supposedly it was a lottery that we won."

My mouth falls open. "What?" Julian gave my parents money?

"At the same time, we received an email," my dad continues, his voice shaking. "The subject was: 'From your daughter with love.' It had your picture. You were lying on a beach, reading a book. You looked so beautiful, so peaceful..." He swallows visibly. "The email said that you were well and that you were with someone who would take care of you—and that we should use the money to pay off our mortgage. It also said that we would be putting you in danger if we went to the police with this information."

I stare at him in bemusement, trying to imagine what they must've thought at that point. A million dollars...

"We didn't know what to do," my mom says, her hands anxiously twisting together. "We thought this could be a useful lead in the investigation, but at the same time, we didn't want to do anything to jeopardize you, wherever you were..."

"So what did you do?" I ask in fascination. The FBI didn't say anything about a million dollars, so my parents couldn't have spoken to them about this. At the same time, I can't imagine my parents simply taking the money and not pursuing this further.

"We used the money to hire a team of private investigators," my dad explains. "The best ones we could find. They were able to track the deposit to a shell corporation in the Cayman Islands, but the trail died there." He pauses, looking at me. "We've been using that money to look for you ever since."

"What happened, honey?" my mom asks, leaning forward in her chair. "Who took you? Where did this money come from? Where have you been this whole time?"

I smile and begin answering their questions. At the same time, I watch them, drinking in their familiar features. My parents are a handsome couple, both of them healthy and in good shape. They had me when they were both in their early twenties, so they are still relatively young. My dad has only traces of gray in his dark hair, though there is more gray now than I remember seeing before.

"So you really were swimming in the ocean and reading books on the beach?" My mom stares at me in disbelief as I describe my typical day on the island.

"Yes." I give her a huge smile. "In some ways, it was like a really long vacation. And he did take care of me, like he told you he would."

"But why did he take you?" my dad asks in frustration. "Why did he steal you away?"

I shrug, not wanting to go into detailed explanations

about Maria and Julian's extreme possessiveness. "Because that's just the type of man he was, I guess," I say casually. "Because he couldn't really date me normally, given his profession."

"Did he hurt you, honey?" my mom asks, her dark eyes filled with sympathy. "Was he cruel to you?"

"No," I say softly. "He wasn't cruel to me at all."

I can't explain the complexity of my relationship with Julian to my parents, so I don't even try. Instead, I gloss over many aspects of my captivity, focusing only on the positive. I tell them about my early morning fishing expeditions with Beth and my newfound painting hobby. I describe the beauty of the island and how I got back into running. By the time I pause to catch my breath, they are both staring at me with strange looks on their faces.

"Nora, honey," my mom asks uncertainly, "are you... are you in love with this Julian?"

I laugh, but the sound comes out raw and empty. "Love? No, of course not!" I'm not sure what gave her that idea, since I have been trying to avoid talking about Julian at all. The more I think about him, the more I feel like the wall of ice around me might crack, letting the pain drown me.

"Of course not," my dad says, watching me closely, and I see that he doesn't believe me.

Somehow both of my parents can sense the truth— that I'm far more traumatized by my rescue than by my abduction.

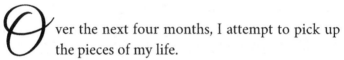 ver the next four months, I attempt to pick up the pieces of my life.

After another day in the Bangkok hospital, I'm deemed healthy enough to travel, and I go home, back to Illinois with my parents. We have two FBI escorts on our trip home—Agents Wilson and Bosovsky—who use the twenty-hour flight to ask me even more questions. Both of them seem frustrated because, according to their databases, Julian Esguerra simply doesn't exist.

"There are no other aliases you've heard him use?" Agent Bosovsky asks me for the third time, after their Interpol query comes back without any results.

"No," I say patiently. "I only knew him as Julian. The terrorists called him Esguerra."

Beth's guess about the identities of the men who stole us from Julian's clinic turned out to be correct. They were indeed part of a particularly dangerous

Jihadist organization called Al-Quadar—that much the FBI had been able to find out.

"This just doesn't make sense," Agent Wilson says, his round cheeks quivering with frustration. "Anyone with that kind of clout should have been on our radar. If he was head of an illegal organization that manufactured and distributed cutting-edge weapons, how is it possible that not a single government agency is aware of his existence?"

I don't know what to tell him, so I just shrug in response. The private investigators my parents hired hadn't been able to find out anything about him either.

My parents and I had debated telling the FBI about Julian's money, but ultimately decided against it. Revealing this information so late in the game would only get my parents in trouble and could potentially cause the FBI to think that I had been Julian's accessory. After all, what kidnapper sends money to his victim's family?

By the time we get home, I am exhausted. I'm tired of my parents hovering over me all the time, and I'm sick of the FBI coming to me with a million questions that I can't answer. Most of all, I'm tired of being around so many people. After more than a year with minimal human contact, I feel overwhelmed by the airport crowds.

I find my old room in my parents' house virtually untouched. "We always hoped you'd be back," my mom explains, her face glowing with happiness. I smile and give her a hug before gently ushering her out of the room. More than anything, I need to be alone right now —because I don't know how long I can keep up my 'normal' facade.

That night, as I take a shower in my old childhood bathroom, I finally give in to my grief and cry.

Two weeks after my arrival home, I move out of my parents' house. They try to talk me out of it, but I convince them that I need this—that I have to be on my own and independent. The truth of the matter is, as much as I love my parents, I can't be around them twenty-four-seven. I'm no longer that carefree girl they remember, and I find it too draining to pretend to be her.

It's much easier to be myself in the tiny studio I rent nearby.

My parents try to give me what remains of Julian's gift to them—half a million with small change—but I refuse. The way I see it, that money had been for my parents' mortgage and I want it used for that purpose. After numerous arguments, we reach an agreement: they pay off most of their mortgage and refinance the rest, and the remaining money goes into my college fund.

Although I technically don't need to work for a while, I get a waitressing job anyway. It gets me out of the house, but is not particularly demanding—which is exactly what I need right now. There are nights when I don't sleep and days when getting out of bed is torture. The emptiness inside me is crushing, the grief almost suffocating, and it takes every bit of my strength to function at a semi-normal level.

When I do sleep, I have nightmares. My mind replays Beth's death and the warehouse explosion over and over again, until I wake up drenched in cold sweat. After those dreams, I lie awake, aching for Julian, for the warmth and safety of his embrace. I feel lost without him, like a rudderless ship at sea. His absence is a festering wound that refuses to heal.

I miss Beth, too. I miss her no-nonsense attitude, her matter-of-fact approach to life. If she were here, she would be the first one to tell me that shit happens and that I should just deal with it. She would want me to move on.

And I try... but the senseless violence of her death eats at me. Julian was right—I didn't know what real hatred was before. I didn't know what it was like to want to hurt someone, to crave their death. Now I do. If I could go back in time and kill the terrorist who murdered Beth so brutally, I would do it in a heartbeat. It's not enough for me that he died in that explosion. I wish I had been the one to end his life.

My parents insist that I see a therapist. To pacify them, I go a few times. It doesn't help. I'm not ready to bare my heart and soul to a stranger, and our sessions end up being a waste of time and money. I'm not in the right frame of mind to receive therapy—my loss is too fresh, my emotions too raw.

I start painting again, but I can't do the same sunny landscapes as before. My art is darker now, more chaotic. I paint the explosion over and over again, trying to get it out of my mind, and every time it comes out a little different, a little more abstract. I paint Julian's face, too. I do it from memory, and it bothers me that I can't quite capture the devastating perfection of his features. No matter how much I try, I can't seem to get it right.

All of my friends are away at college, so for the first couple of weeks, I only speak to them on the phone and via Skype. They don't quite know how to act around me, and I don't blame them. I try to keep our conversations light, focusing mostly on what's been happening in their lives since our graduation, but I know they feel strange talking about boyfriend troubles and exams to someone they see as a victim of a horrible crime. They look at me with pity and disturbing curiosity in their eyes, and I can't bring myself to talk to them about my experience on the island.

Still, when Leah comes home from the University of Michigan, we get together to hang out. After a few hugs, most of the initial awkwardness dissipates, and she's again the same girl who was my best friend all through middle school and beyond.

"I like your place," she says, walking around my studio and examining the paintings I have hanging on the walls. "That's some pretty cool art you've got there. Where did you get these from?"

"I painted them," I tell her, pulling on my boots. We're going out to a local Italian restaurant for dinner.

I'm dressed in a pair of skinny jeans and a black top, and it feels just like old times.

"You did?" Leah gives me an astonished look. "Since when do you paint?"

"It's a recent development," I say, grabbing my trench coat. It's already fall, and it's starting to get chilly. I had gotten used to the tropical climate of the island, and even sixty degrees feels cold to me.

"Well, shit, Nora, this is really good stuff," she says, coming up to one of the explosion paintings to take a closer look. Those are the only ones I have up—my Julian portraits are private. "I didn't know you had it in you."

"Thanks." I grin at her. "Ready to go?"

We have a great dinner. Leah tells me about going to college at Michigan and about Jason, her new boyfriend. I listen attentively, and we joke about boys and their inexplicable need to do keg stands.

"When are you applying to college?" she asks when we're mid-way through dessert. "You were going to go local at first. Are you still planning to do that?"

I nod. "Yes, I think I'm going to apply for the spring semester." Although I can now afford to go to any university, I have no desire to change my plans. The money sitting in my bank account doesn't seem quite real to me, and I'm strangely reluctant to spend it.

"That's awesome," Leah says, grinning. She seems a little hyper, like she's overly excited about something.

I soon learn what that something is.

"Hey, Nora," a familiar voice says behind me, just as we're getting ready to pay our bill.

I jump up, startled. Turning, I stare at Jake—the boy I had been on the date with that fateful night when Julian took me.

The boy Julian had hurt to keep me in line.

He looks almost the same: shaggy sun-streaked hair, warm brown eyes, a great build. Only the expression on his face is different. It's drawn and tense, and the wariness in his gaze is like a kick to my stomach.

"Jake…" I feel like I'm confronting a ghost. "I didn't know you were in town. I thought you were away at Michigan—"

And then I realize the truth. Turning, I look accusingly at Leah, who gives me a huge smile in response. "I hope you don't mind, Nora," she says brightly. "I told Jake I was coming to see you this weekend, and he asked to join me. I wasn't sure how you'd feel about that, given everything—" her face reddens a bit, "—so I just mentioned that we'd be here tonight."

I blink, my palms beginning to sweat. Leah doesn't know about the beating Jake received because of me. That little tidbit is something I disclosed only to the FBI. She's probably afraid that seeing Jake might bring back painful memories of my abduction, but she can't possibly guess at the nauseating swirl of guilt and anxiety I feel right now.

Jake knows I'm responsible for the assault, however. I can see it in the way he looks at me.

I force myself to smile. "Of course I don't mind," I lie smoothly. "Please, have a seat. Let's get some coffee." I motion toward the seat on the other side of our booth and sit down myself. "How have you been?"

He smiles back at me, his brown eyes crinkling at the corners in the way I found endearing once. He's still one of the cutest guys I've ever met, but I no longer feel any attraction to him. The crush I had on him before pales in comparison to my all-consuming Julian obsession— to the dark and desperate craving that makes me toss and turn at night.

When I can't sleep, I often think about the things Julian and I used to do together—the things he made me do... the things he trained me to want. In the dark of the night, I masturbate to forbidden fantasies. Fantasies of exquisite pain and forced pleasure, of violence and lust. I ache with the need to be taken and used, hurt and possessed. I long for Julian—the man who awakened this side of me.

The man who is now dead.

Pushing that excruciating thought aside, I focus on what Jake is telling me.

"—couldn't go into that park for months," he says, and I realize that he's talking about his experience after my abduction. "Every time I did, I thought about you and where you might be... The police said it was like you vanished off the face of the planet—"

I listen to him, shame and self-loathing coiling deep

inside my chest. How can I feel this way about a man who did such a terrible thing and hurt so many people in the process? How sick am I to love someone capable of such evil? Julian was not a tortured, misunderstood hero forced to do bad things by circumstances beyond his control. He was a monster, pure and simple.

A monster that I miss with every fiber of my being.

"I'm so sorry, Nora," Jake says, distracting me from my self-flagellation. "I'm sorry I couldn't protect you that night—"

"Wait... What?" I stare at him in disbelief. "Are you crazy? Do you know what you were up against? There's no way you could've done anything—"

"I should've still tried." Jake's voice is heavy with guilt. "I should've done something, anything..."

I reach out across the table, impulsively covering his hand with my own. "No," I say firmly. "You're in no way to blame for this." I can see Leah out of the corner of my eye; she's twiddling with her phone and trying to pretend she's not here. I ignore her. I need to convince Jake that he didn't screw up, to help him move past this.

His skin is warm under my fingers, and I can feel the vibrating tension within him. "Jake," I say softly, holding his gaze, "nobody could've prevented this. Nobody. Julian has—had—the kind of resources that would make a SWAT team jealous. If it's anybody's fault, it's mine. You got dragged into this because of me, and I am truly sorry." I'm apologizing for more than that night in the park, and he knows it.

"No, Nora," he says quietly, his brown eyes filled

with shadows. "You're right. It's his fault, not ours." And I realize that he's offering me absolution, too—that he also wants to free me from my guilt.

I smile and squeeze his hand, silently accepting his forgiveness.

I wish I could forgive myself so easily, but I can't.

Because even now, as I sit there holding Jake's hand, I can't stop loving Julian.

No matter what he had done.

26

"You know, I think he's still really into you," Leah says as she drives me home. "I'm surprised he didn't ask you out right then and there."

"Ask me out? Jake?" I give her an incredulous stare. "I'm the last girl he'd want to date."

"Oh, I wouldn't be too sure about that," she says thoughtfully. "You guys might've only been on one date, but he was seriously depressed when you disappeared. And the way he was looking at you tonight…"

I let out a nervous laugh. "Leah, please, that's just crazy. Jake and I have a complex history. He wanted closure tonight, that's all." The idea of dating Jake—of dating anyone—feels strange and foreign. In my mind, I still belong to Julian, and the thought of letting another man touch me makes me inexplicably anxious.

"Yeah, closure, right." Leah's voice is dripping with sarcasm. "The entire evening he was staring at you like you're the hottest thing he's ever seen. It's not closure he wants from you, I guarantee that."

"Oh, come on—"

"No, seriously," Leah says, glancing at me as she stops at a stoplight. "You should go out with him. He's a great guy, and I know you liked him before…"

I look at her, and the urge to make her understand wars with my deep-seated need to protect myself. "Leah, that was before," I say slowly, deciding to disclose some of the truth. "I'm not the same person now. I can't date a guy like Jake… not after Julian."

She falls silent, turning her attention back to the road as the light changes to green.

When she stops in front of my apartment building, she turns toward me. "I'm sorry," she says quietly. "That was stupid and inconsiderate of me. You seem so okay that I forgot for a moment…" She swallows, tears glistening in her eyes. "If you ever want to talk about it, I'm here for you—you know that, right?"

I nod, giving her a smile. I'm lucky to have a friend like her, and someday soon, I may take her up on her offer. But not yet—not while I feel so raw and shredded inside.

The next few weeks crawl by at a snail's pace. I exist moment to moment, taking it one day at a time. Every morning, I write out a list of tasks that I want to accomplish that day and diligently adhere to it, no matter how much I may want to crawl under my bed covers and never come out.

Most of the time, my lists include mundane activities, such as eating, running, going to work, doing grocery shopping, and calling my parents. Occasionally, I add more ambitious projects as well, such as applying to college for the spring semester—which I do, as I told Leah I would.

I also sign up for shooting lessons. To my surprise, I turn out to be pretty good at handling a gun. My instructor says I'm a natural, and I start doing research on what I need to do to acquire a firearms license in Illinois. I also tackle self-defense classes and start learning a few basic moves to protect myself. I will never be able to win against someone like Julian and the men who took me and Beth, but knowing how to shoot and fight makes me feel better, more in control of my life.

Between all those new activities, my work, and my art, I'm too busy to socialize, which suits me just fine. I'm not in the mood to make new friends, and all of my old ones are away.

Jake and Leah are both back at Michigan. He pings me on Facebook, and we chat a few times. He doesn't ask me out, though.

I'm glad. Even if he wasn't going to college three-and-a-half hours away, it would never work out between us. Jake is smart enough to realize that nothing good could ever come out of getting involved with someone like me—someone who, for all intents and purposes, is still Julian's captive.

I dream of him almost every night. Like an incubus, my former captor comes to me in the dark, when I'm at my most vulnerable. He invades my mind as ruthlessly as he once took my body. When I'm not reliving his death, my dreams are disturbingly sexual. I dream of his mouth, his cock, his hands. They're everywhere, all over me, inside me. I dream of his terrifyingly beautiful smile, of the way he used to hold and caress me.

Of the way he used to torture me until I forgot everything and lost myself in him.

I dream of him... and wake up wet and throbbing, my body empty and aching for his possession. Like an addict going through a withdrawal, I am desperate for a fix, for something to take the edge off my need.

I am not ready to date, but my body doesn't care about that—and finally, I decide to give in.

Dressing up, I grab my old fake ID and head to a local bar.

The men swarm around me like flies. It's easy, so fucking easy. A girl alone in a bar—that's all the encouragement they need. Like wolves scenting prey, they sense my desperation, my desire for something more than a cold, lonely bed tonight.

I let one of them buy me drinks. A shot of vodka, then one of tequila... By the time he asks me if I want to leave, everything around me is fuzzy. Nodding, I let him lead me to his car.

He's a good-looking man in his thirties, with sandy hair and blue-gray eyes. Not particularly tall, but reasonably well built. He's an attorney, he tells me as he drives us to a nearby motel.

I close my eyes as he continues talking. I don't care who he is or what he does. I just want him to fuck me, to fill that gaping void inside. To take away the chill that has seeped deep into my bones.

He rents a room at the front desk, and we go upstairs. When we get into the room, he takes off my coat and begins to kiss me. I can taste beer and a hint of tacos on his tongue. He presses me to him, his hands hot and eager as they begin to explore my body—and suddenly, I can't take it anymore.

"Stop." I shove him away as hard as I can. Taken by surprise, he stumbles back a couple of steps.

"What the fuck—" He gapes at me, mouth open in disbelief.

"I'm sorry," I say quickly, grabbing my coat. "It's not you, I promise."

And before he can say a word, I run out of the room.

Catching a taxi, I go home, sick from the alcohol and utterly miserable. There is no fix for my addiction, no way to quench my thirst.

Even drunk, I can't bear another man's touch.

---

27

*I*t starts off as another erotic dream.

Strong, hard hands slide up my naked body, callused palms scratching my skin as he squeezes my breasts, his thumbs rubbing against my peaked, sensitive nipples. I arch against him, feeling the warmth of his skin, the heavy weight of his powerful body pressing me into the mattress. His muscular legs force my thighs apart, and his erection prods at my sex, the broad head sliding between the soft folds and exerting light pressure on my clit.

I moan, rubbing against him, my inner muscles clenching with the need to take him deep inside. I'm soaking wet and panting, and my hands grasp his tight, muscular ass, trying to force him in, to get him to fuck me.

He laughs, the sound a low, seductive rumble in his chest, and his big hands grasp my wrists, pinning them above my head. "Miss me, my pet?" he murmurs in my ear, his hot breath sending erotic chills down the side of my body.

My pet? Julian never talks in my dreams—

I gasp, my eyes popping open... and in the dim early morning light, I see him.

Julian.

Naked and aroused, he's sprawled on top of me, holding me down on my bed. His dark hair is cut shorter than before, and his magnificent face is taut with lust, his eyes glittering like blue jewels.

I freeze, staring up at him, my heart thudding heavily in my ribcage. For a moment, I think that I'm still dreaming—that my mind is playing cruel tricks on me. My vision dims, blurs, and I realize that I literally stopped breathing for a moment, that the shock has driven all air out of my lungs.

I inhale sharply, still frozen in place, and he lowers his head, his mouth descending on mine. His tongue slips between my parted lips, invading me, and the hauntingly familiar taste of him makes my head spin.

There is no longer any doubt in my mind.

It's really Julian—he's as alive and vital as ever.

Fury, sharp and sudden, spikes through me. He's alive—he's been alive all along! The entire time while I mourned him, while I tried to mend my shattered soul, he's been alive and well, undoubtedly laughing at my pathetic attempts to get on with my life.

I bite his lip, hard, filled with the savage need to hurt him—to rip his flesh as he ripped apart my heart. The coppery tang of blood fills my mouth, and he jerks back with a curse, his eyes darkening with anger.

I'm not afraid, however. Not anymore. "Let me go," I hiss furiously, struggling against his hold. "You fucking asshole! You bastard! You were never dead! You were never fucking dead..." To my complete humiliation, the last phrase escapes as a choked sob, my voice breaking at the end.

His jaw tightens as he stares at me, the sensuous perfection of his lips marred by the bloody mark from my teeth. He holds me effortlessly, his hard cock poised at the soft entrance to my body. Enraged, I twist to the side, trying to bite him again, and he transfers my wrists into his left palm, restraining me with one hand while grabbing my hair with the other. Now I can't move at all; all I can do is glare at him, tears of rage and bitter frustration burning my eyes.

Unexpectedly, his expression softens. "Looks like my little kitten grew some claws," he murmurs, his voice filled with dark amusement. "I think I like it."

I literally see red. "Fuck you!" I shriek, bucking against him, heedless of our naked bodies rubbing together. "Fuck you and what you like—"

His mouth swoops down on me, swallowing my angry words, and my teeth snap at him in another biting attempt. He jerks away at the last second, laughing softly. At the same time, the head of his cock begins to push inside me. Maddened beyond bearing, I scream—and his right hand releases my hair, slapping over my mouth instead. "Shhh," he whispers in my ear, ignoring my muffled cries. "We wouldn't want your neighbors to hear, now would we?"

At this moment, I couldn't care if the whole world heard us. I'm filled with the primitive need to lash out at him, to hurt him as he hurt me. If I had a gun with me, I would've gladly shot him for the agony he put me through.

But I don't have a gun. I don't have anything, and he slowly pushes deeper into my vulnerable opening, his thick cock stretching me, penetrating me with its heated hardness. I'm still wet from my earlier 'dream,' but I'm also tense with anger, and my body protests the intrusion, all of my muscles tightening to keep him out. It's like our first time again—except that the twister of emotions in my chest right now is far more complex than the fear I once felt. My struggles gradually dying down, I gaze up at him mutely, reeling from the shock of his return.

When he's all the way inside me, he stops, slowly lifting his hand from my mouth.

I remain silent, tears spilling out of the corners of my eyes.

Lowering his head, he kisses me gently, as though apologizing for taking me so ruthlessly. My lungs cease to work; as always, this peculiar mix of cruelty and tenderness turns me inside out, wreaking havoc on my already-conflicted mind.

"I'm sorry, baby," he murmurs, his lips brushing against my tear-wet cheek. "It wasn't supposed to happen like that. You were mine to protect and I fucked up. I fucked up so fucking bad..." He exhales softly. "I never meant to leave you, never meant to let you go—"

"But you did." My voice is small and hurt, like that of a wounded child. "You let me think you were dead—"

"No." He lets go of my wrists and props himself up on his elbows, framing my face with his big hands. His eyes burn into mine so intensely, I feel like he's consuming me with his gaze. "It wasn't like that. It wasn't like that at all."

My hands slowly lower to his shoulders. "What was it like then?" I ask bitterly. How could he have done this to me? How could he have stolen me, taken everything from me, only to abandon me so cruelly?

"I'll explain everything," he promises, his voice low and thick with lust. There's sweat beading up on his brow, and I can feel his cock throbbing deep within me. He's holding on to his control by a shred. "But right now, I need you, Nora. I need this..." He thrusts his hips forward, and I moan as he hits my G-spot, sending a blast of sensation through my nerve endings.

"That's right," he whispers harshly, repeating the motion. "I need this. I want to feel your tight little pussy sheathing me like a glove. I want to fuck you, and I want to fucking devour you. Every single inch of you is mine, Nora, only mine..." He lowers his head again, taking my mouth in a deep, penetrating kiss as he continues thrusting into me with a slow, relentless rhythm.

My own breathing picks up, a rush of heat flooding my body. My fingers tighten on his shoulders, and my legs wrap around his muscular thighs, taking him deeper into me. After months of abstinence, it's almost too much, but I welcome the slight burn, the exquisite pleasure-pain of his possession. I can feel the tension growing inside me, the delicious prickling of pre-orgasmic bliss, and then I explode with a strangled cry, my inner muscles clamping tightly around his thick cock.

"Yes, baby, that's it," he groans hoarsely, his pace picking up, and then, with one last, powerful thrust, he finds his own peak, his shaft pulsing deep within me. I can feel the warmth of his seed releasing inside me, and I hold him close as he collapses on top of me, his large body heavy and covered with sweat.

"Do you want coffee or tea?" I ask, glancing at Julian as I putter around the tiny kitchen in the corner of my studio. He's sitting at the table by the wall, wearing a pair of jeans—the only thing he deigned to put on after his shower. His bronzed, rippled torso draws my eyes, and my hand shakes slightly as I reach for a cup. With his hair cut short, his cheekbones appear sharper, his features even more chiseled than before. Frowning, I take a closer look. He seems thinner than I recall him being, almost as if he lost some weight.

Ignoring my staring, Julian leans back in the flimsy chair I bought at IKEA, stretching out his long legs. His feet are bare and strikingly masculine. "Coffee would be great," he says lazily, watching me with a heavy-lidded gaze.

He reminds me of a panther patiently stalking its prey.

I swallow, placing the cup on the counter and reaching for the coffeemaker. Unlike him, I'm wearing jeans, thick socks, and a fleece sweater. Being fully dressed makes me feel less vulnerable, more in control.

The whole thing is surreal. If it weren't for the slight soreness between my thighs, I would've been convinced that I am hallucinating. But no, my captor—the man who had been the center of my existence for so long—is here in my tiny apartment, dominating it with his powerful presence.

After the coffee is ready, I pour each of us a cup and join him at the table. I feel off-balance, like I'm walking on a tightrope. One second I want to scream with joy that he's alive, and the next I want to kill him for putting me through this torture. And through it all, at the back of my mind is the knowledge that neither of those is an appropriate response for this situation. By all rights, I should be trying to escape and call the police.

Julian doesn't seem the least bit afraid of that possibility. He's as comfortable and self-assured in my studio as he was on his island. Picking up his cup, he takes a sip of the coffee and looks at me, a mesmerizing half-smile playing on his beautiful lips.

I curve my hands around my own cup, enjoying the warmth between my palms. "How did you survive the explosion?" I ask quietly, holding his gaze.

His mouth twists slightly. "I very nearly didn't. When they saw that they were losing, one of those suicidal motherfuckers set off a bomb. Two of my men and I happened to be near the ladder to the basement, and we dove into the opening at the last minute. A section of the floor collapsed on me, knocking me out and killing one of the men who was with me. Luckily for me, the other one—Lucas—survived and remained conscious. He managed to drag both of us into the drainpipe, and there was enough fresh air coming in from the outside that we didn't die of smoke inhalation."

I draw in a shaky breath. The drainpipe... That was the only place I hadn't looked that horrific day when I spent hours combing through the burning ruins of the building. I had been so dazed and shellshocked, it hadn't even occurred to me to check there for survivors.

"By the time Lucas got us both to a hospital, I was in pretty bad shape," Julian continues, looking at me. "I had a cracked skull and several broken bones. The doctors put me in a medically induced coma to deal with the swelling in my brain, and I didn't regain consciousness until a few weeks ago." Lifting his hand, he touches his short hair, and I realize the reason for his new haircut. They must've shaved his head in the hospital.

My hand trembles as I lift my cup to take a sip. He had almost died after all—not that it makes his absence for the past few weeks any more forgivable. "Why didn't you contact me at that point? Why didn't you let me know you were alive?" How could he let my torture continue even a day longer than necessary?

He tilts his head to the side. "And then what?" he asks, his voice dangerously silky. "What would you have done, my pet? Rushed to my side to be with me in Thailand? Or would you have told your pals at the FBI where I could be found, so they could get me while I was weak and helpless?"

I inhale sharply. "I wouldn't have told them—"

"No?" He shoots me a sardonic look. "You think I don't know that you talked to them? That they now have my name and picture?"

"I only spoke to them because I thought you were dead!" I jump to my feet, nearly upending my coffee cup. All of my anger suddenly surfaces. Furious, I grip the edge of the table and glare at him. "I never betrayed you, even though I should have—"

He rises to his feet, unfolding his tall, muscular body with athletic grace. "Yes, you probably should have," he agrees softly, his gaze darkening as we stare at each other across the table. "You should've turned me in at that clinic in the Philippines and run as far and fast as you can, my pet."

I run my tongue over my dry lips. "Would that have helped?"

"No. I would've found you anywhere."

My stomach twists with excitement and a dollop of fear. He's not joking. I can see it on his face. He would've come for me, and no one could've stopped him.

"Who are you?" I breathe, staring at him incredulously. "Why was there no record of you in any of the government databases? If you're a big-time arms dealer, why hasn't the FBI heard about you before?"

He looks at me, his eyes strikingly blue in his darkly tanned face. "Because I have a wide network of connections, Nora," he says quietly. "And because, as part of my interactions with my clients, I occasionally come across some information that the United States government finds valuable—information that relates to the safety and security of the American public."

My jaw drops. "You're a spy?"

"No." He laughs. "Not in the traditional sense of the word. I'm not on anyone's payroll—we simply exchange favors. I help your government, and in return, they make me invisible to all. Only a few of the highest-level officials in the CIA know that I exist at all." He pauses, then adds softly, "Or at least, that was the case before the FBI got their hands on you, my pet. Now it's a bit more complicated, and I'll have to call in quite a few of those favors to get this information erased."

"I see," I say evenly. My head is spinning. The man who kidnapped me is working with my government. It's almost more than I can process right now.

He smiles, visibly enjoying my confusion. "Don't over-think it, my pet," he advises, his eyes gleaming with amusement. "Just because I help prevent an occasional terrorist attack doesn't make me a good guy."

"No," I agree. "It doesn't." Turning away, I walk over to the small window and gaze outside. The sun is just beginning to come up, and there is a light layer of snow on the ground.

The first snow of the season—it must've fallen overnight.

I don't hear him moving, but suddenly he's behind me, his large arms folding around me, pressing me against his body. I can smell the clean male scent of his skin, and some of the residual tension drains out of me. Julian is alive.

"So where do we go from here?" I ask, still staring at the snow. "Are you taking me back to the island?"

He's silent for a moment. "No," he says finally. "I can't. Not without Beth there." There is a tight note in his voice, and I realize that he's missing her too, that he feels her loss just as acutely.

I turn around in his embrace and look up at him, placing my hands on his chest. "I'm glad those mother-fuckers are dead." The words come out in a low, fierce hiss. "I'm glad you killed them all."

"Yes," he says, and I see a reflection of my rage and pain in the hard glitter of his eyes. "The men who hurt her are dead, and I'm taking steps to wipe out their entire organization. By the time I'm done, Al-Quadar will be nothing more than a file in government archives."

I hold his gaze without blinking. "Good." I want them all destroyed. I want Julian to tear them apart and make them feel Beth's agony.

In this moment, we understand each other perfectly. He's a killer, and that's exactly what I need him to be. I don't want a sweet, gentle man with a conscience—I want a monster who will brutally avenge Beth's death.

A faint smile lifts the corners of his lips. Bending down, he kisses me lightly on the forehead, then releases me to walk over to the bed, where the rest of his clothes are.

Frowning, I watch as he pulls on a long-sleeved T-shirt, socks, and a pair of boots. "Are you leaving?" I ask, feeling like a cold fist is squeezing my heart at the thought.

"No," he replies, putting on his leather jacket and walking over to my closet. "We are leaving." Opening the closet door, he pulls out my winter coat and warm boots and tosses them to me.

I catch the coat on auto-pilot and put it on. "Are you kidnapping me again?" I ask, pulling on the boots.

"I don't know." Coming up to me, he cups my face in his hand, his thumb rubbing lightly against my lower lip. "Am I?"

I don't know either. For the first time in months, I feel alive. I feel emotions again, sharp and bright. Fear, excitement, exhilaration.

Love.

It's not the sweet, tender kind of love I always dreamed of, but it's love. Dark, twisted, and obsessive, it's both a compulsion and an addiction. I know the world will condemn me for my choices, but I need Julian as much as he needs me.

"What if I don't want to go with you?" I don't know why I feel the need to ask. I already know the answer.

He smiles. Dropping his hand from my face, he

reaches into the pocket of his jacket and pulls out a small syringe, showing it to me.

"I see," I say calmly. He's come prepared for any eventuality.

He puts the syringe away and offers me his hand. I hesitate for a moment, then I put my hand in his large palm. He curls his fingers around mine, and his eyes look impossibly blue in that moment, almost radiant.

We walk out together, holding hands like a couple. He leads me to a car that's waiting for us—a black car with window glass that looks to be unusually thick. Likely bulletproof.

He opens the door for me, and I climb inside.

As the car takes off, he pulls me closer to him, and I bury my face in the crook of his neck, breathing in his familiar scent.

For the first time in months, I feel like I'm home.

THE END

SNEAK PEEKS

Thank you for reading! If you would consider leaving a review, it would be greatly appreciated. Julian & Nora's story continues in *Keep Me*.

If you'd like to be notified when the next book comes out, please visit my website at http://annazaires.com/ and sign up for my newsletter.

If you enjoyed *Twist Me*, you might like the following books:

- *The Capture Me Trilogy* – Lucas & Yulia's story (*a Twist Me series spin-off*)
- *Tormentor Mine* – Peter & Sara's story (*a Twist Me series spin-off*)
- *The Mia & Korum Trilogy* – A dark sci-fi romance

- *The Krinar Captive* – A standalone sci-fi romance

Collaborations with my husband, Dima Zales:

- *Mind Machines* – An action-packed technothriller
- *The Mind Dimensions Series* – Urban fantasy
- *The Last Humans Trilogy* – Dystopian/post-apocalyptic science fiction
- *The Sorcery Code* – Epic fantasy

Additionally, if you like audiobooks, please visit my website to check out this series and our other books in audio.

And now please turn the page for a little taste of *Keep Me*, *Close Liaisons*, and some of my other works.

EXCERPT FROM KEEP ME

Author's Note: *Keep Me* is the continuation of Nora & Julian's story and is told from both Nora & Julian's perspective. The following excerpt is from Julian's point of view.

There are days when the urge to hurt, to kill, is too strong to be denied. Days when the thin cloak of civilization threatens to slip at the least provocation, revealing the monster inside.

Today is not one of those days.

Today I have her with me.

We're in the car on the way to the airport. She's sitting pressed against my side, her slim arms wrapped around me and her face buried in the crook of my neck.

Cradling her with one arm, I stroke her dark hair, delighting in its silky texture. It's long now, reaching all the way down to her narrow waist. She hasn't cut her hair in nineteen months.

Not since I kidnapped her for the first time.

Inhaling, I draw in her scent—light and flowery, deliciously feminine. It's a combination of some shampoo and her unique body chemistry, and it makes my mouth water. I want to strip her bare and follow that scent everywhere, to explore every curve and hollow of her body.

My cock twitches, and I remind myself that I just fucked her. It doesn't matter, though. My lust for her is constant. It used to bother me, this obsessive craving, but now I'm used to it. I've accepted my own madness.

She seems calm, content even. I like that. I like to feel her cuddled against me, all soft and trusting. She knows my true nature, yet she still feels safe with me. I have trained her to feel that way.

I have made her love me.

After a couple of minutes, she stirs in my arms, lifting her head to look at me. "Where are we going?" she asks, blinking, her long black lashes sweeping up and down like fans. She has the kind of eyes that could bring a man to his knees—soft, dark eyes that make me think of tangled sheets and naked flesh.

I force myself to focus. Those eyes mess with my concentration like nothing else. "We're going to my home in Colombia," I say, answering her question. "The place where I grew up."

I haven't been there for years—not since my parents were murdered. However, my father's compound is a fortress, and that's precisely what we need right now. In the past few weeks, I've implemented additional security measures, making the place virtually impregnable. Nobody will take Nora from me again—I've made sure of that.

"Are you going to be there with me?" I can hear the hopeful note in her voice, and I nod, smiling.

"Yes, my pet, I'll be there." Now that I have her back, the compulsion to keep her near is too strong to deny. The island had once been the safest place for her, but no longer. Now they know of her existence—and they know she's my Achilles heel. I need to have her with me, where I can protect her.

She licks her lips, and my eyes follow the path of her delicate pink tongue. I want to wrap her thick hair around my fist and force her head down to my lap, but I resist the urge. There will be time for that later, when we're in a more secure—and less public—location.

"Are you going to send my parents another million dollars?" Her eyes are wide and guileless as she looks at me, but I can sense the subtle challenge in her voice. She's testing me—testing the bounds of this new stage of our relationship.

My smile broadens, and I reach over to tuck a strand of hair behind her ear. "Do you want me to send it to them, my pet?"

She stares at me without blinking. "Not really," she says softly. "I would much rather call them instead."

I hold her gaze. "All right. You can call them once we get there."

Her eyes widen, and I see that I surprised her. She was expecting that I would keep her captive again, cut off from the outside world. What she doesn't realize is that it's no longer necessary.

I've succeeded in what I set out to do.

I've made her completely mine.

All three books in the *Twist Me* trilogy are now available. Please visit my website at http://annazaires.com/ to learn more and to sign up for my new release email list.

EXCERPT FROM CAPTURE ME

Author's Note: *Capture Me* is the first book in Lucas & Yulia's dark romance series. The following excerpt is from Yulia's POV. This scene takes place in Moscow, when Lucas & Julian were there to meet with the Russian officials.

∾

She fears him from the first moment she sees him.

Yulia Tzakova is no stranger to dangerous men. She grew up with them. She survived them. But when she meets Lucas Kent, she knows the hard ex-soldier may be the most dangerous of them all.

One night—that's all it should be. A chance to make up for a failed assignment and get information on Kent's arms dealer boss. When his plane goes down, it should be the end.

Instead, it's just the beginning.

He wants her from the first moment he sees her.

Lucas Kent has always liked leggy blondes, and Yulia Tzakova is as beautiful as they come. The Russian interpreter might've tried to seduce his boss, but she ends up in Lucas's bed—and he has every intention of seeing her there again.

Then his plane goes down, and he learns the truth.

She betrayed him.

Now she will pay.

He steps into my apartment as soon as the door swings open. No hesitation, no greeting—he just comes in.

Startled, I step back, the short, narrow hallway suddenly stiflingly small. I'd somehow forgotten how big he is, how broad his shoulders are. I'm tall for a woman—tall enough to fake being a model if an assignment calls for it—but he towers a full head above me. With the heavy down jacket he's wearing, he takes up almost the entire hallway.

Still not saying a word, he closes the door behind him and advances toward me. Instinctively, I back away, feeling like cornered prey.

"Hello, Yulia," he murmurs, stopping when we're out of the hallway. His pale gaze is locked on my face. "I wasn't expecting to see you like this."

I swallow, my pulse racing. "I just took a bath." I want to seem calm and confident, but he's got me completely off-balance. "I wasn't expecting visitors."

"No, I can see that." A faint smile appears on his lips, softening the hard line of his mouth. "Yet you let me in. Why?"

"Because I didn't want to continue talking through the door." I take a steadying breath. "Can I offer you some tea?" It's a stupid thing to say, given what he's here for, but I need a few moments to compose myself.

He raises his eyebrows. "Tea? No, thanks."

"Then can I take your jacket?" I can't seem to stop playing the hostess, using politeness to cover my anxiety. "It looks quite warm."

Amusement flickers in his wintry gaze. "Sure." He takes off his down jacket and hands it to me. He's left wearing a black sweater and dark jeans tucked into black winter boots. The jeans hug his legs, revealing muscular thighs and powerful calves, and on his belt, I see a gun sitting in a holster.

Irrationally, my breathing quickens at the sight, and it takes a concerted effort to keep my hands from shaking as I take the jacket and walk over to hang it in my tiny closet. It's not a surprise that he's armed—it would be a shock if he wasn't—but the gun is a stark reminder of who Lucas Kent is.

What he is.

It's no big deal, I tell myself, trying to calm my frayed nerves. I'm used to dangerous men. I was raised among them. This man is not that different. I'll sleep with him, get whatever information I can, and then he'll be out of my life.

Yes, that's it. The sooner I can get it done, the sooner all of this will be over.

Closing the closet door, I paste a practiced smile on my face and turn back to face him, finally ready to resume the role of confident seductress.

Except he's already next to me, having crossed the room without making a sound.

My pulse jumps again, my newfound composure fleeing. He's close enough that I can see the gray striations in his pale blue eyes, close enough that he can touch me.

And a second later, he does touch me.

Lifting his hand, he runs the back of his knuckles over my jaw.

I stare up at him, confused by my body's instant response. My skin warms and my nipples tighten, my breath coming faster. It doesn't make sense for this hard, ruthless stranger to turn me on. His boss is more hand-some, more striking, yet it's Kent my body's reacting to. All he's touched thus far is my face. It should be nothing, yet it's intimate somehow.

Intimate and disturbing.

I swallow again. "Mr. Kent—Lucas—are you sure I can't offer you something to drink? Maybe some coffee or—" My words end in a breathless gasp as he reaches for the tie of my robe and tugs on it, as casually as one would unwrap a package.

"No." He watches as the robe falls open, revealing my naked body underneath. "No coffee."

And then he touches me for real, his big, hard palm cupping my breast. His fingers are callused, rough. Cold from being outside. His thumb flicks over my hardened nipple, and I feel a pull deep within my core, a coiling of need that feels as foreign as his touch.

Fighting the urge to flinch away, I dampen my dry lips. "You're very direct, aren't you?"

"I don't have time for games." His eyes gleam as his thumb flicks over my nipple again. "We both know why I'm here."

"To have sex with me."

"Yes." He doesn't bother to soften it, to give me anything but the brutal truth. He's still holding my breast, touching my naked flesh as though it's his right. "To have sex with you."

"And if I say no?" I don't know why I'm asking this. This is not how it's supposed to go. I should be seducing him, not trying to put him off. Yet something within me rebels at his casual assumption that I'm his for the taking. Other men have assumed this before, and it didn't bother me nearly as much. I don't know what's different this time, but I want him to step away from me, to stop touching me. I want it so badly that my hands curl into fists at my sides, my muscles tensing with the urge to fight.

"Are you saying no?" He asks the question calmly, his thumb now circling over my areola. As I search for a response, he slides his other hand into my hair, possessively cupping the back of my skull.

I stare at him, my breath catching. "And if I were?" To my disgust, my voice comes out thin and scared. It's as if I'm a virgin again, cornered by my trainer in the locker room. "Would you leave?"

One corner of his mouth lifts in a half-smile. "What do you think?" His fingers tighten in my hair, the grip just hard enough to hint at pain. His other hand, the one on my breast, is still gentle, but it doesn't matter.

I have my answer.

So when his hand leaves my breast and slides down my belly, I don't resist. Instead, I part my legs, letting him touch my smooth, freshly waxed pussy. And when his hard, blunt finger pushes into me, I don't try to move away. I just stand there, trying to control my frantic breathing, trying to convince myself that this is no different from any other assignment.

Except it is.

I don't want it to be, but it is.

"You're wet," he murmurs, staring at me as he pushes his finger deeper. "Very wet. Do you always get so wet for men you don't want?"

"What makes you think I don't want you?" To my relief, my voice is steadier this time. The question comes out soft, almost amused as I hold his gaze. "I let you in here, didn't I?"

"You came on to *him*." Kent's jaw tightens, and his hand on the back of my head shifts, gripping a fistful of my hair. "You wanted *him* earlier today."

"So I did." The typically masculine display of jealousy reassures me, putting me on more familiar ground. I manage to soften my tone, make it more seductive. "And now I want you. Does that bother you?"

Kent's eyes narrow. "No." He forces a second finger into me and simultaneous presses his thumb against my clit. "Not at all."

I want to say something clever, come up with some snappy retort, but I can't. The jolt of pleasure is sharp and startling. My inner muscles tighten, clutching at his rough, invading fingers, and it's all I can do not to moan out loud at the resulting sensations. Involuntarily, my hands come up, grabbing at his forearm. I don't know if I'm trying to push him away or get him to continue, but it doesn't matter. Under the soft wool of his sweater, his arm is thick with steely muscle. I can't control its movements—all I can do is hold onto it as he pushes deeper into me with those hard, merciless fingers.

"You like that, don't you?" he murmurs, holding my gaze, and I gasp as he begins flicking his thumb over my clit, side to side, then up and down. His fingers curl inside me, and I suppress a moan as he hits a spot that sends an even sharper pang of sensation to my nerve endings. A tension begins to coil inside me, the pleasure gathering and intensifying, and with shock I realize I'm on the verge of orgasm.

My body, usually so slow to respond, is throbbing with aching need at the touch of a man who scares me—a development that both astonishes and unnerves me.

I don't know if he sees it on my face, or if he feels the tightening in my body, but his pupils dilate, his pale eyes darkening. "Yes, that's it." His voice is a low, deep rumble. "Come for me, beautiful"—his thumb presses hard on my clit—"just like that."

And I do. With a strangled moan, I climax around his fingers, the hard edges of his short, blunt nails digging into my rippling flesh. My visions blurs, my skin prickling with heated needles as I ride the wave of sensations, and then I sag in his grasp, held upright only by his hand in my hair and his fingers inside my body.

"There you go," he says thickly, and as the world comes back into focus, I see that he's watching me intently. "That was nice, wasn't it?"

I can't even manage a nod, but he doesn't seem to need my confirmation. And why would he? I can feel the slickness inside me, the wetness that coats those rough male fingers—fingers that he withdraws from me slowly, watching my face the whole time. I want to close my eyes, or at least look away from that penetrating gaze, but I can't.

Not without letting him know how much he frightens me.

So instead of backing down, I study him in return, seeing the signs of arousal on his strong features. His jaw is clenched tight as he stares at me, a tiny muscle pulsing near his right ear. And even through the sun-bronzed hue of his skin, I can see heightened color on his blade-like cheekbones.

He wants me badly—and that knowledge emboldens me to act.

Reaching down, I cup the hard bulge at the crotch of his jeans. "It *was* nice," I whisper, looking up at him. "And now it's your turn."

His pupils dilate even more, his chest inflating with a deep breath. "Yes." His voice is thick with lust as he uses his grip on my hair to drag me closer. "Yes, I think it is." And before I can reconsider the wisdom of my blatant provocation, he lowers his head and captures my mouth with his.

I gasp, my lips parting from surprise, and he immediately takes advantage, deepening the kiss. His hard-looking mouth is surprisingly soft on mine, his lips warm and smooth as his tongue hungrily explores the interior of my mouth. There's skill and confidence in that kiss; it's the kiss of a man who knows how to please a woman, how to seduce her with nothing more than the touch of his lips.

The heat simmering within me intensifies, the tension rising inside me once more. He's holding me so close that my bare breasts are pressing against his sweater, the wool rubbing against my peaked nipples. I can feel his erection through the rough material of his jeans; it pushes into my lower belly, revealing how much he wants me, how thin his pretense of control really is.

Dimly, I realize the robe fell off my shoulders, leaving me completely naked, and then I forget all about it as he makes a low growling sound deep in his throat and pushes me against the wall.

The shock of the cold surface at my back clears my mind for a second, but he's already unzipping his jeans, his knees wedging between my legs and spreading them open as he raises his head to look at me. I hear the ripping sound of a foil packet being opened, and then he cups my ass and lifts me off the ground. Instinctively, I grab at his shoulders, my heartbeat quickening as he orders hoarsely, "Wrap your legs around me"—and lowers me onto his stiff cock, all the while holding my gaze.

His thrust is hard and deep, penetrating me all the way. My breathing stutters at the force of it, at the uncompromising brutality of the invasion. My inner muscles clench around him, futilely trying to keep him out. His cock is as big as the rest of him, so long and thick it stretches me to the point of pain. If I hadn't been so wet, he would've torn me. But I *am* wet, and after a couple of moments, my body begins to soften, adjusting to his thickness. Unconsciously, my legs come up, clasping his hips as he instructed, and the new position lets him slide even deeper into me, making me cry out at the sharp sensation.

He begins to move then, his eyes glittering as he stares at me. Each thrust is as hard as the one that joined us together, yet my body no longer tries to fight it. Instead, it brings forth more moisture, easing his way.

Each time he slams into me, his groin presses against my sex, putting pressure on my clit, and the tension in my core returns, growing with every second. Stunned, I realize I'm about to have my second orgasm... and then I do, the tension peaking and exploding, scattering my thoughts and electrifying my nerve endings.

I can feel my own pulsations, the way my muscles squeeze and release his cock, and then I see his eyes go unfocused as he stops thrusting. A hoarse, deep groan escapes his throat as he grinds into me, and I know he's found his release as well, my orgasm driving him over the edge.

My chest heaving, I stare up at him, watching as his pale blue eyes refocus on me. He's still inside me, and all of a sudden, the intimacy of that is unbearable. He's nobody to me, a stranger, yet he fucked me.

He fucked me, and I let him because it's my job.

Swallowing, I push at his chest, my legs unwrapping from around his waist. "Please, let me down." I know I should be cooing at him and stroking his ego. I should be telling him how amazing it was, how he gave me more pleasure than anyone I've known. It wouldn't even be a lie—I've never come twice with a man before. But I can't bring myself to do that. I feel too raw, too invaded.

With this man, I'm not in control, and that knowledge scares me.

I don't know if he senses that, or if he just wants to toy with me, but a sardonic smile appears on his lips.

"It's too late for regrets, beautiful," he murmurs, and before I can respond, he lets me down and releases his grip on my ass. His softening cock slips out of my body as he steps back, and I watch, my breathing still uneven, as he casually takes the condom off and drops it on the floor.

For some reason, his action makes me flush. There's something so wrong, so dirty about that condom lying there. Perhaps it's because I feel like that condom: used and discarded. Spotting my robe on the floor, I move to pick it up, but Lucas's hand on my arm stops me.

"What are you doing?" he asks, gazing at me. He doesn't seem the least bit concerned that his jeans are still unzipped and his cock is hanging out. "We're not done yet."

My heart skips a beat. "We're not?"

"No," he says, stepping closer. To my shock, I feel him hardening against my stomach. "We're far from done."

And using his grip on my arm, he steers me toward the bed.

Capture Me is now available. If you'd like to find out more, please visit my website at http://annazaires.com/.

EXCERPT FROM TORMENTOR MINE

Author's Note: *Tormentor Mine* is the first book in Peter's dark romance series. The following excerpt is from Peter's POV.

He came to me in the night, a cruel, darkly handsome stranger from the most dangerous corners of Russia. He tormented me and destroyed me, ripping apart my world in his quest for vengeance.

Now he's back, but he's no longer after my secrets.

The man who stars in my nightmares wants me.

"Are you going to kill me?"

She's trying—and failing—to keep her voice steady. Still, I admire her attempt at composure. I approached her in public to make her feel safer, but she's too smart to fall for that. If they've told her anything about my background, she must realize I can snap her neck faster than she can scream for help.

"No," I answer, leaning closer as a louder song comes on. "I'm not going to kill you."

"Then what do you want from me?"

She's shaking in my hold, and something about that both intrigues and disturbs me. I don't want her to be afraid of me, but at the same time, I like having her at my mercy. Her fear calls to the predator within me, turning my desire for her into something darker.

She's captured prey, soft and sweet and mine to devour.

Bending my head, I bury my nose in her fragrant hair and murmur into her ear, "Meet me at the Starbucks near your house at noon tomorrow, and we'll talk there. I'll tell you whatever you want to know."

I pull back, and she stares at me, her eyes huge in her pale face. I know what she's thinking, so I lean in again, dipping my head so my mouth is next to her ear.

"If you contact the FBI, they'll try to hide you from me. Just like they tried to hide your husband and the others on my list. They'll uproot you, take you away from your parents and your career, and it will all be for nothing. I'll find you, no matter where you go, Sara... no matter what they do to keep you from me." My lips brush against the rim of her ear, and I feel her breath hitch. "Alternatively, they might want to use you as bait. If that's the case—if they set a trap for me—I'll know, and our next meeting won't be over coffee."

She shudders, and I drag in a deep breath, inhaling her delicate scent one last time before releasing her.

Stepping back, I melt into the crowd and message Anton to get the crew into positions.

I have to make sure she gets home safe and sound, unmolested by anyone but me.

Tormentor Mine is available everywhere. If you'd like to find out more, please visit my website at http://annazaires.com/.

EXCERPT FROM CLOSE LIAISONS

Author's Note: *Close Liaisons* is the first book in my erotic sci-fi romance trilogy, the Krinar Chronicles. While not as dark as *Twist Me* and *Capture Me*, it does have some elements that readers of dark erotica may enjoy.

∾

A dark and edgy romance that will appeal to fans of erotic and turbulent relationships...

In the near future, the Krinar rule the Earth. An advanced race from another galaxy, they are still a mystery to us—and we are completely at their mercy.

Shy and innocent, Mia Stalis is a college student in New York City who has led a very normal life. Like most people, she's never had any interactions with the invaders—until one fateful day in the park changes everything. Having caught Korum's eye, she must now contend with a powerful, dangerously seductive Krinar who wants to possess her and will stop at nothing to make her his own.

How far would you go to regain your freedom? How much would you sacrifice to help your people? What choice will you make when you begin to fall for your enemy?

Breathe, Mia, breathe. Somewhere in the back of her mind, a small rational voice kept repeating those words. That same oddly objective part of her noted his symmetric face structure, with golden skin stretched tightly over high cheekbones and a firm jaw. Pictures and videos of Ks that she'd seen had hardly done them justice. Standing no more than thirty feet away, the creature was simply stunning.

As she continued staring at him, still frozen in place, he straightened and began walking toward her. Or rather stalking toward her, she thought stupidly, as his every movement reminded her of a jungle cat sinuously approaching a gazelle. All the while, his eyes never left hers. As he approached, she could make out individual yellow flecks in his light golden eyes and the thick long lashes surrounding them.

She watched in horrified disbelief as he sat down on

her bench, less than two feet away from her, and smiled, showing white even teeth. No fangs, she noted with some functioning part of her brain. Not even a hint of them. That used to be another myth about them, like their supposed abhorrence of the sun.

"What's your name?" The creature practically purred the question at her. His voice was low and smooth, completely unaccented. His nostrils flared slightly, as though inhaling her scent.

"Um…" Mia swallowed nervously. "M-Mia."

"Mia," he repeated slowly, seemingly savoring her name. "Mia what?"

"Mia Stalis." Oh crap, why did he want to know her name? Why was he here, talking to her? In general, what was he doing in Central Park, so far away from any of the K Centers? *Breathe, Mia, breathe.*

"Relax, Mia Stalis." His smile got wider, exposing a dimple in his left cheek. A dimple? Ks had dimples? "Have you never encountered one of us before?"

"No, I haven't," Mia exhaled sharply, realizing that she was holding her breath. She was proud that her voice didn't sound as shaky as she felt. Should she ask? Did she want to know?

She gathered her courage. "What, um—" Another swallow. "What do you want from me?"

"For now, conversation." He looked like he was about to laugh at her, those gold eyes crinkling slightly at the corners.

Strangely, that pissed her off enough to take the edge off her fear. If there was anything Mia hated, it was being laughed at. With her short, skinny stature and a general lack of social skills that came from an awkward teenage phase involving every girl's nightmare of braces, frizzy hair, and glasses, Mia had more than enough experience being the butt of someone's joke.

She lifted her chin belligerently. "Okay, then, what is *your* name?"

"It's Korum."

"Just Korum?"

"We don't really have last names, not the way you do. My full name is much longer, but you wouldn't be able to pronounce it if I told you."

Okay, that was interesting. She now remembered reading something like that in *The New York Times*. So far, so good. Her legs had nearly stopped shaking, and her breathing was returning to normal. Maybe, just maybe, she would get out of this alive. This conversation business seemed safe enough, although the way he kept staring at her with those unblinking yellowish eyes was unnerving. She decided to keep him talking.

"What are you doing here, Korum?"

"I just told you, making conversation with you, Mia." His voice again held a hint of laughter.

Frustrated, Mia blew out her breath. "I meant, what are you doing here in Central Park? In New York City in general?"

He smiled again, cocking his head slightly to the side. "Maybe I'm hoping to meet a pretty curly-haired girl."

Okay, enough was enough. He was clearly toying with her. Now that she could think a little again, she realized that they were in the middle of Central Park, in full view of about a gazillion spectators. She surreptitiously glanced around to confirm that. Yep, sure enough, although people were obviously steering clear of her bench and its otherworldly occupant, there were a number of brave souls staring their way from farther up the path. A couple were even cautiously filming them with their wristwatch cameras. If the K tried anything with her, it would be on YouTube in the blink of an eye, and he had to know it. Of course, he may or may not care about that.

Still, going on the assumption that since she'd never come across any videos of K assaults on college students in the middle of Central Park, she was relatively safe, Mia cautiously reached for her laptop and lifted it to stuff it back into her backpack.

"Let me help you with that, Mia—"

And before she could blink, she felt him take her heavy laptop from her suddenly boneless fingers, gently brushing against her knuckles in the process. A sensation similar to a mild electric shock shot through Mia at his touch, leaving her nerve endings tingling in its wake.

Reaching for her backpack, he carefully put away the laptop in a smooth, sinuous motion. "There you go, all better now."

Oh God, he had touched her. Maybe her theory about the safety of public locations was bogus. She felt her breathing speeding up again, and her heart rate was probably well into the anaerobic zone at this point.

"I have to go now... Bye!"

How she managed to squeeze out those words without hyperventilating, she would never know. Grabbing the strap of the backpack he'd just put down, she jumped to her feet, noting somewhere in the back of her mind that her earlier paralysis seemed to be gone.

"Bye, Mia. I will see you later." His softly mocking voice carried in the clear spring air as she took off, nearly running in her haste to get away.

If you'd like to find out more, please visit my website at http://annazaires.com/. All three books in the Krinar Chronicles trilogy are now available.

EXCERPT FROM THE THOUGHT READERS BY DIMA ZALES

Author's Note: If you want to try something different—and especially if you like urban fantasy and science fiction—you might want to check out *The Thought Readers*, the first book in the Mind Dimensions series that I'm collaborating on with Dima Zales, my husband. But be warned, there is not much romance or sex in this one. Instead of sex, there's mind reading.

～

Everyone thinks I'm a genius.

Everyone is wrong.

Sure, I finished Harvard at eighteen and now make crazy money at a hedge fund. But that's not because I'm unusually smart or hard-working.

It's because I cheat.

You see, I have a unique ability. I can go outside time into my own personal version of reality—the place I call "the Quiet"—where I can explore my surroundings while the rest of the world stands still.

I thought I was the only one who could do this—until I met her.

My name is Darren, and this is how I learned that I'm a Reader.

Sometimes I think I'm crazy. I'm sitting at a casino table in Atlantic City, and everyone around me is motionless. I call this the Quiet, as though giving it a name makes it seem more real—as though giving it a name changes the fact that all the players around me are frozen like statues, and I'm walking among them, looking at the cards they've been dealt.

The problem with the theory of my being crazy is that when I 'unfreeze' the world, as I just have, the cards the players turn over are the same ones I just saw in the Quiet. If I were crazy, wouldn't these cards be different? Unless I'm so far gone that I'm imagining the cards on the table, too.

But then I also win. If that's a delusion—if the pile of chips on my side of the table is a delusion—then I might as well question everything. Maybe my name isn't even Darren.

No. I can't think that way. If I'm really that confused, I don't want to snap out of it—because if I do, I'll probably wake up in a mental hospital.

Besides, I love my life, crazy and all.

My shrink thinks the Quiet is an inventive way I describe the 'inner workings of my genius.' Now that sounds crazy to me. She also might want me, but that's beside the point. Suffice it to say, she's as far as it gets from my datable age range, which is currently right around twenty-four. Still young, still hot, but done with school and pretty much beyond the clubbing phase. I hate clubbing, almost as much as I hated studying. In any case, my shrink's explanation doesn't work, as it doesn't account for the way I know things even a genius wouldn't know—like the exact value and suit of the other players' cards.

I watch as the dealer begins a new round. Besides me, there are three players at the table: Grandma, the Cowboy, and the Professional, as I call them. I feel that now almost-imperceptible fear that accompanies the phasing. That's what I call the process: phasing into the Quiet. Worrying about my sanity has always facilitated phasing; fear seems helpful in this process.

I phase in, and everything gets quiet. Hence the name for this state.

It's eerie to me, even now. Outside the Quiet, this casino is very loud: drunk people talking, slot machines, ringing of wins, music—the only place louder is a club or a concert. And yet, right at this moment, I could probably hear a pin drop. It's like I've gone deaf to the chaos that surrounds me.

Having so many frozen people around adds to the strangeness of it all. Here is a waitress stopped mid-step, carrying a tray with drinks. There is a woman about to pull a slot machine lever. At my own table, the dealer's hand is raised, the last card he dealt hanging unnaturally in midair. I walk up to him from the side of the table and reach for it. It's a king, meant for the Professional. Once I let the card go, it falls on the table rather than continuing to float as before—but I know full well that it will be back in the air, in the exact position it was when I grabbed it, when I phase out.

The Professional looks like someone who makes money playing poker, or at least the way I always imagined someone like that might look. Scruffy, shades on, a little sketchy-looking. He's been doing an excellent job with the poker face—basically not twitching a single muscle throughout the game. His face is so expressionless that I wonder if he might've gotten Botox to help maintain such a stony countenance. His hand is on the table, protectively covering the cards dealt to him.

I move his limp hand away. It feels normal. Well, in a manner of speaking. The hand is sweaty and hairy, so moving it aside is unpleasant and is admittedly an abnormal thing to do. The normal part is that the hand is warm, rather than cold. When I was a kid, I expected people to feel cold in the Quiet, like stone statues.

With the Professional's hand moved away, I pick up

his cards. Combined with the king that was hanging in the air, he has a nice high pair. Good to know.

I walk over to Grandma. She's already holding her cards, and she has fanned them nicely for me. I'm able to avoid touching her wrinkled, spotted hands. This is a relief, as I've recently become conflicted about touching people—or, more specifically, women—in the Quiet. If I had to, I would rationalize touching Grandma's hand as harmless, or at least not creepy, but it's better to avoid it if possible.

In any case, she has a low pair. I feel bad for her. She's been losing a lot tonight. Her chips are dwindling. Her losses are due, at least partially, to the fact that she has a terrible poker face. Even before looking at her cards, I knew they wouldn't be good because I could tell she was disappointed as soon as her hand was dealt. I also caught a gleeful gleam in her eyes a few rounds ago when she had a winning three of a kind.

This whole game of poker is, to a large degree, an exercise in reading people—something I really want to get better at. At my job, I've been told I'm great at reading people. I'm not, though; I'm just good at using the Quiet to make it seem like I am. I do want to learn how to read people for real, though. It would be nice to know what everyone is thinking.

What I don't care that much about in this poker game is money. I do well enough financially to not have to depend on hitting it big gambling. I don't care if I win or lose, though quintupling my money back at the blackjack table was fun. This whole trip has been more about going gambling because I finally can, being twenty-one and all. I was never into fake IDs, so this is an actual milestone for me.

Leaving Grandma alone, I move on to the next player—the Cowboy. I can't resist taking off his straw hat and trying it on. I wonder if it's possible for me to get lice this way. Since I've never been able to bring back any inanimate objects from the Quiet, nor otherwise affect the real world in any lasting way, I figure I won't be able to get any living critters to come back with me, either.

Dropping the hat, I look at his cards. He has a pair of aces—a better hand than the Professional. Maybe the Cowboy is a professional, too. He has a good poker face, as far as I can tell. It'll be interesting to watch those two in this round.

Next, I walk up to the deck and look at the top cards, memorizing them. I'm not leaving anything to chance.

When my task in the Quiet is complete, I walk back to myself. Oh, yes, did I mention that I see myself sitting there, frozen like the rest of them? That's the weirdest part. It's like having an out-of-body experience.

Approaching my frozen self, I look at him. I usually avoid doing this, as it's too unsettling. No amount of looking in the mirror—or seeing videos of yourself on YouTube—can prepare you for viewing your own three-dimensional body up close. It's not something anyone is meant to experience. Well, aside from identical twins, I guess.

It's hard to believe that this person is me. He looks

more like some random guy. Well, maybe a bit better than that. I do find this guy interesting. He looks cool. He looks smart. I think women would probably consider him good-looking, though I know that's not a modest thing to think.

It's not like I'm an expert at gauging how attractive a guy is, but some things are common sense. I can tell when a dude is ugly, and this frozen me is not. I also know that generally, being good-looking requires a symmetrical face, and the statue of me has that. A strong jaw doesn't hurt, either. Check. Having broad shoulders is a positive, and being tall really helps. All covered. I have blue eyes—that seems to be a plus. Girls have told me they like my eyes, though right now, on the frozen me, the eyes look creepy—glassy. They look like the eyes of a lifeless wax figure.

Realizing that I'm dwelling on this subject way too long, I shake my head. I can just picture my shrink analyzing this moment. Who would imagine admiring themselves like this as part of their mental illness? I can just picture her scribbling down Narcissist, underlining it for emphasis.

Enough. I need to leave the Quiet. Raising my hand, I touch my frozen self on the forehead, and I hear noise again as I phase out.

Everything is back to normal.

The card that I looked at a moment before—the king that I left on the table—is in the air again, and from there it follows the trajectory it was always meant to, landing near the Professional's hands. Grandma is still eyeing her fanned cards in disappointment, and the Cowboy has his hat on again, though I took it off him in the Quiet. Everything is exactly as it was.

On some level, my brain never ceases to be surprised at the discontinuity of the experience in the Quiet and outside it. As humans, we're hardwired to question reality when such things happen. When I was trying to outwit my shrink early on in my therapy, I once read an entire psychology textbook during our session. She, of course, didn't notice it, as I did it in the Quiet. The book talked about how babies as young as two months old are surprised if they see something out of the ordinary, like gravity appearing to work backwards. It's no wonder my brain has trouble adapting. Until I was ten, the world behaved normally, but everything has been weird since then, to put it mildly.

Glancing down, I realize I'm holding three of a kind. Next time, I'll look at my cards before phasing. If I have something this strong, I might take my chances and play fair.

The game unfolds predictably because I know everybody's cards. At the end, Grandma gets up. She's clearly lost enough money.

And that's when I see the girl for the first time.

She's hot. My friend Bert at work claims that I have a 'type,' but I reject that idea. I don't like to think of myself as shallow or predictable. But I might actually be a bit of both, because this girl fits Bert's description of my type to a T. And my reaction is extreme interest, to say the least.

Large blue eyes. Well-defined cheekbones on a slender face, with a hint of something exotic. Long, shapely legs, like those of a dancer. Dark wavy hair in a ponytail—a hairstyle that I like. And without bangs—even better. I hate bangs—not sure why girls do that to themselves. Though lack of bangs is not, strictly speaking, in Bert's description of my type, it probably should be.

I continue staring at her. With her high heels and tight skirt, she's overdressed for this place. Or maybe I'm underdressed in my jeans and t-shirt. Either way, I don't care. I have to try to talk to her.

I debate phasing into the Quiet and approaching her, so I can do something creepy like stare at her up close, or maybe even snoop in her pockets. Anything to help me when I talk to her.

I decide against it, which is probably the first time that's ever happened.

I know that my reasoning for breaking my usual habit—if you can even call it that—is strange. I picture the following chain of events: she agrees to date me, we go out for a while, we get serious, and because of the deep connection we have, I come clean about the Quiet. She learns I did something creepy and has a fit, then dumps me. It's ridiculous to think this, of course, considering that we haven't even spoken yet. Talk about jumping the gun. She might have an IQ below seventy, or the personality of a piece of wood. There can be twenty different reasons why I wouldn't want to date her. And besides, it's not all up to me. She might tell me to go fuck myself as soon as I try to talk to her.

Still, working at a hedge fund has taught me to hedge. As crazy as that reasoning is, I stick with my decision not to phase because I know it's the gentlemanly thing to do. In keeping with this unusually chivalrous me, I also decide not to cheat at this round of poker.

As the cards are dealt again, I reflect on how good it feels to have done the honorable thing—even without anyone knowing. Maybe I should try to respect people's privacy more often. As soon as I think this, I mentally snort. Yeah, right. I have to be realistic. I wouldn't be where I am today if I'd followed that advice. In fact, if I made a habit of respecting people's privacy, I would lose my job within days—and with it, a lot of the comforts I've become accustomed to.

Copying the Professional's move, I cover my cards with my hand as soon as I receive them. I'm about to sneak a peek at what I was dealt when something unusual happens.

The world goes quiet, just like it does when I phase in… but I did nothing this time.

And at that moment, I see her—the girl sitting across the table from me, the girl I was just thinking about. She's standing next to me, pulling her hand away from mine. Or, strictly speaking, from my frozen self's hand —as I'm standing a little to the side looking at her.

She's also still sitting in front of me at the table, a frozen statue like all the others.

My mind goes into overdrive as my heartbeat jumps. I don't even consider the possibility of that second girl being a twin sister or something like that. I know it's her. She's doing what I did just a few minutes ago. She's walking in the Quiet. The world around us is frozen, but we are not.

A horrified look crosses her face as she realizes the same thing. Before I can react, she lunges across the table and touches her own forehead.

The world becomes normal again.

She stares at me from across the table, shocked, her eyes huge and her face pale. Her hands tremble as she rises to her feet. Without so much as a word, she turns and begins walking away, then breaks into a run a couple of seconds later.

Getting over my own shock, I get up and run after her. It's not exactly smooth. If she notices a guy she doesn't know running after her, dating will be the last thing on her mind. But I'm beyond that now. She's the only person I've met who can do what I do. She's proof that I'm not insane. She might have what I want most in the world.

She might have answers.

If you'd like to learn more about our fantasy and science fiction books, please visit Dima Zales's website at www. dimazales.com and sign up for his new release email list. The book is now available at all retailers.

ABOUT THE AUTHOR

Anna Zaires is a *New York Times, USA Today,* and #1 international bestselling author of sci-fi romance and contemporary dark erotic romance. She fell in love with books at the age of five, when her grandmother taught her to read. Since then, she has always lived partially in a fantasy world where the only limits were those of her imagination. Currently residing in Florida, Anna is happily married to Dima Zales (a science fiction and fantasy author) and closely collaborates with him on all their works.

To learn more, please visit http://annazaires.com/.